Louis Zangwill

An Engagement of Convenience

Outlook

Louis Zangwill

An Engagement of Convenience

1. Auflage | ISBN: 978-3-73261-736-4

Erscheinungsort: Paderborn, Deutschland

Erscheinungsjahr: 2018

Outlook Verlag GmbH, Paderborn.

Louis Zangwill

An Engagement of Convenience

Outlook

An Engagement of Convenience

A Novel

By

Louis Zangwill

Author of "The World and a Man,"
"One's Womenkind," &c., &c.

London

Brown, Langham & Co., Ltd.

78 New Bond Street, W.
1908

> "In tragic
> life,
> God
> wot,
> No villain need be!"

GEORGE MEREDITH.

An
Engagement of Convenience

I

Miss Robinson had first seen Wyndham and fallen in love with him on the day that he appeared in the road as a neighbour and set up his studio there. But that was years before, and she had never made his acquaintance. He was the Prince Charming of the romances, handsome, of knightly bearing, with a winning smile on his frank face. From her magic window in the big corner house where the road branched off into two, she had narrowly observed his goings and comings, had watched eagerly all that was visible of his romantic, mysterious profession—the picturesque Italian models that pulled his bell, the great canvasses and frames that, during the earlier years at least, were borne in through his door, to reappear in due course as finished pictures on their way to the exhibitions—and it was sometimes possible to catch glimpses of stately figure-paintings and fascinating scenes and landscapes.

Then, too, there was the suggestion of his belonging to a brilliant social world: she had indeed felt that at her first sight of him. Smart broughams and victorias in which nestled stylish people not unfrequently drew up at his studio about tea-time, and in the season he could be seen going off every night in garb of ceremony; not to speak of his occasional departures—to important country-houses, no doubt—with portmanteaus and dressing-bags stacked on the roof of his hansom.

And not less eagerly had Miss Robinson followed his work, scanning the magazines for his drawings, and haunting the galleries in the search for his paintings. No one guessed how much he was the interest of her life: her parents had no suspicion at all, though they knew of their unusual neighbour, and spoke of him occasionally at table. But Alice Robinson was the humblest of womankind. Her youth lay already in the past: she accounted herself the plainest of the plain. So she idealised and worshipped her hero at a distance, feeling immeasurably farther from him than the hundred yards of respectable Hampstead pavement that separated their lives.

One morning at breakfast her father read out from his paper the news of a sensational bankruptcy. A world-famous house of solicitors had fallen, and some of the first families in England were losers. Immense trust funds had gone for building speculations, and amongst the fashionable creditors who had been hit the worst were Mr. Walter Lloyd Wyndham, the artist, of Hampstead, and Miss Mary Wyndham, his sister. It seemed a curious little fact to Mr. Robinson that this affair should vibrate so near to them, and a mild and not unpleasant stimulation was thereby imparted to the breakfast-table. But Miss Robinson was hard put to it to dissimulate her deeper interest in the announcement. Her agitation was profound, shattering: she was glad to escape, and sit alone with her secret. It seemed a sacrilege that earthly vicissitude should touch this brilliant existence. And thereafter she watched her hero more narrowly than ever, reading in his bearing a stern defiance of adversity.

At first indeed there was little difference visible in Wyndham's outward seemings, and Miss Robinson was thankful that the calamity had ruffled him so imperceptibly. Yet, as the year went by, it began to dawn upon her that things nevertheless were changing. She had learnt to read with consummate skill all the little activities that beat around the studio, and it did not escape her attention that he was going into society rarely, that smart visitors were fewer, and that pictures were being returned to him after astonishingly brief intervals. And gradually, as if in corroboration of her own conclusions, she found his work missing from the exhibitions, and knew with a sinking of her heart that his brilliant days were waning.

And as time further passed, and one year merged into another, she realised definitely that his vogue had ended. She could not even find anything of his in the magazines, though she purchased them prodigally, and searched them through with a hope that was desperation, and a fear that was well-nigh frenzy.

The last year or two a dead unnatural calm had settled over the studio. Pictures were neither despatched nor returned: if models rang the bell, it was only to turn away the next minute with disappointed faces. Of fashionable visitors there was never a sign now: not even a comrade or fellow-artist came to look him up. But only a tall, sad-faced girl, who somehow resembled him, called there at long intervals, and Miss Robinson envied this sister the sympathy she could bring him.

He did not leave London now. All through the summer he kept in town, lying low, as Miss Robinson could well see from the pallor of his face on her return from her own conventional holiday at the seaside. She could cherish no delusions—he was a beaten man!

Time and again she brushed close to him, passing him by chance in the street, and observed the languor of his step, the growing sadness of his features. Other details did not escape her. There was no one to attend on him; no one to care for him. Even a charwoman was a rarity at last, and Wyndham could be seen shopping almost furtively in the adjoining streets, and bearing back his own provisions to the studio. Miss Robinson divined, under their wrappings, the tin of sardines, the potted tongue, the loaf of bread. She knew that he never took a meal out now, and that, if he left the studio in the daytime, it was only to escape from the misery of solitude and hopelessness.

She alone observed him so minutely. Her mother had in some degree shared her interest in his work, and had sometimes accompanied her to the galleries; but the common interest of the family in their neighbour was casual and fitful. Miss Robinson hardly dared mention his name now: it seemed to her that to draw attention to his poverty was to humiliate him. Besides, she feared to reveal her own emotion.

One day Miss Robinson's own life caught her with a breathless upheaval. An honoured and intimate friend of her father's, successful, opulent, came forward with an avowal of esteem for her; deferentially desired her association with him in his second essay in matrimony! Mr. Shanner seemed to spring it on her with untempered abruptness; though the attentive courtesies that had preceded the crisis might have glimmered some little warning. But Mr. Shanner's footing in the house was as old-established as the rest of his appertainings; and Miss Robinson's spirit was ever at the nadir of diffidence. Men as a rule shunned her: women cared as little to talk to her. That anybody might ever wish to marry her had seemed impossible, inconceivable. Mr. Shanner had many pretensions to style, yet, to her spoiled eye, he seemed merely of clay indifferent.

She strung herself to the ordeal of refusing him, though her real strength knew no faltering. For he proved insistent; wooed her—soberly—decorously—as became the dignity of five decades completed; wooed her with reasons of urgency, and implications of sentiment. He was to depart on a mission to the New World; wished to bear her promise with him. He would treasure it; would think of the new light to shine in his household. But within her lay an unfailing inspiration, and her innermost soul stood like a tower impregnable; though she was all wounds and distress, and quivered with the hurt. Was not her heart with her Prince Charming? her one dream in life the privilege of helping him?

Mr. Shanner had to sail away disconsolate!

But, though Miss Robinson's mind was occupied day and night with this problem of Wyndham's salvation, she could arrive at no plausible solution. For how should she ever dare to give him a sign? She who would have yielded her life for him could only watch him drifting downwards with an agonised sense of her helplessness.

And he all the while unsuspecting of this obscure, loving historian of his existence; of the warm heart that beat for him in these evil days on which he had fallen!

II

For hours the rain had beaten against his windows, and at last, now that a lull had declared itself, Wyndham dragged himself to the door, and looked out into the gray afternoon. His eye took in the familiar vista, but, as it rested on the great bow-windowed house at the corner where the road branched into two, he turned away with a shudder. For years the sight of that house had irritated him: its ugly brick bulk had been symbolic of all Suburbia, of everything in life to which he was instinctively hostile as an artist and a gentleman.

But presently he laughed: it had struck him as comic that he should have preserved in its freshness his full youthful contempt for all this Philistine universe!—he, a half-starved devil of an artist, down in the mouth, with a solitary half-crown in his pocket, speculating with bitter humiliation whether his hard-worked sister had yet a little to spare for him, after all the life-blood which, leech-like, he had sucked out of her! Nay, more, he was conscious that his distaste for this surrounding wilderness of affluent homes, in the midst of which he had so long dwelt as an isolated superior intelligence, had grown more marked in direct proportion as he had become poorer and poorer.

The prosperous figure of the owner of the bow-windowed house rose before him. Immersed in his own existence, Wyndham had deigned to notice very few indeed of his neighbours. But old Mr. Robinson was one of the few, not only because of the regularity with which he passed the studio every day at six o'clock as he came home from business, but also because he invariably bore something in a plaited rush-bag that had a skewer thrust through it, suggesting visits to Leadenhall Market, and purchases of game or salmon for the good wife according to season. But Mr. Robinson's mild aspect, benevolent white beard, and gentle amble had never impressed Wyndham with much of a sense of human fellowship. He might concede that the old man was "a decent sort, no doubt, in his own way"; but they were creatures belonging to different planets.

Still amused at his own disdain, though the corners of his mouth were set a trifle grimly, Wyndham turned back into the studio with the idea of making himself presentable and going to see his sister—since it now seemed possible to get across town without the prospect of an absolute drenching. Happily his wardrobe had substantial resources: in the old days he had kept it well replenished, and his simple life of late here in the studio had made small demands on it. Thus he could still go out faultlessly clad and shod. Nobody need suspect his poverty, he flattered himself, if he ever chose to dip into his own world again. Only he did not choose; there was always so much questioning to face. "We've seen nothing of yours in the last two or three Academies—when are you going to give us another masterpiece?" "Still on the big picture? How is it getting along?" However genially thrown out, such usual interrogation annoyed him beyond measure. It was so long since anything had been "getting along." On all sides he was regarded as a doomed man, and suspected it: suspecting it, he was morbidly sensitive. His life was unnatural and not worth the living. Months and months had been wasted in apathy. Each day he dreamt of a new lease of energy and courage to begin on the morrow; but, after making his bed and clearing away his breakfast and purchasing his food for the day, he would find himself dejected and incapable of a single stroke.

And yet he could not wholly realise the change that had come over the scene. He rubbed his eyes sometimes, as if expecting to awake from an unhappy dream. Was not the flourish of early trumpets still in his ears? The dazzle of admiration still on his retina? The gush of extensive and important family connections still tickling his self-esteem? The sweeter approval of a superior art-clique still flattering his deeper vanity?

He had been born with a silver spoon; his childhood and youth had been ideally happy. From the playing-fields of Eton he had passed to the quadrangles of Oxford. A distinguished student of his college?—not in the ordinary grooves; yet favourably known as an intellect with enthusiasms. Phidias was more of an inspiration to him than Aristotle; Titian more actual than Todhunter. Ruskin, Pater, Turner, had stirred him; left his mind subdued to their colours. From boyhood had been his the swift skill with pencil that ran as easily to grace as to mockery. And, left early arbiter of his own existence, with gold enough for freedom, he had made for the one career that called to him.

Genius cannot prove itself at a stroke: it has its adventurings to make. Seldom it realises at the outset that it is adventuring in the dark, therein to grope as best it may to self-discovery. Even this first stage may be long deferred; yet, however sure of himself at last, the artist has still to tread the unending road with the great light of self-realisation ever in the distance. There are the years of strenuous search, of faithful labour; of bitterest failure on failure to bring the deep, mysterious impulses to bloom and fruition. But there is yet another, if independent, adventuring. The great light that crowns the artist's journey shines only in his own spirit. The world sees and knows nothing of it. He has none the less to find his way into that other light—the lurid, mocking limelight of the world's acceptance; to seek a place beside or beneath the charlatan. This is the bitterest stage of all— to stand shivering in marketplaces that are knee-deep with dung and offal; to be upholding precious things to the vision of swine. What wonder if in the course of so harsh a journeying, as he lives and breathes in his own universe of striving, his precise moral relation to things external grows dim, intangible; and, if money one day give out, he clutches at any crust for sustenance.

Wyndham began his journeyings. His advantages were many and obvious; his disadvantages subtle and unseen. There was the danger that facile talent and social prestige might bring him an early delusive success; a failure, rightly seen, however tricked out with glamour.

His beginnings, indeed, were pleasant: it was great fun throwing himself into this new queer Bohemian world of art. He worked hard as a student, the sheer interest of his labours lightening them astonishingly. And, after some preliminary swayings in varying directions, he at last "found himself," as he supposed; developing a dexterous imitative craft, and joining an advanced crowd with Whistler and Sargent for his deities.

Wherever he pursued his studies—in London, or Paris, or Italy—there he was remarkably popular. Everybody said: "Wyndham belongs to very good people. They're swells—tip-top!" And indeed he had obviously the stamp of being "the real thing," and even the elect of Bohemia were flattered and fascinated by personal association with him.

When ultimately he set up his studio here in Hampstead, he had his policy definitely before him. With the means and the leisure to aim at a high career, he would make no concessions to popularity or the market. He had chosen the locality deliberately. It was London, and within reach of the world; but not so near the world as to endanger his labours. The little tide of fashion that rolled up to his door was not a tribute to fame, but merely the fuss and interest of his non-Bohemian circle pleased for a time with the novelty of having a studio and a genius connected with them.

So in the early years he worked enthusiastically, and was able to win some footing in the galleries. But, in the eyes of his numerous family connections, he was seriously launched; especially when a couple of his pictures at last attracted buyers, and he moreover found himself earning guineas from the patronage of friendly editors whose humbler commissions he carried out in the same spirit of the dignified, ambitious worker.

Then the financial crash came, leaving brother and sister entirely dependent on their labours. Both met the crisis with commendable philosophy. Mary, who had long before taken up educational work as an amateur, was soon able to establish herself as a professional, and had taught ever since at a high school in Kensington; picturesquely settling herself in a tiny flat in an artisan's building, and living as a homely worker. The dignity and serene simplicity of her life had of late furnished the one ideal thing for Wyndham's contemplation.

Wyndham himself had stood up straight and felt very strong; had reassured his fussy, frightened folk that he could rely on his profession. He felt in himself an endless ardour for achievement, a confidence of triumph in the contest with men. Nay, more, he would gain his bread without descending from his high standpoint! The task was fully as difficult as he had anticipated; but at any rate he contrived to live for a couple of years. Then, somewhat to his surprise, the Academy began to return his pictures; and somehow, to his greater surprise, everything else went against him at the same time. He could not even get "illustrating" to do. Those who had acclaimed him before because he was a "swell" were now turning against him apparently for the same reason. Your aristocrats were never to be taken seriously; they were necessarily amateurs! It was all so unanimous, so settled and persistent, that it had almost the air of a conspiracy. Wyndham saw well enough that everybody had tired of his work, that he had had his hour and his vogue; his career lay like a squib that had blazed itself out. All bangs and fizzings, and then a blackened bit of casing, silent, extinguished! Yet he had the discernment to recognise that the dying-down had been really inevitable; that his present relative poverty had little or nothing to do with it. He had been dexterous on the surface, but the sameness of his note—without even the saving grace of convention—had destroyed him commercially.

Well, he believed in himself, and he refused to accept this erasure. On the contrary, he would launch out more daringly than ever. An end to facile imitation of other people's styles! He must express his own deeper self. The strict Whistlerian creed was much too narrow. Art was not merely a bare abstract aesthetics: humanity counted for something after all. Was woman's loveliness something really apart from woman herself? True that art meant beauty—in the largest sense, of course; but why should not humanity and beauty fuse together?

So, scraping together all he could command in the way of money, he set himself to work out a large dramatic idea, suggested by the sight of a May-day demonstration. The canvas was gigantic, and he strove to depict a mob of strikers straggling out of the Park after their great meeting, with elements of fashion caught in this *mêlée* of labour. The pictorial irony had greatly interested him, and he felt that this painting on the grand scale was being sincerely born out of his own emotion, that it would trumpet out a warning to the age.

The beginnings were full of promise, and he decided to stake everything on it.

But for so realistic a representation of Hyde Park Corner he needed to make a great many sketches on the spot. So, through the friendly offices of an amiable acquaintance, he obtained access to a convenient window in Grosvenor Place, and made free use of the privilege. The master of the house, a nobleman of the old school, who at first sight seemed stately as the portraits in his own dining-room, proved on acquaintance to be singularly bluff and genial, sometimes almost slap-dash. He had made Wyndham welcome and at his ease, bidding him come and go as he pleased, and "never to mind a bit about turning the room into a studio." And this charming nobleman had likewise a charming daughter, who sometimes came for a minute or two to talk to Wyndham and interest herself in the sketches. Lady Betty was a brilliant figure of a girl; had travelled a good deal and knew the world. She was sunny and friendly, yet naturally on a pedestal. She was clear-headed and capable; in the home supreme mistress. Wyndham was the subject of many graceful little attentions. If he came in the morning she saw that his glass of sherry and biscuit was never neglected; in the afternoon she presided over tea in the drawing-room and expected him to appear there.

Of course poor Wyndham never dared tell himself that he was in love with her. A girl like that must naturally be reserved for a great match, as regards both position and fortune. He could not think of her save as presiding over a plurality of palaces or voyaging in a magnificent yacht. Palaces and yachts were not the rewards of painters, so Wyndham kept his mind sternly fixed on the purpose for which he was there. Even so, the intervals between his appearances grew wider and wider. And when, after some couple of years of toil, discipline, searching, it had come home to him that in this terrible picture he had undertaken a task beyond his strength and experience, he found himself too shamefaced to "abuse" further the courtesy that had been extended to him. The consciousness, too, of his growing poverty was becoming acuter and acuter. Already he was drawing back into his shell, and, once he had ceased going to Grosvenor Place for the sake of his work, he had not the heart to continue his visits as an ordinary acquaintance. More than a year afterwards he read of Lady Betty's engagement in the papers—it was the very match one would naturally look for. Yet the news "shattered him to bits"—absurdly enough, he told himself, since he had known her at best irregularly, and not in the ordinary course of social intimacy. He was really half-surprised at receiving an invitation to the wedding. He could not prevail on himself to go; but, remembering she had once admired one of his Academy pictures, he sent her a photograph of it on a miniature silver easel as a trifling wedding gift. She wrote back a gracious acknowledgment, which had since remained one of his treasures.

Meanwhile he had been struggling on with the picture, determined to conquer.

But its difficulties and problems were endless. After all his toil it stood on his easel in a terribly unfinished condition, though he had stinted his own body to lavish his money on it. At last, gulping down the humiliation, he was forced to accept of Mary's little store of savings to pay his rent and his models. It was his first step of the kind, and he paid the full proverbial cost of it. But he had still the hope of returning the loan a thousandfold. Was not his success to redeem her life as well as his?

Certainly Mary believed in him and the picture, and looked forward to its scoring a great triumph. The whole heart and hope of the sister centred on that vast canvas. She sometimes ran across town to see it, though—poor child!—Hyde Park Corner always looked the same to her at every stage of its long creation. But the picture was Wyndham's backbone; it was his stock-in-trade before his world. He was more and more of a recluse now, refusing all invitations, discouraging his friends from coming to interrupt him—as he put it. Certainly Wyndham would rather have died than confess to failure after all the magnificent trumpeting. Even as it was, the time came soon enough when the big picture no longer served to protect his dignity. He imagined half-pitying glances and ironic smiles, and so eventually he found himself avoiding everybody without exception.

It was only on Lady Betty's wedding day, after more than three years of futile striving, that he had the resolution to remove the great canvas from the easel and stand it with its face to the wall.

He was tired now, but he must make an effort to emancipate himself from Mary's exchequer. Till then he could not hold his head up. So he painted some smaller and pleasanter pictures, but again he could do nothing with them. The Academy sent them back, the minor galleries sent them back, the Salon sent them back the following year. The dealers offered less than the cost of the frames. Meantime he had ceased to count up the five-pound notes Mary had starved herself to keep for him. He knew he was a coward and dared not. He had reached that stage of moral confusion which Nietzsche registers as in the natural history of the artist-type, and which may not be eyed too harshly from the point of vantage of ordered and organised existence in this outer universe. One idea stood clear beyond all others; grew into his mind; grew till it became his mind. He must cling to his studio, hold desperately to this atmosphere of paint and canvasses.

He was getting on in years now—past thirty-three. It was like the striking of a pitiless clock, this adding of swift year after year to his unsuccessful life. His hand began to fail him. The necessity of now doing his own house-work; of bothering with coals and cinders, preparing his makeshift monotonous meals, pouring oil into lamps, and boiling kettles, and washing plates and teacups, had begun by encroaching on his time and energies, and ended by absorbing them altogether. The care of ministering to his own primary needs had at last superseded art as his profession. Even so, the cobwebs multiplied and the dust lay thick.

Months now slipped by, he scarcely knew how; he was astonished to realise how time might elude one, how a colourless day might be trifled away without appearing to hold the possibility of even a morsel of achievement. Yet he still grasped the hope that something would "arrive"—an unexpected magazine commission, a request from a dealer. Ideas for a new start would teem in his head as he lay tossing on the narrow iron bed up in the gallery at the end of the studio. Why not do some pretty little things—to fetch ten guineas apiece, say—Cupids playing amid wreathed flowers with pale Doric structures in the background? If Mary could manage just another few pounds for him, he would have time to turn out a number of such decorative trifles. Such things were in constant demand and were a sure source of livelihood. He had stood out long enough, much longer indeed than he had had the right. He had consistently worked on a basis of high endeavour, but now he must withdraw his dignity and enter on the pot-boiler phase. Better that than this abominable leech-like existence. Continued misfortune had befogged his wits, and this last year certainly he had been half mad.

So be it! He must wake up now, and no longer lose his days in this stupid pottering about!

Every dog had his day, and his own turn would come in time. He was an artist. He felt it in his bones and blood. Art was his life and destiny. He had blundered in attempting too big a feat too early in his career, but he did not intend that that should wreck his existence. No, no! he would never throw up the sponge. He would rather die than admit defeat, with all those who knew him looking on at the game.

III

He dressed himself carefully to go to Mary's, trying hard not to think of the real purpose of his visit—he had merely informed her that he would be in the neighbourhood and would look in for a cup of tea. But, though it was distasteful to dwell on these unending demands on her earnings, he was anything but profligate in spending them. He had spun out her previous five-pound note so that it had kept him going for weeks and weeks, and he had grudged himself even a newspaper. In view of the newly-projected work to tickle the dealers, he regretted more than ever that he had not been able to pull himself together sooner: in these past precious weeks he might have knocked off half a dozen of such pretty-pretty things.

A series of omnibuses took him across London to Kensington Church, where he descended, presently turning out of the High Street. The "Buildings" where Mary resided were in a side alley at the back, and Wyndham made direct for them. He walked straight in through the large front door that stood perennially open, and followed the trail of muddy footmarks up the worn stone stairway. On the third landing he came to a stop, and pulled a bell half hidden in the obscurity of a corner. The door opened, and Mary stood before him. He could not help seeing how unnaturally slim she appeared to-day; how her simple stuff dress seemed to hang loosely on her.

"This is so good of you. I am so glad to see you, dear." Her earnest face brightened with a wistful yet pleasant smile.

He stooped and kissed her, then followed her into her tiny sitting-room. It was evidently the home of a gentlewoman. With the shelf or two of books, the escritoire, the few prints, and the little trinkets and photographs she valued, she had contrived to make a dainty little nest of it, and all these simple things gave the place a peculiar personal stamp. The table was laid for tea, and the kettle sang on the fire.

"You have had a dreary journey," she said, as she gave him a chair.

"No, the weather has been unexpectedly kind," he reassured her. "The sun peeped out just for one moment. I believe I was the only person in London that noticed it: the rest of the world were intent on other things. Have you been keeping well?"

"You forget I am just back from vacation."

"Of course—I had forgotten," he laughed. "How did you spend your time?" "I passed the first three weeks with Aunt Eleanor, as I told you I should. We were a big, merry party, and everybody made a great fuss of your little sister." Again that wistful smile. "They all spoiled and petted me shamefully."

"Ah, that was good for you."

"I am not so sure about that," she returned thoughtfully. "I am certainly not used to the sort of thing, and I really found it restful and refreshing to go on to old Lady Glynn, who had me to herself."

"So that's your idea of a holiday—taking care of paralytic, deaf old people whom everybody else shuns like the plague." He shook his finger at her. "And you call it restful and refreshing."

"Service is the greatest of all happiness," she answered gently. "Even as it is, I'm sadly afraid I'm a sham and a fraud. I'm not really a worker—in the same sense as others I know. They have no fashionable friends with big houses in the country."

She brewed the tea and gave him his cup.

"Do people inquire much about me?" he asked, as the uncomfortable thought recurred to him.

"Certainly not of me," she returned. "You neglect them, you refuse their invitations, they never hear a word from you, and naturally they suppose you wish to be quit of them all. And so, no doubt, they feel it the proper thing not to appear to wish to discuss you with your sister." There was a pause. Both seemed lost in thought for the moment. "And so you, poor Walter, have had no holiday at all!"

"Ah, well," he sighed. "I try to content myself with the thought that I'm saving it up. One of these days I daresay I shall go off to Rome or Venice, and recuperate from several points of view. I daresay a bit of luck will be coming my way presently, and I'm keen on getting back to Italy again. I've often planned it out. A month or so at Paris, a couple of months in the South of France, three at Rome, and three at Venice—with a look-in at Naples some time, of course."

"What a lovely holiday that would be!" He did not surprise her quick flash of longing. Both remained pensive.

"But tell me about everybody," he said at last. "You see I take more interest in them all than they suppose."

"That's natural enough. After all, Hertfordshire's your home."

He winced visibly, half sorry that he had set her mind in that direction. She, however, proceeded to draw for him various pictures, and he presently found himself listening with a deeper eagerness than he had foreseen. She brought him close again to his own world, uplifted him in his own eyes: he had almost the sensation of being restored to a sphere which it had been more painful to abandon than he had ever admitted. The minutes passed, bringing him a warm, happy sense of social comradeship with his sister. The little fire burned brightly, and the feeling of the well-ordered nest was fragrant and exquisite. He felt his bitterness softening under its influence; a deep peace seemed to surround him, filling the little haven, radiating from Mary's wistful face, from her gentle smile and voice. How thankful he was this terrible London yet held her sympathy!

"It is a great thing for me to have you to come to, Mary," he broke in on her suddenly. "It helps me tremendously."

"Poor Walter!" she breathed. Her eyes filled with tears.

For a moment both were too moved to speak again. But abruptly, as with a courage and firmness long since resolved upon, she looked straight at him.

"Why don't you give it up, darling? This art is ruining your life."

He did not seem surprised at this sudden turn of the conversation, though such a suggestion had never before fallen from her lips. He took her words as a cry of despair rather than an attempt at a stern reckoning.

"Why don't I give it up?" he echoed. "That's an easy question to ask. The answer is difficult. But I can't give it up. It is impossible."

"It is not so impossible as it seems."

"What can I turn to? I am fitted for nothing."

"Go to the Colonies. Labour on the soil—or work with hammer and saw."

"I am willing to labour, willing to face anything in life. But, Mary—the confession of failure—you don't see how deep, how mad the pride is in me."

"You have nothing to confess. The whole world knows you are a failure. They talk about it openly. They spare me as much as possible, but I can't shut my ears."

It was a staggering blow. "They despise me!" he breathed.

Her lips hesitated, clenched together, the corners convulsed with pain.

"They despise you!"

He found his defence. "Because I have not succeeded commercially." His voice was full of scorn. "It matters little that these gross Philistines misjudge me. They will yet regret it. I shall yet show them that I am not so self-deceived as they imagine. I am an artist—art was born in my blood, art is my whole existence. I shall stick to it till I fall dead. I ask you, Mary, to believe in me a little longer."

"Heaven knows I have never wavered in my belief a moment. But it is not my belief that can save you. You have made a brave attempt, but you have been defeated. I am only facing the simple facts. The present position seems to me a hopeless one to start from. You have no means behind you now, so what is there before you save to go on in the same miserable way as you have lived the last year or two? I see no possibility of anything but repetition of the same unhappy experience—the world is not going to step out of its way for your sake. And remember it has already made up its mind about you."

"Then I have lost your sympathy!" he exclaimed. He stared gloomily into the fire.

She saw now that the morbid sensibility of the man who had failed would never face clear, cold reason, however gently administered.

"No, dear; you have not lost my sympathy. Please don't think that," she pleaded. "Don't you see I want to be a real friend to you; don't you see that you are more to me than your art?"

"I must fight it out," he insisted. "To-morrow I am starting a fresh lot of things—to sell! I have always stood out for the big accomplishment, but now I offer my labour in the market. Pretty designs, prettily coloured—Cupids and pearly clouds and wreaths of flowers. The dealers will take them. You will see, Mary, I shall manage to pull through yet."

She shook her head incredulously. "Better to give it up altogether before it is too late."

"You can't mean it," he exclaimed. "You have stood by me so long that I can't believe you are going to turn against me."

"I repeat that I care for you more than for your art, and I cannot see you sacrificed. No, I have not turned against you. I have been against you all this long, unhappy time. To-day I am your friend for the first time. Listen, darling. When I got your letter yesterday, I knew that things were as bad as ever, that you were at your wits' ends again for money."

He maintained a shamefaced silence, not daring to make any pretence to the contrary. She looked straight at him as she continued: "I am sure you will be the last to think I have ever considered the few pounds I have been able to put aside for you—my heart's best affection has always gone out to you with them. But the whole of last night I kept awake, and prayed for strength to refuse you any more money."

He held his head down; he was too abased to speak.

"Strength has been granted me at last. You are dear to me, and I will not help to continue this unhappy state of affairs. Sell off your studio, try your fortune in the Colonies, and you will yet pull your life out of the mire."

He rose, and took up his hat. "I daresay you are right, Mary. But I am an artist. Art is my life. Outside that there is nothing for me. Don't think I am ungrateful for all you have done. Goodbye!"

"Goodbye, darling. Perhaps you will yet think it over."

He shook his head wearily and turned away, not seeing that she had held her lips to him. The next moment he was descending the muddy staircase, slipping and stumbling on the bare stone. He was conscious that Mary was standing in the doorway a moment, but he did not see the convulsive working of her face, nor know that as soon as he was out of sight she had thrown herself on her bed, heart-broken, her body shaken in a terrible burst of sobbing.

IV

In the High Street Wyndham waited impatiently for an omnibus to take him home again. Instinctively he turned for refuge to the bleak studio, from whose loneliness he had so often been impelled to escape. But it was his own corner, and all he had. He would not light his lamp; he would lie there in the gloom till his pain and self-abasement should have worn themselves out. Merciful sleep might come; perhaps—and the idea seemed sweet to him—the sleep of all sleeps.

So he possessed his spirit as best he could, while the vehicle lumbered along through the endless streets; shivering a little in the autumn dusk as now and then a gust of wind arose. The sky clouded heavily, and, when finally he descended, the rain was falling swiftly again.

At last he was at home! He thought of the studio now with affection, and quickened his pace feverishly. Then he became aware that a familiar figure, holding a familiar rush-bag with a skewer thrust through it, was trudging just ahead of him in the growing darkness. But he was not surprised at catching sight of Mr. Robinson, since it was the regular hour of the merchant's appearance after his homeward journey from the City. As usual, Mr. Robinson's house filled the centre of vision, looming vast at the cross-roads, and softened in the evening mist; and for the first time the figure plodding towards it under the dripping umbrella struck Wyndham as interesting and strangely human.

Steadily, steadily, Wyndham gained on his neighbour; then, acting on some vague instinct, slackened his step so as not to have to pass him to get to his own door. But just outside the studio Mr. Robinson slipped, swayed, then came to the ground heavily. Wyndham at once hurried forward, and helped him to his feet.

"You are not hurt, I hope?" he inquired.

"I think not," returned the old man. He leaned against the studio door, whilst Wyndham took the rush-bag from his clenched fingers, and gathered up the umbrella from the gutter into which it had rolled. Mr. Robinson surveyed his soiled garments ruefully, and shook his head sadly.

"It *is* beastly," assented Wyndham.

"It can't be helped," said the old man; "though mud like this on a new suit of clothes puts a hard strain on a man's philosophy." There was a good-natured gleam in his eye and a brave smile on his face. Wyndham found himself unexpectedly attracted, and was much concerned when Mr. Robinson tried to take a step or two, but was pulled up painfully.

"Pray, don't alarm yourself, sir," said Mr. Robinson, as Wyndham caught at his arm solicitously. "I am only a little bruised, and have had rather a wrench. I must just breathe for an instant."

"Won't you come into my studio, and rest for a moment or two?" suggested Wyndham. "I shall be delighted if you will."

He produced the key from his pocket, turned it in the lock, and threw open the door. Then he offered Mr. Robinson the support of his arm.

"It is very kind of you, sir," said the old man, as he linked his arm in Wyndham's. "My name is Robinson. I live just up the road. I daresay you may have noticed me: I have often noticed you."

"I am enchanted to make your acquaintance, though I regret the particular circumstances," said Wyndham, as they passed through the little ante-room into the dim interior.

"I cannot share your regret," returned Mr. Robinson, with a touch of suave conviction. "No, not even if the accident were more serious, since I have been afforded the pleasure of knowing you."

Wyndham was surprised at the sweetness and old-world courtesy revealed in the old man's personality. "You are very kind," he said with a smile. "I hope indeed I am worth so pretty a sentiment. But please take this arm-chair."

He pushed it forward, then set the rush-bag down on the table, hastily throwing a serviette over the litter of his last meal, which he had not had the energy to clear away, and which now brusquely offended his fastidiousness. But as Mr. Robinson, good careful soul, hesitated to soil the chair, Wyndham got a rag and wiped away the more lurid splashes from his garments. Then, whilst the old man rested, Wyndham trimmed his lamp; and presently the glooms vanished before a cosy illumination. Mr. Robinson at once began to scrutinise the studio on all sides with amusingly deep interest. The old Normandy presses, the model's throne, the giant easel, the well-worn Persian carpet, the hosts of canvasses of all sizes standing with their faces to the wall, the disorder and informality everywhere—all seemed to strike for him a note of youth and gaiety, to animate him with a sense of a new romantic universe. His face lighted with pleasure. He gazed up at the lofty roof and the oak cross-beams that supported it, and finally his eye rested on the little stairway and gallery at the far end, now almost lost in the shadows.

"Is your bedroom up there?" he hazarded, his naïve interest slipping out on his tongue.

"Yes," smiled Wyndham, as he tackled the dying fire. "It's the traditional arrangement."

"What a fascinating place you've got here! It's all a new world to me."

"Ah, it's a very ordinary sort of world—when once you've settled down to work."

"I have never known an artist before," pursued the old man, "and it is all fresh to me. I think that if I were a youngster again, I shouldn't at all dislike having a place like this, and making my home of it. Not that I mean I should ever have made anything of an artist," he added with a smile. "It's the spirit of the thing that appeals to me. You must be very happy here."

"Not necessarily," said Wyndham. He saw the old man's eyes fixed on him gravely. "You see, I'm not one of your successful artists, and the years have a way of passing on." He struggled with the fire, making the sticks blaze, then piled up the coals unsparingly. Mr. Robinson was the only person in the world to whom he had ever admitted failure, but somehow it did not seem to matter.

The old man gazed at him in frank astonishment. "Why, you are in the prime of early manhood!" he exclaimed. "Really it is most extraordinary to hear a splendid young man like you complain of the years passing!"

"I'm thirty-three," volunteered Wyndham. "And an unlucky devil of thirty-three, who has as much trouble in getting rid of his work as I, feels old enough in all conscience."

"But you artists have to expect these adverse experiences," said Mr. Robinson. "Art of course isn't like other things—it isn't exactly a business or profession in the ordinary sense, and so long as a man has the gift, he ought not to get disheartened. In our business world, of course, pounds, shillings and pence are everything, but in the world of art it wouldn't do to set up a standard of that kind."

Such sentiments on the part of a Philistine who came home every evening from the City at six o'clock struck Wyndham speechless.

"The struggle of genius is proverbial," Mr. Robinson added, before the younger man could find his tongue; "and genius wouldn't be genius without it."

"Ah, if I were only a genius!" said Wyndham, laughing.

"I am sure you are a genius," said the old man very gravely. "I have often thought what a clever face yours was. At home we have often spoken of you."

"I suppose then I must be a conspicuous figure in the road. I had no idea of it!" Wyndham laughed again.

"You've been in the neighbourhood some years now," said Mr. Robinson half apologetically; "and neighbours naturally notice one another. Besides, if I may say so, you are quite unlike the ordinary run of people. You are not the sort of man one sees in the City."

"You interest me. In what way do I differ from others?"

"You have the stamp of belonging to leisured people; it is plain from your walk and bearing, from your voice and manner of speech. And then there is something about your clothes even—I don't quite know what." The old man's eyes rested on him with a sort of approval and satisfaction.

Wyndham was amused. "You are really an original character," he exclaimed. "I like you."

Mr. Robinson smiled with gratification. "I more than return the compliment, I can assure you."

"But pray go on," said Wyndham. "I believe you're a wizard. I must get you to cast my horoscope."

Mr. Robinson raised his hands. "I don't think I could manage that," he laughed. "I am only a quiet observer of my fellow-men. In the present case it is very easy to see that yours is the face of a gentleman by birth. There is a certain composure in your whole style. Whatever you had to face, you would never have that appearance that men get in the City—of wearing themselves out."

"Better to wear out than to rust out," said Wyndham meditatively. "I rust out."

He was astonished at his own frankness. But there was a deep pleasure in being natural for once, in throwing off the cover of sham and pretence that had characterised his intercourse with his kind in the past. He did not even consider it was strange that the person he should be baring himself to so freely was one whose existence hitherto he had merely deigned to notice. But nothing could exceed Mr. Robinson's amazement at this last profession of his.

"Rust out!" The old man's eyes opened wide. "Why, you have done an immense amount of work!" He waved his hand significantly towards the army of canvasses ranged against the walls.

Wyndham affected to be impressed by the consideration. "Yes," he admitted; "I have used up a considerable amount of material in my time, I must admit." He had suddenly perceived that Mr. Robinson was largely discounting his ingenuous frankness, and was really taking his profession of failure, which, as it happened, he had thrown out in an offhand way, as rather affectation than literal truth.

"And no doubt will be using up still larger amounts in the future." The old man smiled and rose. "But I am taking up your time!"

"No, indeed," Wyndham assured him. "I hope you have quite recovered now."

"Oh, quite," returned Mr. Robinson. "I had altogether forgotten the little accident in the pleasure of our conversation."

There was a pause. "I am sorry there's no light," said Wyndham; "else I should show you some of my work—that is, if you cared to see it."

The old man looked eager. "Couldn't you make the lamp do?" he exclaimed. "I'm sure it would give me a very good idea of your pictures. But I am presuming on your kindness."

"Oh, no," protested Wyndham.

He began to move about the studio, conscious of a new energy. Somebody was here to appreciate him; somebody desired to see his work, was looking up to him in admiration! He felt strangely rejuvenated—it was as if he had taken a dose of some wonderful elixir. He selected half a dozen of the smaller pictures, and brought them forward. Then, as he wheeled the great easel into position, the whim took him to see how his huge "masterpiece" looked after all this long interval of time.

For, since he had stood it with its face to the wall on Lady Betty's wedding-day, he had never had the heart to glance at it again. Not merely failure and wasted years were associated with it, but it stirred memories of the hours he had spent at Grosvenor Place in the first freshness of his hopes, when he had worked with the passion of youth. Then, too, there was the silent drama that had played itself out in the depths of his own spirit. Looking back, it seemed to him that no man could ever have cherished a more hopeless love, or have encountered a more inevitable one. Nor had the lapse of time softened the bitterness of that strange romantic chapter. Lady Betty's figure and personality would remain with him as his ideal of woman for the rest of his life; and he clung to the memory of his hurt as typical of his whole fortune.

But though the thought of the picture to-night inevitably stirred up some of these old emotions, there was joined to them a sudden overwhelming curiosity. What would be his impression at the first glance? Would all its deficiencies and crudities stand out in relief, and make him turn away from it in sickness and loathing? Or would it strike him, however unfinished it might be, as having yet promise in it, as justifying some at least of the time—nay, even life-blood—he had consecrated to it?

"What a huge thing!" ejaculated Mr. Robinson, as Wyndham tilted it back from the wall.

"It *is* tremendous," smiled Wyndham. "I'm afraid I shall have to ask you to give me a hand with it."

Together they carried it to the easel, and Wyndham hoisted it to its old place. "I don't know whether we shall be able to make head or tail of it," he said; "but I'll do what I can with the lamp. As you see, it's a powerful one."

"Of course I don't profess to be a connoisseur of oil paintings," Mr. Robinson warned him. "But I know what I like, though I daresay you will think me extremely benighted."

"No, indeed," protested Wyndham; "I shall value your opinion highly." He worked away at the little wheel at the back of the easel as he inclined the canvas at the most favourable angle, whilst the old man watched the process fascinated.

The next moment Wyndham was holding the big lamp high in the air, and carefully illumining the surface of the picture. For a moment everything before his eyes was blurred, and he could see nothing at all; but he stood his ground firmly, and gripped the lamp heroically. And before the mist could clear he heard Mr. Robinson's voice rise in admiration.

"Wonderful!" exclaimed the old man, his tone vibrating with an immense conviction; and at that moment Wyndham received the picture full on his vision and felt at once he had there a basis that could be worked up into a splendid achievement.

"The crowd of strikers with their banner is the most life-like thing I've ever seen. Wonderful!" Mr. Robinson gazed and gazed, his interest overflowing into a running comment. "It's Hyde Park Corner! Why, of course—there's the Duke of Wellington's house, and there's Lord Rothschild's. Marvellous! What a variety of faces and characters! And the old fellow there in the corner— what powerful features full of despair! And the old woman with the red shawl —she hasn't had a morsel of food, poor creature, for twenty-four hours, I'll wager. Why don't you leave her alone, you old ruffian of a policeman! And then that fashionable lady in her brougham with her over-fed poodle—what contempt on her face for all these artizans! How real everything is—the perspective is grand! Why, you could take a walk out there in the distance! Marvellous! It doesn't need an art education to see that's a work of genius."

Wyndham stood listening in elation, though, in his own perception of the work just now, he felt as aloof from it as if it had sprung from another's labours. His brain seemed emancipated from the tangle of its old problems and all his old flounderings. And as Mr. Robinson continued his admiring ejaculations, Wyndham put in now and again a word of explanation, drawing attention to a point here and there, though this was at first rather by way of soliloquy than conversation. But, presently, as he moved the lamp to and fro, up and down, he warmed to the occasion; even enlarging on his pet ideas, and pointing out where he had failed to realise his own scheme and formula. Mr. Robinson listened, wholly absorbed and fascinated by these new horizons that opened before him. His respect and worship for art was contagious: Wyndham began to worship it more himself.

And the younger man grew eloquent, expatiated on the old art and the new, on academies and masters, on realism and symbolism, on plein air and sunlight, on colour and technique. And as he spoke, he was enchanted with his own voice. It was splendid to feel himself speaking again after all this long suppression—he was realising the strength and infallibility of his own artistic convictions. Never before had he felt so sure of his conceptions; his former humility had only led to confusion and hesitation. In future, his own mind should dominate—he would not be blown about by all these conflicting schools and critics.

He was conscious of standing more vigorously upright; and, as he enlarged on the picture, he seemed to get a new and sure hold of it, seeing more and more the potentiality of a great and powerful structure that no Academy could dare refuse to recognise. He saw now that his long interval of hibernation had not been unfruitful. And it had made a necessary sharp division between the two parts of his life—the first, uncertain, stumbling, unsuccessful; the second, confident, mature, triumphant.

The picture before him was transformed. Problems that had baffled him seemed to solve themselves in a flash. Effects he had vainly sought through maddening months stood at once revealed, flowing naturally out of what he had already set down. His hand longed to be wielding the brush again.

"But if I may make the remark," interposed Mr. Robinson at length; "it seems matter for surprise that a gentleman like you should be attracted to the choice of such a subject. I should hardly suppose that you have ever come into any real contact with labour, and workmen on strike would therefore scarcely come within the sphere of your sympathy."

"The artist is of universal sympathy," said Wyndham gravely, and himself believed it. At that moment he felt his endless sympathy spreading itself out, embracing all creation. "And then it was not only the humanity of the scene that touched me, and inspired me to attempt to put it down finely and greatly; there was also the pure art part as it appealed to the trained vision—the splendid difficulties to be vanquished, the opportunities for draughtsmanship and subtle colour, the sense of far-stretching space to be produced from only a narrow gamut of light and shade."

"Marvellous!" echoed Mr. Robinson again.

"But if I may make the remark in my turn," said Wyndham, "your sympathy with labour surprises me equally."

"Why so?" asked Mr. Robinson.

"The natural antagonism between capital and labour!" smiled Wyndham.

"Oh, I started as a poor boy—right at the foot of the ladder," explained Mr. Robinson. "My father was a carpenter. Wages were low in those days, and prices of all necessaries were high. I remember in my childhood we had a pretty hard time of it. In my own firm we share the profits with all the employees. So you see I'm rather partial to labour so long as it's decent and reasonable. When I think of my own struggles, I like to see every man get fair opportunities. When a man has no particular talent—such as myself, for instance—it is ever so much the harder to go through discouragements. But, at the worst of times, it must be a great thing for a gifted man like yourself to be conscious of his own powers."

"So you set up to have no particular talent!" explained Wyndham. "You amuse me. Haven't you made your fortune unaided? I confess that that seems to me the most difficult thing in the world—immensely cleverer than anything in the way of art or painting."

Mr. Robinson laughed. "Now you're making fun of me."

"I was never more serious in my life," insisted Wyndham, now wheeling forward a smaller easel, in order to display the pictures he had at first selected. "I consider it frightfully clever to make money."

"My dear sir, fools often make money," Mr. Robinson assured him.

Wyndham shook his head incredulously. "Do you care much about this landscape?" he asked.

"Very much indeed. It is so green and fresh and airy, and those are grand old trees."

"It's our old home in Hertfordshire. I lost the property and a modest fortune through a rascally set of lawyers."

Mr. Robinson's face expressed deep concern. "Yes, I remember the affair well," he said. "I remember reading it over the breakfast-table to my wife and daughter. We saw your name among the creditors. It was a bad business."

"They had managed all our family concerns for thirty years."

Wyndham was now wound up to enter into more personal matters than he had so far touched upon. As before, he was perfectly frank, recounting in the intimacy of the moment all the details of this financial catastrophe. He spoke freely of his relations in the country, and of his sister Mary, and the independent way in which she was earning her bread; passing from canvas to canvas the while, and breaking off frequently to discuss the paintings.

At last they had gone through all the selection, but the unfailing appreciation of his visitor was so pleasant to the artist that he could not help bringing forward two or three more, and then finally another. And still yet another after!—like the preacher's "one word more."

"I have passed a very happy time here with you," the old man declared, as Wyndham restored the lamp to its usual place on the table. "You see I was right; the occasion was well worth the accident that brought it about."

"Happily you were not really hurt. So all's well that ends well."

The old man took hold of his rush-bag. "I mustn't forget my middle of salmon," he smiled. "I generally fetch something home for my wife—some game or fish fresh from the market."

"You make me wish *I* had a husband in the City," sighed Wyndham.

Mr. Robinson laughed. "Well, I suppose I must make up my mind to be off, else my wife and daughter will be wondering what has become of me."

Wyndham came forward hurriedly. "I hope I have not been keeping you," he murmured. Somehow he did not like being left alone now. The old man's coming had saved him for the time being from the clutch of a terrible despair, and he saw it waiting to descend swiftly on him. The half-hour of self-respect would vanish like an illusion.

But Mr. Robinson's voice was breaking in on his mood again.

"Would it be presuming too much on our slight acquaintance if I suggested ——" The old man hesitated with an evident shyness that was very winning.

"Pray suggest anything you like," said Wyndham.

Thus encouraged, Mr. Robinson launched out boldly. "Would you come home and dine with us—quite without ceremony. We're the simplest of people, but we shall offer you the heartiest of welcomes."

"That is very kind of you," said Wyndham. "I should not be deranging your household?"

"I am sure my wife and daughter will be as delighted to see you as I am. Will you not come home with me now—in a simple, friendly way?"

"Since I am to meet ladies," smiled Wyndham, "I should like to make myself presentable. I have just been across town, and in this filthy, murky atmosphere one gets to feel so utterly unclean."

"Oh, yes; am I not in the same plight myself?" smiled Mr. Robinson.

Wyndham escorted him to the door, and the old man again thanked him for the pleasure the visit had afforded him.

"We dine at half-past seven," was his parting reminder, and Wyndham, promising faithfully to be punctual, closed the door after him.

V

But his visitor had no sooner departed than Wyndham experienced a sharp revulsion of feeling. How stupid to have accepted this invitation! His isolation in this suburban wilderness had always afforded him a certain satisfaction— he had consistently maintained his magnificent want of interest in all this Philistine population. His studio was his castle, and if he chose to starve therein it was at least a mitigation of his misery to be able to do so without the sense of others' eyes prying at him. And now he had surrendered his privacy. The indiscretion was really inexplicable! And he had let his tongue run on so recklessly and confidentially! He might even have drawn back at the very last —alleged an engagement, and cut short the acquaintanceship there and then. Perhaps it was not yet too late!

In his annoyance he started pacing the length of the studio. But the great canvas, still glistening there on the easel, suddenly claimed his attention again, and brought him to a standstill. Impulsively he caught up the lamp, and once more directed its light on to the surface. The picture took deep hold of him, and he stood absorbed in it. And somehow Mr. Robinson's wondering voice began to sound its praises. "Marvellous!" the old man seemed to be saying. "It doesn't need an art education to see that's a work of genius." And as he recalled each stroke of admiration, he nodded his head in agreement.

Was not the old man's appreciation of good augury? Surely it foreshadowed a popular Academy success. Whatever one's personal art ideals, it did not detract from their worth if one could carry them out and please the crowd at the same time—incidentally, of course—without deliberate intention. Did not Molière first try his comedies on his housekeeper? Mr. Robinson's tastes were the tastes of the great public—nay, of even the better classes that went to the galleries. Like him, they dwelt entirely on the illustrative aspect of painting, and were altogether swayed by the humanity of a picture, by its dramatic or anecdotal interest. No wonder some of his fellow-craftsmen had been driven to the opposite extreme, and tried to rule out humanity altogether. But the human side of art need not be necessarily on a low plane, or descend to mere anecdote. In his hands art should be the vehicle of real intellect and emotion.

If only he were not forced to do those idiotic trifles! After holding out so long, to capitulate absolutely for want of bread! No, he would not dine with Mr. Robinson—he would starve rather!

"Better to starve than stoop to inferiors!" he exclaimed, as he set down the lamp again. How little, indeed, he had eaten all that day! And with the thought a distressing weakness came over him. There was a humming at his temples: the studio disappeared in a mist, then reappeared oscillating. He was constrained to steady himself by clutching at the table.

In a minute or two the vertigo passed off, leaving him with a dull craving for food and drink. He might make some sort of a meal from such poor provender as his larder afforded—a portion of a loaf, the remainder of a tin of sardines, a hunk of cheese; but somehow the prospect was singularly uninviting. He might, indeed, add variety to the store by laying out his last shilling in the streets adjoining, but the shilling was too precious, and anyway he had not the energy to go shopping. There swam up before him the picture of a well-lighted, comfortable dining-room with a heavily laden table, and of a middle of salmon, piping hot, that was being served with a dainty white sauce. And then there were hosts of bottles on a mahogany sideboard: fat, gold-tipped bottles; tall, long-necked bottles; fantastic twisted bottles. Good well-cooked food was nourishing him, a delicate wine was moistening his feverish palate, touching his whole dull self to a lighter mood.

He had accepted the invitation. The Robinsons were expecting him, would be troubled and put out if he did not arrive. He carried the lamp up to the gallery, and began his preparations. And then the whim took him to change his clothes again. Not that he supposed the Robinsons affected to be fashionable of an evening, but the pride of the half-starved man rose in irrational self-assertion.

So he dressed carefully, tying his bow to perfection, and arranging the set of his waistcoat fastidiously. It was so long since he had put on evening clothes, and as he saw himself in the glass, well set up, and bearing himself exquisitely, the fact of his poverty seemed absurd and incredible. His face, too, seemed to have recovered some of its olden confidence as he scanned it critically. True the cheeks were a trifle thin and shrunken, but the lines of dejection and sadness had lightened at the new stirring within him.

Then for the first time in all these years he made his way up the road to the ugly house at the corner that had stamped itself upon him as the symbol of all Suburbia, as the stronghold of a type of life that Bohemia mocked at and Belgravia waved aside as impossible.

If he had not yet entirely overcome his distaste, it was at least mitigated by a splendid sense of condescension.

VI

A handsome Phyllis, in cap and apron, opened the door, and Wyndham stepped into a broad corridor, carpeted in red, and hung with popular engravings that he had seen in the windows of all the carvers and gilders in London. Next, he was ushered under a crimson door-hanging into a resplendent drawing-room, lighted by a dazzling crystal chandelier, and sensuously warmed by a great red-hot fire. There was nobody to receive him yet, and he was left to amuse himself with the show-books on the tables— padded photograph albums full of old-fashioned naïve people posing against rococo backgrounds, collections of views of the Valley of the Thames and of the Lake District, and richly bound volumes of Tennyson and Sir Walter Scott.

The interest of these treasures was soon exhausted, and Wyndham, sinking into a remarkably soft arm-chair, impatiently beat with his foot at a cluster of roses on the brand-new "Aubusson" carpet. The room was almost triangular, a large bow window commanding the vista of the main road, and pairs of other windows, straight and tall, overlooking the streets that branched on either hand. And all these windows were elaborately draped in a would-be Renaissance style, with many loops and festoons, and with big gilt cornices above. And between each pair of them stood a gilded consol table surmounted by a mirror that reached to the ceiling. Oval mirrors with lighted candles in sconces glittered from several points of vantage, and crimson couches and the immense piano completed the tale of splendours.

At length the door opened softly, and Mr. Robinson entered. Wyndham rose, not displeased to observe that his host was likewise in evening clothes; as he had been already regretting the self-assertion to which he had yielded.

"Ah, you are in good time," said the old man, coming forward in his quiet, gentle way, and shaking hands again. "I am sorry to say that my wife and daughter are not down yet."

His tone was apologetic, and Wyndham smiled, readily understanding that the announcement of a guest to arrive had scared the ladies to a more elaborate toilette than usual.

"They were enchanted when I told them you were coming," Mr. Robinson continued. "As for commiseration over my fall—not a word!"

The two men had conversed for some few minutes before the hostess and her daughter came sweeping into the room; and, as he had half expected,

Wyndham found he knew them more or less vaguely by sight. Mrs. Robinson was a tall dame, fully sixty, with gray hair, and a most amiable expression; stately, even handsome, in her black silk dress with its tasteful lace at the throat and wrists. The daughter who followed rather shyly behind her gave Wyndham the impression that he was beholding the most simple, homely person he had ever met; and this despite the complexity of her costume, which seemed to be built up almost entirely of old lace that lay over itself in thick folds and rich creamy masses. Timidity of temperament and modesty to the verge of self-distrust were at once suggested by the almost awkward constraint of her bearing and the quiet, half-averted glance of her dark eyes. He could see that she hardly dared look at him. He gallantly supposed that she was a year or two younger than himself, and as he met her desperately friendly smile (intended for him but hardly bestowed in his direction) with his choicest bow, he received a further impression that was distinctly more favourable than the first of unrelieved plainness. For, once his eye had taken in her features, the artist in him was ready to do justice to her throat and arms, which were really good: and her dark hair, her greatest glory, lay in a superb coil, which, with a surprising touch of coquetry, was set off by a velvet band and some lilies of the valley. It was curious that the figure of Lady Betty should swim up before him just then, as if to emphasise his real ideal of woman's beauty, and to make him feel once for all how impossible it was ever to step down from that standard. But he could not help smiling covertly at the thought that the family were making such a serious business of so casual an invitation—these toilettes were really so very much more elaborate than anything he might conceivably have looked for; though at any rate it reassured his pride in the fullest degree—evidently, his frank admissions to Mr. Robinson notwithstanding, they were not taking him as a poor devil of an artist, but were looking up to him with a perfect appreciation of the respect that was his due.

Wyndham's presentation to the ladies over, there followed an instant of general embarrassment. Mrs. Robinson smiled again, and quickly tried to make conversation.

"How pleasant to become acquainted at last, after being neighbours so many years!" she murmured. "And so unexpectedly, too."

"When the unexpected does happen," said Wyndham, "it generally is delightful. I suppose that's because most of us in this hard life get into the habit of expecting only the opposite sort of thing."

Miss Robinson laughed shyly, whilst her mother seemed somewhat puzzled.

"They say that the unexpected always happens," ventured the younger woman tremulously. "I'm sure the proverb must be wrong, because nice things happen so seldom." Her voice was soft, vibrating with gracious amiability.

"I disagree with Mr. Wyndham," said her father. "I was not at all expecting to slip down. When the unexpected happened, I am bound to say I did not find it delightful."

They all laughed; and then Mrs. Robinson resumed the interrupted tenour of her discreet, agreeable way. She herself had often thought how pleasant it would be to know him; but in London one could live for ever so many years and yet know absolutely nothing of one's next-door neighbour. In the country, of course, things were different: there etiquette was more human, and people called of their own accord. Was Mr. Wyndham exhibiting anything just now? They had seen pictures of his in the Academy in past years, and were great admirers of his. Wyndham was by now too faint and exhausted to do more than hold his own in a smiling, conventional way: the splendours of the room, too, dazzled him to the verge of confusion. He was thankful when Phyllis appeared with the announcement that dinner was served; and Mr. Robinson, giving his arm to his daughter, led the way across the hall, under another crimson door-hanging, and into a long dining-room, wherein was set out a great table with flowers and fruit and silver. The covers were laid at one end, which gave the dinner an air of informality and family intimacy.

A glass of sherry at the start revived Wyndham considerably, and soon he fell to conversing at his ease. Presently he found he was somehow taking the lead, and their evident respect and admiration for his lightest word made him clearly perceive that he was an important and brilliant figure for them. Such grains of resentment as he still cherished at having entered on the acquaintanceship were dying away. Meanwhile the seductive prevision of material joys that had risen before him at the studio at that moment of physical weakness was being literally realised, almost comically so. There on the immense mahogany sideboard stood bottles and decanters galore, and now up came the middle of salmon with a piquant sauce accompanying it! God! how delicious it tasted, after all these months of bread and cheese! Wine gave him inspiration, and food the strength to live up to the rôle they were allotting to him. He was good-looking and knew it; his voice, his bearing, his choice of words, were alike distinguished; his experiences were of worlds that were to them far-seeming and romantic. He was the sort of hero they had read about in novels—a handsome guardsman nonchalantly looking in at a Park Lane dance at midnight, or a brilliant attaché to an embassy in touch with wonderful horizons.

Meanwhile the supply of dainty food continued; a leg of lamb, spinach, fat, luscious asparagus, a melon from a Southern clime, a chicken, and the juiciest of French lettuces. The hock was of the most delicate, the champagne subtle and sparkling. Even so he felt himself sparkling in the eyes of the others. He was the lion to whom all this homage was his rightful due, holding them fascinated with his wide knowledge of men and cities, of social life in European capitals. He drew upon his wanderings in by-ways known only of artists; fascinated them with sketches of the art life of Rome and Paris. Reminiscences bubbled up of his student days, and with them were mingled deft touches of Eton and Oxford, and charming cameos of county life; this last developing insensibly into discussions of Anglo-Saxon character, its comparison with the Latin, relative estimations of intelligence, industry, ambition. Mr. Robinson here had many shrewd observations to offer, for they had now wandered into the domain of affairs. Wyndham was genuinely interested in his host's experiences, in his accounts of unusual men of business from strange, even barbarous parts of the world, with whom he had had personal relations. They even touched upon financial operations; and Wyndham felt perfectly at ease amid complications in which millions were bandied about like tennis-balls, and the credit of banks and States was pawned as simply and swiftly as he might pawn his own watch. At last, over the dessert, there was a perceptible slackening. Wyndham, who so far had taken care not to let his eye rest on the many heavy-framed "oil paintings" that hung on the walls, for fear some discussion of them might thence arise, was now incautious enough to fix his gaze markedly on some sheep pasturing just opposite him. But Mr. Robinson seemed to welcome the opportunity thus afforded.

"Oh, of course I know you won't find any of *those* things worth glancing at," he threw out with a laugh; and the others chimed in, highly amused at the thought of the impression "the things" must be making on their guest.

"Oh, some aren't at all half bad," conceded Wyndham politely, his eye now promenading freely. "The girl with the mandoline is laid in with rather a charming touch, and the fruit-and-flower piece is really decorative."

"We always considered those two the best," declared Mr. Robinson. "I bought them at an auction in the City, many years ago now—more, in fact, than I care to remember."

Wyndham still affected to be examining the collection.

"Now, of course," resumed Mr. Robinson, "that Highland scene is the merest pot-boiler—a stream in the middle, a mountain on one side, and a cow on the other. I've seen hundreds of them for sale. But it's not likely I shall ever be taken in again that way, especially after examining the work I saw at your studio, Mr. Wyndham."

Wyndham inclined his head smilingly, and Mr. Robinson duly proceeded to describe to the others the great masterpiece which that afternoon he had had the privilege of inspecting. His memory of the details proved to be extraordinarily minute, and his face glowed all over again with the wonder and enthusiasm he had displayed at the studio. "The figures, the faces," he wound up, "were simply marvellous. I can't give you the faintest idea of how magnificent it all is. I could spend hours looking at it."

Wyndham could do no less than suggest that the ladies should come and see the picture for themselves, though just then a whiff of unpleasant thoughts urged on him again the imprudence of such further social developments.

"We shall be only too delighted; it will be a great pleasure," exclaimed Mrs. Robinson, and Miss Robinson's eyes shone with unmistakable excitement.

"We must really take down that Highland scene, my dear," proceeded Mrs. Robinson, addressing her husband. "It is altogether too bad. We ought to have something better in its place."

It passed through Wyndham's mind that one of his projected panels would do excellently, but of course it was far too below the dignity of the brilliant lion to appear to snatch at the opportunity of turning a few honest guineas through the grace of his humble entertainers.

"Let us have the Highland scene down by all means," said Mr. Robinson. "And I've an idea! If we can induce Mr. Wyndham to paint our Alice's portrait, why, then we should have something first-rate to hang in its place."

Miss Robinson turned fiery red; the quick glance she flashed at her father was the more conspicuous. "How splendid!" she exclaimed breathlessly. Her bosom heaved. Wyndham was almost painfully aware of the thumping of her heart.

But he himself was caught quite unprepared. True that the unexpected had happened again, but that very quality of the event was in this instance disconcerting. No doubt they observed his slight hesitation.

"Of course it would be a great privilege for us," interposed Mrs. Robinson; "but it seems to me we are counting without Mr. Wyndham's authority."

Wyndham inclined his head graciously with a smile; swiftly master of the situation again, and improving the occasion with a compliment.

"Oh! I shall be most delighted." He gave his proposed subject the professional glance that the occasion authorised. "Miss Robinson will afford me the opportunity of a most distinguished piece of portraiture."

Miss Robinson gazed at her plate, nervously peeling a banana. She had not spoken much during the dinner, but she had hung on Wyndham's words with a naïve, unconscious admiration, which, from a prettier and more brilliant woman, he would scarcely have passed with so little a sense of appreciation.

"Thank you for the compliment, Mr. Wyndham," she said simply. "I am afraid the distinction will be due more to your work than to your sitter."

"No, indeed, Miss Robinson," he protested, with a suave gravity that made his polished assurance the more impressive and charming. "I did not intend any compliment—I spoke only as the artist." He was rather surprised that a woman should display so little vanity. And, in a subtle way, it did not enhance his estimation of her.

Miss Robinson's banana occupied her more earnestly than ever; but her mother came to the rescue by raising the important question of costume. Wyndham, after further professional consideration of his client, preferred to paint Miss Robinson as he saw her now. And with a ready sense of detail he saw, too, that certain rings she wore, though he had not observed them closely at first, would make excellent spots in a scheme of decoration. These rings were unusually chosen, and were more artistic than extravagant. The one on her right hand was a small, subtle cat's-eye surrounded by fine pearls. On her left hand were an aquamarine, and a scarab that shone like the patina of an ancient bronze. Almost without a pause he dashed at once at a scheme, which he elucidated there and then, much to their overwhelming. He would pose her on an Empire chair. In a blue and white Oriental vase on a high stand at the side should be arranged three tall arum lilies amid some vivid carnation blossoms. Why, the Nankin bowl on the mantelpiece was the very thing! The background of the picture should be vague and of an olive-grey tone, laid in with free brushwork, against which the masses of creamy lace would show deliciously decorative. The great surmounting coil of hair would give character to the whole scheme, and the lilies of the valley in the velvet band afford a final contrast of lightness and graciousness against the intense note of the coiffure.

The parents were radiant with pleasure, though poor Miss Robinson looked more and more scared each instant. In her trepidation she could only echo stammeringly the elder people's wonder at his great skill and cleverness. The scheme unfolded itself before them richly beautiful—not one of your dull black portraits, but a canvas glowing with exquisite light and colour.

"There, Alice, you ought to be proud of yourself," said her father, rallying her good-naturedly as a parting shot, when the women rose to retire; and Wyndham attended their exit under the crimson hanging with his most engaging air.

Left alone, the men drew their chairs to the fire, and Mr. Robinson brought forward boxes of fragrant-smelling cigars, large and rotund. The atmosphere of comfort enveloped Wyndham soothingly: the sense of unlimited abundance seemed a miracle after his long privation. Fortunately he had not been tempted to have his glass filled too often: he had appreciated all these good and luscious things with commendable moderation, and had been stimulated to brilliancy without losing cool command of himself. He lighted his cigar at the little silver smoker's lamp that just then came in with the coffee, and, as he puffed, a splendid warm feeling of well-being took possession of him. He helped himself to cream and sugar with the masterful calm and something of the gesture of a stage hero.

Presently Mr. Robinson raised the subject of Wyndham's fee for the portrait, approaching the point apologetically.

"Of course, we could hardly discuss this side of the matter before my wife and daughter," said the old man. "But I must insist on your accepting a fair remuneration for the work—shall we say two hundred guineas?"

"To be frank," said Wyndham, "if you had left it to me, I should hardly have mentioned so large a sum."

"Naturally a gentleman of your disposition would think more of the artistic pleasure of the work than of the money it brought. Still, in this life money has to be considered. In all things, sublime or humble, the labourer is worthy of his hire. I do not for a moment suggest that the sum I have named in any way expresses our appreciation of the work, even in anticipation, and certainly not in any way our sense of the privilege and honour you are bestowing upon us."

"I shall endeavour to merit your kind words," said Wyndham, not to be outdone in polished courtesy, though he conceded that, by force of simple sincerity and good feeling, Mr. Robinson seemed a past master in the delicate art. "At any rate," he pursued, "the work is developing in my mind. The more I dwell upon it, the better and better I like the scheme, and I shall work at it enthusiastically from start to finish."

It being thus assumed that two hundred guineas were to be the artist's reward, Mr. Robinson seemed by no means loth to wander from a point which he had approached with great hesitation and an immense sense of its difficult delicacy. As yet Wyndham did not measure the radical change in his personal situation; nor did he display any undue elation. But his cool demeanour was no mere pose. Indeed, he was surprised himself at the ease with which he was accepting the transaction, as if it were commonplace in his experience. But he merely supposed that he was meeting good fortune with the natural dignity of the artist—to whom commissions are due as a matter of right, however long they may be deferred.

They did not linger in the dining-room, but joined the ladies after their first cigar; though not before Mr. Robinson had sedulously inquired as to his liking for the particular brand, which, he assured Wyndham, was not readily obtainable in London, and had made, him promise to take a box away with him.

In the drawing-room Miss Robinson played to them, at first tremulously, but gaining confidence with the experience. She displayed a degree of trained taste and a certain individual choice, favouring the tenderer and gentler works of Mendelssohn and Mozart. She sang also one or two of Heine's love songs in the German with a touch of passion and regret, whilst Wyndham accompanied her; and he himself wound up the evening in more jovial mood with a rousing student's song from his old Munich days.

Their parting with him had almost a touch of affection; and the final understanding was that he was to plan out the arrangements for the sittings, and to communicate with them in the morning.

He was forgetting his box of cigars at the end, but Mr. Robinson carefully caught it up from the hall table, and brought it after him just as the servant was opening the door.

VII

The next morning early Wyndham jumped out of bed with a bewildered sense of some change in his life, and it was an instant or two before his faculties cleared and he remembered his adventure of the previous evening. His next thought was one of pleasure that he had at last carried out his resolution of rising early. The autumn had developed with unusual severity, but the morning was intensely clear, and the studio full of a strong light. He pushed aside the hanging, and looked down from the gallery on the familiar scene below. Ordinarily, on rising, the sight had filled him with disgust and apathy, but now a freshness and vigour pervaded him, a new imperious desire, not merely in his mind but in all his limbs and muscles, to enter again on the contest with men. As his thought ran back through the past intolerable year or two, his inaction and sloth seemed almost incredible. He saw himself rising at midday, suffering moral tortures before the work he was powerless to begin, letting the barren hours drift away into the deep, then regretting them passionately. Was it not all a nightmare from which he had been curiously released?

He dressed, and, whilst his little kettle was boiling, took careful stock of his professional materials. Colours, brushes, varnishes—all needed renewing; there seemed nothing but impracticable odds and ends, mere bits of wreckage from his disastrous life's venture. Then, too, the filth and disorder all around him struck him brusquely, stung him to annoyance. On every surface where dust might accumulate it lay in serene possession. Wherever spiders could spin, there the webs hung thick, amazing and complicated citadels, prodigious masses and networks.

He felt he could not endure it a day longer. There must be a thorough physical cleansing at once. And he must return to the luxury of a daily bed-maker. This preoccupation with household things took off the keenest edge of one's first energy and enthusiasm; he must reserve himself jealously for his high calling.

As he sipped his coffee he mused over the little financial difficulties that immediately beset him. Now that at last he had a valid ground for appealing to Mary, he felt reluctant; anxious to bring her only the sense of his success without alloy. He might explain the situation to Mr. Robinson, and ask for money in advance; but that seemed as impolitic as it was repugnant in this new rapture of fine upstanding dignity. Payment of the quarter's rent that was already due could be easily deferred—for the bare humiliation of making the request. But he needed something for equipment, and must face the sacrifice of some of the older pictures to which he had clung so long, accepting any sum in exchange, if only shillings.

He still felt no disposition to invest the accident that had turned the tide for him with any touch of superstition or romance. He regarded the whole matter in the same dry light as at his first acceptance of it the evening before. He had sat waiting for clients, and at last they had turned up. But he did not at all dislike the Robinsons: they were very much better than the great run of their class—they had evidently ideals, and aspired to a higher degree of refinement than they as yet possessed, or, perhaps, were capable of possessing. They were neither smug nor self-satisfied, and, in giving him this work, they had avoided indulging in any semblance of bourgeois patronage, whereas other people of their class, even if well meaning, might easily have been gross and intolerable.

He had studied his sitter pretty closely. The profile, as is not unfrequently the case with "plain" women, had a curious individual interest. He felt it offered scope for "construction," and he could import subtly into the drawing a certain distinguished sentiment that was not really in the original, though somehow it might easily have been there, and, in moments of enthusiasm on the part of the observer, might even be conceived to be there. Yes, the profile was undoubtedly the thing: that way, too, the great coil of hair could be handled the more effectively. Indeed, it seemed to him that, taking into consideration her dark eye with its soft lashes, and the long shapely arms, and the exquisite ivory tones of the old lace dress, the scheme should really turn out, as he had so promptly put it to Miss Robinson herself, "a most distinguished piece of portraiture." He was shrewd enough to understand the essential shyness of her disposition, and he felt he might well invest her expression with some suggestion of this, though it should come out as a sort of gentle spiritual modesty.

And now his imagination returned to the contemplation of his own fortunes, and went soaring skywards. His luck having once changed, who could say what might not turn up next? Another sitter might appear, one of your great heroines, stately and brilliant—a sort of Lady Betty, in fact: he might as well admit he *had* Lady Betty in mind! Such a portrait, appropriately conceived, would form a remarkable pendant to this one. Then, too, he might make another dash at his masterpiece! Such a display of versatility in the next year's exhibitions must place his name on everybody's lips, must surely pave the way to his reputation not only as a great decorative portrait painter, but also as a modern of the moderns, touched to inspiration by all the stress and striving of his age!

This roseate flight was abruptly disturbed by the advent of the postman. The rat-tat, one of the double sort, imperiously summoned him to the door. Had the "something else" already turned up? He rather prided himself on the coolness with which he rose to meet it. The postman handed him a packet and a letter. But at a glance he saw that the packet was a rejected drawing and the letter Mary's, and he went straight down into the depths again. He, however, affected a cheerful good morning to the postman; then, no sooner alone, tore open the letter, with the bitter taste of yesterday's scene with his sister full in his throat. To his astonishment, he pulled out two five-pound Bank of England notes, and only a few words accompanied them. "DEAREST," she wrote,— "Since you left me to-day I have suffered beyond endurance. That you will ever forgive me for my harshness I cannot hope. I am the only soul you have to turn to, and yet I struck at you as with a whip. Your face as you turned away will haunt me for the rest of my life. I have been sobbing and sobbing, feeling my heart must break. I ask you to be good to me now, and take this little money. Darling, don't punish me by sending it back. Better times are coming presently, and, if God is good, this little help now may bring you the best of fortune.— Your loving sister, MARY."

Wyndham was unnerved; realising to the full the torture her gentle, sympathetic nature was inflicting on her. What it must have cost her to gather up her strength for that critical interview he could only remotely surmise. Yet it had failed her after all!

However touched he was by her sweetness, however much he was moved to respond to this prostration and surrender, he yet saw only too clearly that at bottom it *was* a failure of strength. The idea of using the money was singularly distasteful; even though he told himself he would have his hand cut off rather than doubt her perfect goodness and sincerity in sending it.

This necessity of a difficult decision disturbed the nice cool balance with which he had started out to face the day. There was nothing for it but to put aside the letter for the present in the hope that counsel would come to him later. And in the meanwhile he went on with his programme. He tidied his papers, went to hunt out his old charwoman, and, ultimately leaving her in possession of the studio, he ran into town to get his new materials, and look up the various accessories for the scheme of the picture.

His first visit was to a shop in Oxford Street, where he had dealt ever since his student days, and where he could order what he needed without immediate payment. A burly man in a Norfolk jacket and knickerbockers was making purchases at one of the counters, and his back seemed not unfamiliar. Wyndham brought out his list and was going through the various items with one of the assistants when a heavy hand was placed on his shoulder, and, turning, he beheld the big powerful head and pointed beard of one of the old gang of his Latin Quarter days.

"Sadler!" he exclaimed.

The big head was convulsed with laughter, and Wyndham's hand wrung in a mighty grip.

"How jolly! I was coming to look you up! I've just ferreted out your address; you're still fixed out there at Hampstead?"

"Oh, do come—I shall be delighted," said Wyndham genially. "Have you been in London long?"

"Three weeks. After knocking about for five years—what do you think of that, my boy? First went all over Spain—made scores of studies. Gee! First- rate! Cheapest place in Europe—exchange thirty-five to the sovereign—and lots of good eating. Went to see a bit of Velasquez down at Madrid. Gee- rusalem! And the Titans, stuck up in a funny little room! You never see anything so fine in your life."

"Oh, I've been there," smiled Wyndham.

The vigour and enthusiasm of his old friend, the nasalities of the deep voice, had almost a complete freshness for him, after the long interval since their last meeting. He was pleased at the encounter—it brought him whiffs of old days of happy comradeship. He felt the stirring of the war-horse.

"Then I put in a nice couple of years at Munich; saw some Boecklin. Gee! He's great!"

"I once saw some wretched things of his, though," said Wyndham. "I remember—at a modern exhibition at Venice."

"I grant there are one or two rotten ones," conceded Sadler; "but they're interesting, if you take them in the right way—experiments that failed, though they were fine as he had them in him. Well—then I did a bit of a tour all over the shop—came along through Holland—made cart-loads of sketches; and then I came right along here. Been getting lots of fun in London; been round with the boys, and had a rattling good time. Taking the opportunity, too, of getting some nice suits of clothes." And here Sadler turned abruptly from art, and plunged into sartorial details. His interest in such matters was astonishing, almost touching. He revelled in fancy waistcoats and rioted in tweeds and broadcloths. London was the only place in the world where you could get the rakish cut. He, Sadler, had never suspected what a lovely figure he had, till this latest cutter had revealed him to himself!

He paused at last for breath.

"Anything particular on with you?" he was presently impelled to ask, observing that Wyndham was exercising a marked fastidiousness in the choice of his canvas.

"A portrait," said Wyndham. "Not a bad little commission."

"Good!" ejaculated Sadler, his face shining enthusiastically. "A lady?"

"Yes," answered Wyndham, "and I've rather a charming scheme."

"Good!" roared Sadler again. "I heard you hadn't been doing much of late. They were running your work down—some of the boys, and I said they were talking rot. We nearly came to blows about it. I think I fairly shut them up."

Wyndham had at first winced a little. Then he felt like shrugging his shoulders. After all, the past had to be lived down. Besides, Sadler's championship was genuine and influential.

"That was very kind of you. You always did stick up for me."

"Don't you mind 'em a bit, my boy. You just go ahead, and you'll come out at the top of the tree."

"I'll do my best," said Wyndham, smiling.

"That'll be good enough, I guess," said Sadler. "Perhaps this portrait will open up other things for you."

"How so?" inquired Wyndham.

"It all depends on the crowd you strike—I heard you came a bit of a cropper, and I daresay you're not too well off now to despise a job or two—you can always put decent work into them. Now there's Jim Harley—he struck a rich middle-class lot ten years ago, rotten out-and-out Philistines, twenty guineas apiece—and they've been keeping him going ever since. Does fifty of 'em a year."

"The prospect hardly tempts me. After all, the main thing is to get back to big work."

Sadler smiled. "I guess I should be the first to drag you back again—after a while. But Jimmy married young. A boy and girl affair. His wife's family weren't satisfied with his financial position, and there was a mighty row at the time. Of course the girl had only her pretty eyes."

"Ah, you don't approve of idealistic love affairs."

"Not of that kind. I'm forty, and I've seen something in my time."

Wyndham had finished his purchases, and was telling the assistant to send the parcel to his studio. As they left the shop presently, Sadler pressed Wyndham very hard to lunch with him at a particular restaurant he mentioned, and Wyndham could not do otherwise than accept the invitation, though he confessed the place was unknown to him. Whereat Sadler expressed great astonishment. It was one of the very few places in London where the food was fit to eat! Why, the cooking was even better than at Lavenue's in the Quarter, and that was saying a great deal. He, Sadler, could not endure any other place during his sojournings in London. Wyndham let the dear fellow gallop on to his heart's content. Sadler was a fine painter, and in the old days Wyndham as the junior had sat at his feet, and in the matter of technique had been greatly indebted to him. But he had observed with covert amusement at a very early stage in the acquaintanceship that Sadler, like so many others in the hard-working, hand-to-mouth world of the arts, had an amiable weakness for "being in the know" anent the good things of life, and affected a lavishness in public that was off-set by a sharp economy in the less visible phases of his existence.

At the restaurant Sadler scrutinised the carte with the confident eye of a man about town, grumbled a little, held a fussy colloquy with the waiter, and finally ordered oysters and chablis to begin upon, the while a chateaubriand was being prepared for them.

Over the meal Sadler talked a great deal of old times. He seemed to have kept himself well in touch with scores of men they had known in common, despite scatterings and vicissitudes. His mind kept leaping across the world, beating them all out of their lairs for Wyndham's enlightenment. Did he remember Pycherley—the biggest duffer of them all? Well, he had married an heiress on the strength of his genius, and was painting awful stuff out in California; and Snyders, who had shared his studio, had built himself a Moorish house high up on a mountain-side overlooking the Gulf of Salerno; a third had settled down to "black-and-white" in a queer little creeper-clad house in St. John's Wood; a fourth was decorating a municipal building at Toronto. Marlowe was still in the avenue du Maine, where the fascinating American actress he had wed had since borne him a sheaf of daughters: and the beautiful Mrs. Smith they had known at Fontainebleau, the summer they had spent there together, had long ago divorced her husband, and married the Italian sculptor, in whose studio she had made such sensational progress. She now exhibited regularly, and had already received a gold medal of the second class.

And so the conversation continued—for the most part about men who were now pretty well getting on into middle life, whose destinies had found definite declaration and were visible to all Wyndham expressed his pleasure that his own future, on the contrary, still lay wrapped in mystery; that, though the curtain was full up, the interest of the drama was by no means played out.

"You can afford to talk like that, Wyndham," shouted Sadler. "What are you? You're only a boy! But I'm forty, and I tell you I'd give up the interest of the drama for a safe income, and think it a damned good bargain. I get along, I sell my stuff, but I tell you I sweat and groan."

"I admit I should like my old income back again," said Wyndham; "not for itself, but for the sake of the splendid freedom to work."

"That's just my point," shouted Sadler. "What the hell do I care about money for itself? And I tell you what, my boy, the right thing for an artist is to marry a woman with money." He struck the table hard with his big fist, making the whole restaurant rattle.

Wyndham almost jumped. "Good gracious! So that's what you were driving at! The idea to me is perfectly loathsome."

"That's just what I used to think," exclaimed Sadler. "But you can't go on for ever with your head in the clouds."

"The thing's so awfully brutal and sordid," insisted Wyndham, shuddering visibly. "It makes my blood run cold."

"You make me tired," snapped Sadler pettishly. "Where's the sordidness? I don't say a man ought to run after a fortune—but enough to steady things. Taking it all round, we artists have less chance of making money for ourselves than other men of the same worth; and since most of us do marry some time or other, we ought to look to marriage to help our work, and not to drag it down."

Wyndham was unconvinced. "If you take away the poetry out of life, the rest of it is too hideous to bother about. If a man marries to make himself comfortable, he's no better than a contented pig wallowing in muck. Rather than surrender the ideal, I'd give up marriage altogether, stand by my guns, and die fighting."

"We artists are a damned sentimental lot," shouted Sadler. He lifted a juicy morsel to his mouth. "This chateau's jolly good, isn't it?"

"Excellent," admitted Wyndham.

"Now you see I wasn't exaggerating when I said it's as good here as at Lavenue's." Sadler swallowed his mouthful. "We all begin with your idyllic ideas—Rossetti, Meredith, and all the rest of it. But I tell you it's hell! You dig the work out of yourself with sweat, with blood!" The veins began to swell in Sadler's mighty forehead. "And when you're not one of the lucky ones, what does the world do to help you to work for it?" He had wrought himself up to a tense excitement, and put the question with a hoarse shout. "Nothing! It prints your name in the papers, it talks about you at dinner parties! Painting is starvation—painting is death! By the time you've worried along till you're forty, you begin to see a bit straight, my boy. Look around you—what do you see on all sides? You see the best of us and the luckiest of us fixing up some pretty little nook here in town or in the country, and then trying to clear a few hundreds or so by tempting somebody to buy it for double what it cost. We begin with ideals, and afterwards we are glad to come down to the level of the common speculator. Let us have no delusions about it —there's nobody keener for necessary money than we artists when we begin to feel the years slipping by. I tell you it's hell!" He gulped down a glass of wine and wiped his lips.

"I see your point of view," said Wyndham; "but I detest it. Better to fight to the end, and stand alone."

"You make me tired," snapped Sadler again. "There are plenty of women of the right sort who'd prefer an artist with a name to some damned bore of a booby who hasn't an idea in his head. They're not fools, those women, I tell you. They know there's no money in the profession; they know you can't get everything in life. Life's a compromise. You've got to give and take. And when women have money, you'll find they understand these things better than when they haven't. A romantic boy runs after a rosy-cheeked, bread-and- butter miss with nothing. The chit gives herself airs, expects what they call 'an establishment'—the rotten Philistines!—and then starts out to please herself in every way, places her whims and caprices first, and the happiness of the household nowhere. The brute exacts every sacrifice, and if she has to make the tiniest concession, it rankles in her all her life."

Wyndham dissented. The same things might happen even if the chit were a millionaire.

Sadler dissented in his turn. He insisted that in woman money and good sense somehow went together. It was a fact. "Look how much happier French marriages are; look how the husband and wife are comrades and stick together. I tell you the French system is the best in the world. Every girl brings her husband a dowry of some kind, and they both work together for the common good. When the time comes it is easier to pass on the money to their own daughter in their turn."

Wyndham contended that these things were all a matter of temperament. "Even at the best you'd have to keep your mind very elastic as to the type of person, whereas, for my own part," he declared, with the Lady Betty type in his mind, "I not only hold on to my poetic standpoint, but there are certain personal ideals I couldn't possibly surrender."

"If you stick out too much for ideals, you'll never get anywhere at all," said Sadler.

"There are things one must stick out for," insisted Wyndham. "For instance, I could never marry a woman who wasn't intelligent, and certainly never one who wasn't beautiful."

"Intelligent—yes. But what is beauty?" asked Sadler, shrugging his shoulders. "And if you get a woman too obviously beautiful, you'll have every man a mile round making love to her, like flies round a honey-pot. It's a sort of primitive law of the universe, and it'll hold good for all time, I suppose."

"Oh, I should chance all that," said Wyndham.

"But what is beauty?" insisted Sadler.

"I know when I see it," laughed Wyndham.

"Give me character," said Sadler. "Unselfishness and loyalty are the chief points, and a sort of sweet reasonableness, of course. If a woman's features aren't quite classical, it's wonderful what a good dressmaker can do to set them off. Waiter! Cigarettes!"

When ultimately the waiter brought the bill, Sadler produced a silver sovereign purse, saw with unconcealed horror that it contained only half a sovereign, then felt in his pockets for loose silver. "It's rather awkward," he said, pulling the longest of faces. "I'm afraid I haven't enough left on me after paying for my colours and materials this morning. I shall have to ask you to lend me a little."

A flash of surprise, an imperceptible raising of the eyebrows; then swiftly Wyndham accepted the situation, and threw down one of Mary's banknotes. "Sorry I've nothing smaller," he said, smiling.

"All right, old fellow," said Sadler. "You pay this time, I'll pay next time."

By the time the waiter brought Wyndham his change, the conversation had passed on to the last exhibition of the New English Art Club.

Wyndham arrived home, after completing all his business calls, late in the afternoon, and found that the charwoman had finished her work, and was replacing the furniture. A not unpleasant tinge of turpentine permeated the atmosphere. The oak presses, newly polished with beeswax, shone and glowed even in the shadow of the afternoon. For the first time for months the hearth was clear of ashes and cinders, and the stone scoured and whitened.

When the woman had gone he devoted a few minutes to wandering about his domain, enjoying this new sensation of spotlessness, appreciating the professional hand, the skill of which had never before seemed so legitimate a theme for admiration. Then he sat down and wrote to Mary as follows:—

"MY DEAR LITTLE MARY,—Your sweet little letter came this morning, and at a moment to be of the greatest service to me. Fortune has already smiled on me again. For the immediate present I have a portrait commission for a couple of hundred guineas! A great fortune—is it not?—after all these seasons of leanness! You will guess that I am now ambitious of getting to grips again with the big picture. I have taken a deep and engrossing look at it again, and I see how to resolve all its difficulties, I daresay, by the spring. I know this letter will make you happy, so, for Heaven's sake, don't give another thought to yesterday afternoon. I have been a great trial to you for so long, and I want to recognise your goodness and kindness in the only way I can, and that is by—succeeding. My heart is in the work, and your belief in me shall find justification.

"I am keeping your money; it will remove my last anxiety and enable me to work at ease. I want you to come here as soon as I have made some headway with the new work, as I should like you to carry away the impression on your next visit of something real that has been accomplished.

"Your loving brother,
"WALTER."

VIII

The first sitting was eminently satisfactory. Miss Robinson and her mother were punctual to the very stroke of the clock, the new canvas stood waiting on the smaller easel, and everything was ready for an immediate start. Wyndham had been able to obtain on hire a most lovely Empire chair, with swans' heads for armrests, and exquisitely mounted with chiselled garlands. It did not take him long to find his arrangement, and he saw now how shrewd had been his idea of the Empire chair. It was remarkable how Miss Robinson and the chair composed together: it gave her distinction, heightened her personality, and the profile at once seemed to take precisely the quality which he considered essential to his scheme. Her right arm rested lightly along the swan's neck, and the subtle cat's-eye, with its border of tiny pearls, showed deliciously against the long hand and fingers that emerged from the lace lying loosely about the wrist. Her left hand lay on her lap, and here the ancient green scarab and the aquamarine made important decorative spots amid so great a mass of lace-work. The nankin vase had been sent to the studio during the morning, so that Wyndham was practically able to build up his picture before him. Indeed, so interesting was the result that it promised to lessen by half the labour of creation.

And, now that he had taken the measure of the Robinsons, he was easily master of the situation. They were not merely in his hands as clients who were availing themselves of his skill; but surrendered as to one naturally high above them. In posing Miss Robinson, he had once or twice given utterance to his satisfaction in so spontaneous a way that the tremulous sitter had no easy task to maintain her immobility. And then the kind and condescending explanations with which he accompanied the many little changes and refinements in the arrangement from moment to moment were so clever and penetrating! It was really wonderful how points struck him, and what surprising improvements he accomplished with a wave of the hand and imperceptible subtle shiftings of Miss Robinson's position. At last, after many scrutinisings of his sitter from varying standpoints he suddenly expressed the conviction "Splendid!" Then— "Wait; the left hand slightly forward, I think; so as to soften the bend of the elbow.... Ah, that's better. Now it couldn't possibly be improved upon. Don't you think so, Mrs. Robinson?"

And the mother was as fluttered as her daughter at this sudden appeal. "Alice looks lovely," she broke out. "You know so well how to make the best of people. I've never seen her so beautiful."

"It's the beautiful accessories that produce the effect," stammered Alice.

"They certainly produce some effect," conceded Wyndham. "That is why they are there. But it's you I'm painting, Miss Robinson. You are the picture, and the picture will be you—and not the surroundings."

He had arranged his palette, and fell to with the brush in earnest, bidding her speak the moment she felt fatigued. And, indeed, he insisted on her resting frequently, though she struggled bravely to keep the spells of work as long as possible, and confessed to cherishing ambitions in that direction.

Altogether the ladies were enchanted with their experience. Like Mr. Robinson, they had never before visited a studio, and it stirred them with a sense of play rather than of work, suggesting to them endless fun and merriment. Pleased with the promise of the picture itself, Wyndham chatted to them charmingly. Miss Robinson, reassured and encouraged by his gracious suavity, soon felt at her ease, and spoke more freely than was her wont at any time. A shade of animation came into her features, and she was ready to break into a laugh at a jest, or to listen to a more serious little disquisition with the intensest absorption. They were not infrequent these charming little disquisitions of Wyndham's, and his visitors thought it wonderful (and told him so with engaging frankness) that he should be able to go on speaking so beautifully, and yet never relax his attention from the painting.

He did not prolong the whole sitting beyond two hours, when he expressed himself delighted with this beginning, and offered them tea.

They accepted eagerly. "Will you be making it, Mr. Wyndham?" they asked, their eyes shining with amusement.

"Oh, I'm an old hand at it," he assured them. He threw open a door which they had imagined to indicate a cupboard. "Kitchen, scullery, and every kind of domestic office rolled into one," he explained, and promptly disappeared inside it. They came peeping in gleefully, fascinated by the rough white-washed doll's interior with its miniature dresser, and they watched him fill his kettle and put together the tea-things. Then he emerged, set the kettle over the fire, spread the table with a fresh cloth, and emptied a large bag of cakes on to a fascinating plate of old-seeming majolica.

"How nice!" said Miss Robinson, her face shining with make-believe gluttony.

"There are some chocolate fingers among them—just the sort you like," said her mother.

"And tiny cream-cakes—just the sort you like, mamma," returned Alice.

"How much tea do you put in the pot?" inquired Mrs. Robinson.

"One spoonful for the pot, and one for each cup," quoted Wyndham promptly. "And I am always careful to warm the pot first with a little of the hot water, and, in scalding the leaves, I am equally careful to catch the water at the exact moment it boils."

"If only our cook were as careful!" sighed Mrs. Robinson.

Wyndham asked them if they would like their tea in the Russian style. They didn't quite know what it was, but it sounded interesting, so they said they'd certainly like to try it. Whereupon he fished out a large lemon, and, cutting it up, put slices into their cups. They were in a happy mood. They kept him sternly to the rôle of host, refusing to spoil the fun by moving a finger to help him. And when he had completed all the processes, and poured the tea for them, they praised its fragrance and delicacy to the skies, and in a trice he was called upon to renew the supply. They likewise declared the cakes delicious, and ate them with affected greed. Meanwhile he let them see some of his pictures; showing off his tall, handsome figure, and occasionally balancing his cup to a nicety, as he talked and manipulated the canvasses from his point of vantage. And when tea was over, he kept them some little time further, whilst he exhibited his overwhelming masterpiece, which he had kept to the end with its face turned away from them. As he wheeled the big easel round, and the picture came into view, a cry of admiration broke from their lips. They were indeed surprised to learn that it was "impossibly" unfinished; to them it seemed that, if justice were done, it should go straightway into the National Gallery. Their pleasure and gratification were extreme: they made not the least attempt to hide their sense of the privilege of sitting at his feet.

And, when they rose to depart, they were absurdly grateful for the lovely afternoon he had given them. Still staggering under the magnificent impression of his brilliancy as an artist, Mrs. Robinson summoned her courage, and suggested that, if he hadn't any other engagement that evening, he might as well dine with them as dine alone. The argument struck him as forcible, and he accepted with an unhesitating simplicity that won her heart still further. He was thanking her for her kindness, but she raised her hands in horrified deprecation to check him.

"Kindness," she cried. "Not at all, Mr. Wyndham. We know we are not worthy of the honour you do us."

"Yes, it is very good indeed of you to come," chimed in Miss Robinson, as they shook hands. She smiled at him quite frankly now, and her soft fingers lingered a friendly moment in his.

He shut the door and turned back into the studio; then, as the thought struck him for the first time, his lips murmured almost involuntarily, "I do believe

Miss Robinson's half in love with me." But he checked himself abruptly. "Good heavens! what a caddish thing to say." For, with his innate chivalry, he had certainly never been addicted to the habit of imagining that this or that woman was immediately enamoured of him.

He returned to the portrait, lingered over it a moment or two, putting in here a stroke, there a touch or a smear. And somehow the train of "caddish" thought persisted in his mind; mastered his will and desire to suppress it. Suppose Miss Robinson should fall in love with him! He recognised her worth as a human being, but instinctively he placed her beyond a certain pale. It was not with that kind of woman that one connected the idea of loving or falling in love; the true type had been fixed for him once for all. The person, too, perhaps! As he had all but felt in his discussion of the subject with Sadler, matrimony was really excluded from his mind. His business in life was work, achievement— his spirit was almost one of revenge for the past.

Yet, suppose she *should* fall in love with him! The speculation persisted, and again he tried to brush it aside. Well, he hoped to goodness that she would not, and brusquely wielded his paintbrush. In any case, it was all in the day's work. Take his own case, for instance! Had he not suffered atrociously during all the time he had known Lady Betty? In his bitter poverty he had hardly dared say even to himself that he had met the woman of his aspirations!

Thus reflecting, he wheeled forward his masterpiece again, and worked on it tentatively, though he did not hope to make serious headway till he should be able to do some fresh sketches on the spot, and have a few at least of the models pose to him over again. But it was a pleasure to feel himself so eager- spirited and hopeful. The Academy dare not refuse it! The picture must establish his reputation!

He went on till the light failed, then, after reading an hour or two, he dressed for his engagement with the Robinsons.

He found the family had in no wise relaxed from the pitch of ceremony to which his first acquaintanceship had wrought them up. But he reflected that, however indifferent the point might be to him, it was just as well they should feel it the right thing to meet him on his own plane—as they understood it. Certainly it was not without its amusing side—the spectacle of a good honest family stimulated out of their customary simplicity merely because a starving artist was to regale himself at their table! And fare sumptuously again the artist did with a vengeance!

He ate, too, with the satisfied contemplation of a good day's work behind him. He had somehow earned this provender, and the meal had on that account an extra subtle relish. Besides, he felt so much more at leisure and at ease than on the former occasion. Then, his visit had been an uncertain and not over-willing experiment; now, he was acclimatised, his impression of everything was cooler. The greater self-possession of the family, too, made the evening distinctly less of an effort for him. Miss Robinson had largely got the better of her distressing shyness, and her personality was more in evidence. In her gentle way she was rising to fill her important position as daughter of the house.

Wyndham's impression of the Robinsons was thus definite and final; as much derived from their surroundings as from themselves. He noticed, for example, that the house itself and everything in it was of an extreme solidity. Indeed, the substantial walls and solid wood-work were so unusual in suburban construction, which was associated in Wyndham's mind with jerry-building, that he could not help remarking thereon when he and Mr. Robinson were left to their coffee and cigars. The old man was greatly pleased at this piece of discernmentand observation. He explained that he had had the house built for him twenty years before, and this solidity represented his dearest philosophy. He hated nothing so much as a superficial appearance which affected to be superior to the underlying reality. "Soundness and sincerity" had been his motto throughout his life, and on that principle his prosperity had been founded. Wyndham grew infected with this unmetaphysical philosophy. The ground he had trodden these last years seemed hideously unstable to look back upon: there was really a wonderful comfort in feeling himself here, supported on so sure a flooring, surrounded by these strong walls, and seated on this thickly-cut mahogany arm-chair that was framed to last three generations. The entire furniture of the house was of the like soundness— even the crimson couches of the drawing-room were of a massive build, and the grand piano, like this great dining-room table, had the fattest of legs, and was resonant of strength and durability.

And in tune with all this solidity was the solid prosperity of Mr. Robinson himself: his banking account seemed an embodiment of his life-principles, supporting all this substantiality on its imperturbable back, like the fabled Buddhistic tortoise nonchalantly supporting the world. Wyndham's own existence seemed feeble by contrast, ready to go down before the merest puff of wind. He stretched himself luxuriously, half incredulous, as if to assure himself it was all no vain imagining; permitted Mr. Robinson to recharge his glass with port; and lighted another of those fragrant unpurchasable cigars. It was so good to savour to the full this sensation of prodigious security! Here one might repose one's head: might hear the trump of doom ring out, and pity the rest of the universe.

After all, was there not more than a grain of truth in Sadler's gospel? In boyhood you could be adventurous; life stretched before you so endlessly that you could afford to gamble with it. But, when the years were racing by, you longed for a little peace, a little happiness. This constant uncertainty of outlook, this perpetual wear of heart and brain, how it sapped life at the very foundation!

To be "safe!" To be solidly established! The import and significance of the conception sank deep into him. Sadler was an older man, had gone through all these phases. "Safety!" No wonder his friend would not hesitate to barter romance for all that the magic word doubtless meant to him.

IX

It was this keynote of "safety" that sounded more in his mind, this appreciation of the stability and comfort of the house at the corner that grew upon him as his visits to the Robinsons continued; for it naturally came to be the settled thing that he should dine with the Robinsons on most of the evenings that he was not engaged elsewhere or otherwise. The argument at first had been the same simple one that he might as well join them as dine alone, and there seemed no reason for refusing their excellent fare and their admiring society. On the other hand, as his ever-insistent pride demanded that they should not suppose he was cut off from his own world; and as, too, he felt subtly required to live up to the social rôle which he fancied they as yet attributed to him, he was thus stimulated to pick up again some of the old threads of his existence. He called on remote aunts in Eaton Square; on retired military uncles in South Kensington. And as the winter advanced he began to find a pleasure in renewing old acquaintanceships, enjoying everybody's surprise at his turning up again, smiling and prosperous. It almost amounted to a self-vindication, and he chuckled in secret, imagining to himself their confusion.

And since he *was* emerging from his retirement, there seemed no longer any reason why he should not mix again in the art world, and Sadler, who had come up to his studio on one or two occasions, induced him to show himself at some of the clubs. At the same time he began to cultivate again some of the smaller coteries of which he had once been so popular a light. Other men, too, began to look him up, and, best of all, an editor one day sent him an unhoped- for commission—half-a-dozen drawings for a magazine story by a widely- read author.

On the whole he was well satisfied to get back into the world. It raised, or rather confirmed, him in his own esteem, and saved him—as he put it—from attaching too cheap a price to himself. He was thus able to meet the Robinsons from a real plane of vantage, and to purge his mind of that slight consciousness of charlatanism which had haunted him at the outset.

Were he not taking ultimate success for granted, without a renewal of the more bitter side of the struggle, he would scarcely have resumed all these old relationships. Yet the precariousness of the future, summon his coolness and confidence as he might, was a thing to be actively, even desperately, reckoned with. The editor's cheque was a god-send, relieving him of immediate anxieties, but he dared not relax his efforts. His mornings were entirely devoted to the big canvas now, and he rose early to avail himself of every minute of light during these short wintry days. He worked with a passion and a concentration that he had never yet known. Every fibre of his body bent to the strain; every drop of his blood seemed to drain its life into this frenzy to achieve. Withal, a delightful sense of emancipation from the old tired vision; a splendid consciousness of some rich new store that had gathered in him during the long period he had lain fallow!

Yet he shuddered and grew sick at the possibility that the Academy might still reject him! In that case, what had he to build upon beyond the coming fee for Miss Robinson's portrait? As the weeks went by, something of a panic began to overtake him; the future seemed to be bearing down on him grim and remorseless.

It was then that the well-garnished atmosphere of the house at the corner seemed more and more desirable and alluring. The flow and abundance, the great glowing fires in this raw winter, the naïve burning of incense at his altar —all these things wooed him, wrapped him in a certain balm. Ensconced with Mr. Robinson, and sipping his after-dinner coffee, he felt the load of his anxieties falling away from him, The heavy decanters of cut glass glowed richly at him—the softness of old whiskey, the ruby and golden glint of wines, the clear light of cunning distillations. The great pineapples, the clusters of grapes, the baskets of peaches, all the fragrant store of Nature's bounty set out on a table that yet, by no stretch of imagination, could be conceived as "groaning"—all seemed to shine fatter and finer than at the houses of his society friends. And here, too, his footing was of an unique, admirable character. He had his place at the board practically as a matter of right. They ranked him as a god; yet felt that the balance of debt was heavily against them. Whereas, elsewhere, he was one of a crowd, a merely casual figure among others not less important even where he had been most intimate. He knew that his own world, despite its breeding and traditions, would yet at bottom despise him and his art if he could not earn an excellent livelihood by its practice. But the Robinsons worshipped him for himself; and money was almost a vulgarity sullying the high artistic universe in which he moved and breathed and had his being.

X

Meanwhile the sittings were progressing in a manner to gratify the artist beyond his hopes. Miss Robinson seemed to find some mysterious inspiration in this decorative scheme, seemed to fuse into it, to lend herself to design and draughtmanship. Her face, too, took on subtler phases, was touched to a measure of nobility! Her dark eyes shone softly under their long lashes; her expression was full of goodness and charity. Wyndham prided himself that he had put on the canvas something remote from the lines of ordinary portraiture —a simple soul, a gentle Lady Bountiful, yet not less dignified in her way than the heroines of the grand portraiture.

Mrs. Robinson did not insist on uninterrupted chaperonage of her daughter; the ladies evinced little fanaticism on this head. Often they brought knitting or needle-work with them, which occupied the mother in a peaceful, old-fashioned way that Wyndham even found himself admiring. Sometimes Mrs. Robinson would appear only towards the end of the sitting, and sometimes she considerately announced that Alice would have to come alone for the next occasion as she herself was otherwise busy. They both showed a tact and a good taste in the matter which he fully recognised, and for which in a way he was grateful.

In the natural resulting intimacy between artist and sitter, Miss Robinson expanded, opened out her mind; at first timidly and tentatively, ultimately with freedom and confidence. She confessed that her experience of life had been nothing at all, since she had always lived in quiet shelter. Her unsophisticated simplicity was certainly engaging; he could see that she was a sheet entirely unwritten upon, that her soul was as naïve and trusting as her outward being. She was refreshingly a child of nature—no bewildering complexity here—no shadow of affectation. She spoke without reserve of the poverty of her childhood, and admitted that she had disagreeable qualms of conscience about their present riches. Was it right to enjoy so much when one thought of the state of the world generally? They debated the subject endlessly; considering it elaborately from every conceivable standpoint: and his personal authority went far to allay her disquietude. His theories, backed up by high philosophy and poetry, fascinated her with their harmony and originality; he had such a charming way of arranging the order of things into a beautiful artist's scheme, whilst yet his sympathies were deep, true, and universal!

Sometimes he was conscious of his sophistry, and felt ashamed of it afterwards. Was he playing a comedy of sentiment? he asked himself. Well, why not? Men and women made a careful toilette for an evening party: why not a spiritual toilette for their sentimental relations?

The last words of his own thought, startled him. Then it *was* a sentimental relation. "By Jove, I must be careful!" he murmured to himself. "She's an awfully good soul, and it isn't fair to either of us." But the next moment he shrugged his shoulders. Why trouble his mind at all? Every relation between a man and a woman who came into such close personal touch was in a way sentimental—for the time being! That was only the game of life, and everybody had to play at it: the main thing was to bow to the rules. Such temporary relations might well be made as pleasant as possible; but, when they were at an end, it was incumbent on both parties to realise that.

Yet he could not help being increasingly conscious of his power over her; it was so pathetically visible. Their conversations were often amusingly like those of kindly tutor and obedient, inquiring child; she hanging on his words in entire self-surrender, as he discoursed so graciously and brought his points so lightly and simply within the range of her comprehension. Sometimes, in following up an explanation, he would be carried away by the flow of his own ideas and his personal interest in the matter, and then he would almost seem to be addressing an equal in knowledge and experience. But whenever that happened; whenever, for example, he had let himself go too far into the subtle mysteries of technique, he would find himself regretting the unchecked surrender to impulse, and remain strangely vexed about it long afterwards. It was really soaring right outside her limitations! She was not a Lady Betty!

Lady Betty was so often in his mind now: she seemed to have established herself more definitely there than ever before, as if to keep him up to the proper pitch in his judgments of women. He bowed his head low to Lady Betty, recognised her as his full intellectual equal—in some aspects his superior. She was brains and beauty. She was stateliness itself. She was sunshine and sweetness. What was Miss Robinson by the side of her? And as he asked himself the question, an impression of Miss Robinson, as he had recently come upon her suddenly in the streets, blotted out the more dignified version on his own canvas. How plain and homely she had seemed in her unobtrusive walking-costume; how insignificant her whole meek bearing! Yes, that was the true Miss Robinson; caught photographically in the act of being herself, and fixed by his vision for always—extinguishing the gorgeously-dressed person of these incessant festal evenings no less than his own artistic edition of her.

In no respect could she claim to come up to his measure. He appreciated all her virtues, recognised her exceptional womanhood: by the side of Lady Betty she was insipid, *bourgeoise*, monotonously amiable.

Yet he could never arrive at so harsh a verdict without relenting at a rebound. "It is curious," was his thought, "that in proportion as I get more friendly with her and really like her, I yet get harder and harder on her, poor child! She's a jolly good sort! What a decent world it would be if only there were ever so many more women like her!"

And, by way of atonement, his manner at their next meeting would warm and soften sensibly; and it came upon him always with a degree of surprise that, however he might feel about Miss Robinson theoretically, her actual society was always pleasant and comrade-like.

XI

By mid-December the portrait needed only the finishing touches, and, at his invitation, several of his artist-friends came to see it. Commendation of the work was general, combined with a certain admiration of the unknown sitter. Wyndham could not help feeling that there was much speculation as to her identity, and he gave himself all the more credit as an artist for the qualities with which he had endowed her, and which alone bestowed upon her this interesting individuality.

Wyndham, who made it a point never to have his work interrupted, had so arranged these visits that none of his friends had stumbled upon the Robinsons. To the not infrequent query of "Who is she?" he usually responded, with a half-humorous gleam in his eye, "She might be Brown or Jones: as a matter of fact she is Robinson—the daughter of a respectable citizen of that ilk." Yet what more, in sober truth, could he tell them about her? He might have put it differently, but it was the information he supposed they wanted. Yet one day he was to learn that this conciseness had been construed as reserve. Sadler lounged in one Sunday afternoon, when, as it happened, Wyndham was awaiting his sister, whose long-deferred visit had at last been arranged for that day. And, in the course of conversation, the visitor soon let slip out a word that struck Wyndham like a blow. Sadler had begun by referring to Miss Robinson as "your friend;" but, presently, as he still reviewed the painting, out came "your *fiancée*."

"My *fiancée*! What the devil——?"

Sadler apologised; a shrewd meaning smile clung about his massive jaws. "Of course everybody understands that it's a secret, but when you've heard of a thing, it's difficult to keep it from slipping out, don't y'know."

"This is all too absurd!" Wyndham was suddenly impelled to laugh.

"What's absurd about it? It seems likely enough to me; else I shouldn't have believed it."

"An artist cannot accept a commission without being engaged to his sitter?" urged Wyndham indignantly.

"Things have a way of getting about, you know," maintained Sadler.

"They have indeed," said Wyndham.

"Well, what are you so annoyed at?" shouted Sadler. "You make me tired. There's nothing discreditable in being engaged by rumour to a wealthy and beautiful woman."

Wyndham laughed again. Beautiful! he thought. If only Sadler had met the everyday Miss Robinson shopping with her mother in the Finchley Road!

"Seriously, do you consider her beautiful?" he asked in a more genial tone, suddenly curious to hear Sadler's real impression.

"What is beauty?" demanded Sadler. "The moment you can define it, it ceases to be beauty. Its essence is elusiveness. A touch, a flash—and you've got it! The lines here are not classical, but your Miss Robinson has distinct individuality. The eyes are fine. She looks the sort that would stick to a man. Gee-rusalem! I shouldn't mind having a shot at her myself. Look here, old fellow, will you introduce me to her? If there's nothing in it for you, give me a chance."

"Goodbye," said Wyndham sweetly. "You won't think me rude, but I've an engagement in a minute or two."

"Right!" said Sadler. "I'll be off. Goodbye, Wyndham, old chap. You're a real damned old swell. Gee-rusalem! you're just great at getting rid of people."

Left alone, Wyndham gave way to annoyance again. It was a fine thing! Artists themselves ought to know better than to indulge in tittle-tattle of that kind. He worked himself up into a towering rage. Then Mary rang the bell, and he had abruptly to recall his graciousness.

It was her first visit to the studio since the new turn of affairs; her multifarious duties as worker among the sick and poor after her day's teaching leaving her so little freedom. They had of course seen each other in the interim; for Wyndham had himself looked in at the "Buildings" in Kensington whenever his engagements had taken him that way, and he had been fortunate enough just to catch her at home for a few moments on several occasions. The poor girl had been overflowing with happiness—had not a window on the skies been opened, too, for her? And though both had so far delicately avoided all reference to that old painful interview, she had yet often been impelled to throw herself at his feet in contrition. Only she felt that he, in his great magnanimity, would be hurt by such an abasement.

When he brought the picture well into the light, her first exclamation was, "Oh, how beautiful!" Then she kissed him impulsively.

The tribute gave him more pleasure than all the professional praise that had been showered on the portrait.

"What a charming girl! I should like to know her," were her next words. "She has such a good face, and I'm sure she's every bit as beautiful as you've painted her."

Wyndham's vexation at his rumoured engagement seemed to take wing and be off into the airs. He even felt a shy pride in Miss Robinson. "I'm sure you'll like her," he said. "Shall I arrange a tea here one of these days before Christmas?"

"That would be lovely." Mary's voice was full of enthusiasm. "School breaks up in a day or two, and I shall have so much more time to myself," she added, still gazing at the picture.

"Any criticism?"

"None," she returned. "You have caught the character with rare genius. She is so simple and unaffected; one could repose absolute trust in her.... You see," she continued, smiling, "I feel so strong an interest in her as being the beginning of your good fortune. I have a sort of conviction—don't laugh at me, please—that it has come to stay."

When he poured out her tea, she suddenly laughed, remembering she had a message for him which she had forgotten to deliver in the absorption of contemplating Miss Robinson; in fact, there was a heap of things she had wanted to talk over. The most important, at any rate, was the question of his Christmas holiday. Aunt Eleanor wanted Mary to spend the two or three weeks with her, but she was anxious that Wyndham, too, should join their little party over the New Year—since she now understood that he had emerged to some extent from his austere seclusion. A refusal Aunt Eleanor would take to heart—she naturally regarded her own home as his, as the place to which his mind should spontaneously turn at such a season.

Wyndham welcomed the invitation. It was more than two years since he had passed any time in Hertfordshire, and the visit itself, which last Christmas he had sullenly avoided, would afford him the greatest satisfaction. Much as he appreciated the Robinson housekeeping, it was a relief to feel definitely that he was not staying the year-end at his studio, with no resource save their cordial hospitality.

Mary went off in great elation. "I don't know when I have felt so happy as to-day," she declared, as she kissed him. "I leave my best love for the work— and for the lady as well," she added, smiling.

It was arranged on the door-step that they should travel down to Hertfordshire together, and Mary insisted he must leave her to look up the trains, and make all the arrangements.

"It is just the sort of task I enjoy," she assured him. "Looking up trains to get into the country always sends me into a sort of happy excitement; it is part of the joy of anticipation."

Wyndham was left, somehow, a greater admirer of Miss Robinson. He studied her again in his own picture, and accepted her as a far finer creature than he had realised—even allowing for this idealisation of her in paint. "My feeling against her must be purely morbid, and it's really too bad when she likes my society so much!—she has no idea how much she shows it." Her unsophistication, hitherto a deficiency, began to take on a certain charm. How refreshing this womanly simplicity in a world of showy coquettes and chattering, feather-headed females! Even Mary, who was so shrewd and fastidious, had been compelled to pay her homage. The Robinson family was charming! What fine old-world courtesy in the father—many a born aristocrat might well take a lesson from him! How unassuming, too, the mother, full of quiet virtues and womanly excellencies!

And Mary's significant smile remained with him. Good gracious! was she, too, taking the sort of thing for granted? This power of suggestion from every side was annoying: still—it would not be right to let that prejudice him!

Wyndham paced to and fro feverishly. Why should he not——?

It was the first time he was impelled to put the question to himself in clear seeking. Obscure in his mind these last weeks, it crystallised itself brusquely —surprised him with its swift definiteness: but he broke it off, all unprepared to meet it yet. He had a shamefaced remembrance of his matrimonial conversation with Sadler, of the lofty convictions he had then expressed.

Well, he had spoken honestly, he argued, and his convictions had changed not a jot. "Only now that I am face to face with the actual possibility, I see aspects of the case that then escaped me. Till now I have always viewed marriage as the great central fact to which the whole of life has to converge, from which everything else takes its significance. Hence it was a case of the ideal or nothing—there seemed no other choice. But now I recognise that matrimony that is not ideal may yet take its place as an accessory to life, may be accepted as a good without filling the whole horizon."

He resumed his feverish pacing. Well, why should he not seize an opportunity which presented itself so favourably? By the loss of his money he had become reduced in his own world to the rank of a mere "detrimental." Had he not already felt that sufficiently? He laughed harshly at the memory. No, no, a Lady Betty he could not hope to marry. Such wondrous beings did not grow on every bush; nor did life permit of his setting out in search of one. This holding out for the perfect ideal only meant humiliation and sadness in the end. The world—the hard world of fact—was like that, and you had to take it as you found it. No folly could be greater than to forget that life was as it was, and not as you thought it ought to be!

Yet he vacillated again. Did he really want to marry at all? Had he not decided —wholly, absolutely, irrevocably—that his business in life was work? Though he would never have spoken of it to another, he was proud in his heart of his sentimental loyalty to Lady Betty, and marriage seemed almost an unfaithfulness. Better perhaps to bend himself sternly to the task before him!

Yes, but this task before him—unaided, he could never accomplish it. Let him confess it now, since he was master again of his full sanity. He had been beaten, smashed! But for this timely piece of good fortune all would have been at an end by now. The Robinson support once withdrawn, he would not be strong enough to stand. He had gauged his powers in the great contest, and, in this moment of supreme lucidity, he foresaw he must be conquered again. One portrait could not suffice for the rebuilding of his future; even on the money side his fee would be absorbed immediately. And the finishing of the great picture meant more outlay. To try to "fake" it without proper models would be a folly of follies—far better to abandon it altogether. His blind optimism at the turn of things had certainly been of benefit to him, had stimulated him to his best; but with this first piece of work practically accomplished, the moment for estimating and facing the situation with mathematical exactitude had certainly arrived.

He could not fight the world alone. However he might desire nothing in life save self-consecration to work, he could not even achieve that much without reinforcing his own strength by means that were unexceptionable and honourable.

He came to an abrupt stop as the words swept from his brain. "By Jove, that hits the nail pretty square!" he murmured, his lips ashen. Naked and ugly, his primary motive stood before him as in a mirror. For one clear moment he saw himself brutally, and shuddered. "I am not in love with her. If she were dowerless, I should never have worked myself up to this stage of appreciation; I should never have dressed up the Robinson menage to make it palatable. The portrait would never have come out like this. I should have dashed in a brutal modern study of a plain woman, full of bravura passages. If I am going in for a thing of this kind, let me at least be honest with myself."

And then he laughed with the irony of it all. He, the lover of poesie; he, the fastidious gourmet in things of the spirit; who had followed the cult of all that was lyrical and exquisite; he planned to mate beneath him for the sake of crude money. Faugh! A vulture hovering over a heap of carrion!

But the violence of the metaphor brought a reaction. "Rubbish!" he murmured, and paced again. The pacing grew into a striding. Up and down the length of the studio he stamped, face and eyes working intensely. "I am exaggerating. I am morbid about it all; I am rushing to the other extreme. When have I ever hidden from myself that the thing would be primarily a means to my great impersonal end—I may as well admit it has been in my mind all along! What could be a greater degradation than my old way of living? Poor Mary! Why, I owe it to her as a duty to put an end to all this misery. I'd face anything on earth now to make up to her for the past! Besides, the idea is not at all so inhuman as I am trying to make out. In a mildish sort of way, of course, I am really fond of Miss Robinson. Her virtues *are* a reality! She is plain, I admit—very plain; but my eye has learnt to see her its own way—the way of the portrait!"

Brusquely he flung his hesitations from him. Why should he not marry Miss Robinson? Even in the driest aspect of the case, the match was not inequitable. The "crude money"—yes, let him use the words deliberately— the "crude money" on her side; on his a full equivalent in his personal self, his no doubt brilliant career once sordid matters were disposed of, and a sphere of existence that was obviously interesting to her. If he brought no immediate fortune himself, his future earnings, once he were free to work without anxiety, might well be considerable. What was there in the idea to wound his pride? How absurd his metaphor of the vulture!

And then he turned to dwell again with relief at the pleasanter aspects of the case. Even if he were not attaining to passionate poetic dreams, he would yet be carrying into effect a charming domestic ideal of peace and tranquillity. And the very poetry of marriage began to invest Miss Robinson with something of its own glamour. He saw her in a bridal veil holding a big bouquet. His enthusiasm mounted.

And Mary's voice seemed to echo again in the studio: "What a charming girl! She has such a good face, and I'm sure she's every bit as beautiful as you've painted her." He almost felt himself blushing in embarrassment; it was as if he himself were being commended. "She is so simple and unaffected," went on Mary's voice with its unmistakable ring of conviction. "One could repose absolute trust in her."

How shrewd and true was his sister's reading of the character! Moreover, Mary had confessed to an almost superstitious thrill at gazing on the features of the woman who had been the beginning of his good fortune. Could he say that he was entirely free from the same sort of superstitious sentiment? Alice Robinson had begun his good fortune; why should she not complete it? If only that confounded set of fools hadn't started their silly tittle-tattle!

Undoubtedly there was a substratum of truth and good sense in the views so stoutly and passionately maintained by Sadler; only Sadler imagined it was possible to compromise, to step down from the ideal and yet find great happiness. He himself would give up the dream of happiness in the ideal sense: his would be frankly a case of convenience, though were it not for the many virtues of Miss Robinson, his mind would never have become reconciled to it. No! not even were she as rich as Croesus. He must do that amount of justice to himself. At his age he could appreciate the importance of the rarer qualities of character in his life's mate—loyalty, modesty, devotion! He would be making a wise marriage! not a sordid one. He would be choosing the deep calm of life instead of the elusive and often mocking flash of superficial passion and beauty.

And, on his part, he was prepared to be the best and most dutiful of husbands!

XII

When, that same evening, Wyndham was ushered into the Robinsons' drawing-room, he was mildly surprised to find a sedate gentleman there in familiar conversation with the family. The stranger vibrated with neuter lights; yet dry, clean lights. Tall spare figure, hair and close-trimmed beard, tailed morning coat and sharp-creased trousers, brow and visage, air and movement—all a chiaroscuro in grey; accentuated curiously, too, against the host's correct black and white, and the laces and chiffons and shimmering brilliance of the ladies.

"My friend, Mr. Shanner," said Mr. Robinson, introducing them; and Wyndham remembered at once that the Robinsons had mentioned Mr. Shanner occasionally as an intimate of the house who was away in the New World for the interests of the concern in which he was junior partner.

But Mr. Shanner, though he shook hands cordially, yet gave him a swift look up and down that had something of antagonism in it. And in Wyndham, too, arose some obscure enmity, likewise masked by the conventional friendliness of greeting.

"As I was just telling Mr. Robinson," said Mr. Shanner, with an obviously forced smile that yet illumined the man, broke through and flashed away the greyness for an instant, "I hadn't the least idea that I was going to stumble on an evening party. I feel quite out of it." His voice was full of affable vibrations, and he smiled again, with a general nod that indicated all this ceremonial get-up around him.

"I am sure we shall do our best to amuse you," returned Wyndham, naturally associating himself with the family, but feeling hopelessly out of sympathy with the new-comer.

Miss Robinson had reddened as the two men approached each other, but on her father's again mentioning that Mr. Shanner was just back from his tour in the New World, she came into the conversation bravely, and rose above her shade of embarrassment.

"Have *you* ever crossed to America, Mr. Wyndham?" she asked, smiling at him.

"No," he confessed; "though America has largely crossed to me."

Mr. Shanner looked puzzled.

"How do you mean—America has crossed to you, Mr. Wyndham?" he asked.

"Oh, I hope I did not seem to suggest that I have been a centre of pilgrimage," laughed Wyndham. "Only, in past years, when I was running a good deal about the Continent, I often used to live with New York, Chicago, and Boston, for considerable periods."

"Mr. Wyndham has often given us charming sketches of the Americans," chimed in Miss Robinson.

"Oh, I don't pretend to be much of a hand at that sort of thing," said Mr. Shanner, with pleasant humility. "I can only just give my impressions as a plain observer. But then I'm a man of affairs, and nothing at all of an artist or a literary man." Wyndham observed how careful and honeyed his delivery was; it seemed to advertise a perpetual self-consciousness of being a gentleman.

"Mr. Shanner is unduly modest," put in Mr. Robinson. "His descriptions are most entertaining."

"Well, of course, I can speak of things within my experience, and make myself fairly clear—in my own way, of course. But, from all that you people have been telling me, I shouldn't attempt to emulate Mr. Wyndham."

Mr. Shanner gave a strange little laugh, full of insincere echoes; which failed in its implication of good-fellowship, and only emphasised the ill-nature it was meant to cover. Wyndham was not a little bewildered; conscious of some suppressed excitement in the man, some ruffling of the ashen chiaroscuro. This impression was deepened when dinner was announced, and Mr. Shanner made what was perilously like a dart to the side of Miss Robinson and offered his arm. Wyndham stepped out of their way, bowing as they passed him.

At table Mr. Shanner gave no undue signs of modesty or self-distrust, but talked about "things within his experience" with the utmost unconstraint. An unmistakable note of assurance animated the honeyed voice, which soared away occasionally, yet sedulously recollected itself; drew back within bounds, reverted to the lesser pitch and the deliberate pace. Mr. Shanner was at pains to let it be seen that he was a man of affairs on the grand scale, one to be ranked with diplomatists and ambassadors. In the course of business he had come into contact with exalted personages of almost every kingdom, and had corresponded voluminously with some of them. He carried an assortment of their letters in his pocketbook, which lay on the table as a perpetual source of illustration. He spoke of some of these great ones of the earth with extreme familiarity—he had been closeted with them on confidential business, and he flattered himself he had counted for something in certain important decisions of policy. And, as he warmed to the conversation, far from being "out of it," he was king of the table, his honeyed words emerged endlessly. There was a distinct flash of challenge in his occasional glances at Wyndham—he was not to be overborne by the presence of any aristocrat on earth. And not content with all this insistent implication of his personal importance, he even related by way of pleasant interlude how, with ear to one private telephone and mouth to another, he had smartly seized a sudden opportunity, and, buying an incoming cargo through the first telephone and selling it through the second, had netted twenty thousand pounds for his firm. Whereas Wyndham amused himself trying to measure the depths of Mr. Shanner's contempt should he suspect that the sole resources of his vis-à-vis were the guineas to be paid him from Mr. Robinson's treasury.

It was evident, too, that Mr. Shanner was more familiarly at home in the house than Wyndham. He called its master "Robinson"; most significant of all, Miss Robinson was Alice to him. Indeed, his manner, as he sat next to her, was almost proprietorial; at any rate it had easy, affectionate suggestions about it. She, however, had fallen back into a shy constraint; though she emerged at moments, lifting her deep-glancing eyes to Wyndham and flashing him the friendliest of messages. Wyndham understood by now; knew also that it was clear to Mr. Shanner that they were rivals—that a mutual detestation lurked beneath their pleasant amenities. He had gathered also that Mr. Shanner meant to show that he did not concern himself one jot about the new star that had appeared in the firmament during his absence. But Wyndham came off easily the victor, displaying for Mr. Shanner a charming deference, and pursuing the unruffled tenour of his entertaining conversation without manifesting in the slightest degree any of the emotions that the evening had raised in his breast. Such perfect unconsciousness of matters intensely present, Mr. Shanner could not hope to emulate. It was clear he was uneasily alive to the contrast—that he had the growing consciousness of defeat. His note of self-emphasis rang louder, though smothered continuously.

The war continued after dinner; Mr. Shanner eagerly turning the pages of Miss Robinson's music, and so entirely appropriating her that Wyndham could scarcely contrive to approach her during the rest of the evening. However, Wyndham smilingly kept his place in the background, disdaining to assert himself or to enter openly into emulation; though there were opportunities he, the socially experienced, might have seized adroitly. After all, why annoy this admirable, upright gentleman? Even as it was, poor Mr. Shanner was fated to receive one or two sharp slashes; as when, in the course of describing the sittings, Mrs. Robinson let it be clearly seen that she was not always present to chaperone her daughter in the studio. At that moment Mr. Shanner's face was an extraordinary face to look upon; although he affected to laugh and smile, and packed even more honey into his voice. All of which forced sweetness notwithstanding, it began to be evident that the topic of the picture, and of Wyndham's work in general, bored him considerably. At last, when Mrs. Robinson innocently suggested that Wyndham should ask him to come to see the portrait at the studio, he deprecated the idea with some degree of vehemence. He really was very busy in the daytime now. Besides, he added pleasantly, on principle he never cared to see an article whilst yet on order; time enough to examine it when it was tendered for delivery. He smiled meaningly at Wyndham as if to accentuate that these commercial metaphors were merely by way of pleasantry.

"And then it's so extremely difficult for an outsider to get any idea of an unfinished picture, and of course I don't profess to be a judge of art in any case, though I know what I like."

So, if Mr. Wyndham would excuse him, he added, he would rather wait till the portrait had come home, and had been hung in the house.

It was not without difficulty that Wyndham found his opportunity of arranging the little tea-party at which the ladies were to meet his sister. Miss Robinson was to give him the final sitting on the Tuesday; so it was therefore agreed that the tea should take place on that day after work was over. The sitter herself crimsoned deeply at learning that Mary "had admired her immensely," and her eyes glistened in a way that showed her pleasure and rapturous appreciation.

XIII

The definite figure of Mr. Shanner with his magnificent appropriation of Miss Robinson merely impelled Wyndham to smash up this rival at once and have done with the business. The evening had obscured all the repugnance that lay in the depths of him; had stimulated roseate conceivings of possible felicity.

On the Tuesday he found his opportunity. Miss Robinson came alone, explaining that her mother would not appear till the time fixed for the tea-party. The weather was rigorously wintry now, and a biting wind blew in as the door was opened. A new layer of snow had fallen during the last hour, and Miss Robinson had come across wrapped in a big, heavy cloak. He ushered her through the ante-room with a charming air of solicitude, to which she vibrated like a struck harp, and gave him the softest and tenderest intonations of her voice. He helped her off with the cloak, and hung it away carefully, the whilst she stooped and warmed her long hands at the lavishly heaped-up fire. Her throat and arms now showed at their best, and her face had some strange, almost mystic undertone of happiness. As she bent down there before his eyes, she completely blotted out the impression of the insignificant plain woman whom he had suddenly come upon in the streets; of the everyday Miss Robinson that at one time had almost become an obsession. At that moment she was well-nigh the idealised figure he had painted. Yet there was something even subtler in her which he had missed, and knew that he had missed. But, studying his own work again, he saw that that was just as well; for the picture existed as a separate creation, a piece of painting first and foremost, in which he had exhibited the cleverness of his brush. It was paint —distinguished, intellectual paint—more than it was human portraiture; in spite of all the significance with which he had tried to invest it. As this new truth dawned upon him, he kept glancing from sitter to canvas, and from canvas to sitter, with a strange, surprised interest. But her hands suddenly arrested his attention, and he became aware that, for the first time since he had known her, they were absolutely bare of rings.

"You have no rings to-day," he remarked, his voice showing his surprise. "I might have wanted to touch up the hands."

Her colour deepened unaccountably. "I thought the hands were finished," she breathed, all of a flutter. "Shall I go back for them?"

"What a goose it is!" he said lightly, and she smiled again, as if pleased they were on so charmingly intimate a footing.

"Shall we not need them?" she asked.

"I think not," he answered, studying the hands a little. "You were perfectly right; they had best remain as they are."

She took the pose, and for a minute or two he worked silently; she maintaining the perfect stillness that had at first been her cherished ambition. He was still pondering about her bare hands and her confusion at his having observed them, and light came to him. Was it to show him that no man—not even Mr. Shanner—had any claim on her? After the close attentions he had witnessed the other evening, was she afraid he might infer that some understanding existed between herself and Mr. Shanner?—that one of these rings, even if not a formal pledge, might be his and worn for his sake? Her neglect of such favourite trinkets to-day was then to indicate that no one of them had any special sentimental interest for her!

"You are sitting perfectly to-day," he presently remarked. "It doesn't tire you?"

"What an unkind suggestion! I thought I had got beyond the amateur stage long ago."

"I'm sorry. You didn't hear, though, the beginning of my remark."

"I agreed with that," she answered with a sly humour.

"So that it hadn't to be reckoned. Do you know all women are like that?"

She considered. His brush made strokes. "Like what?" she asked at last.

"If you pay them the greatest of tributes, but are incautious enough to hint the tiniest of qualifications, the tribute dwindles to nothing, and they remain tremendously annoyed at the suggestion of imperfection."

"Am I like that?"

"You were just now."

"I was such a bother and a hindrance to you when we started," she explained. "I used to get tired every few minutes. And now at last, just when I am flattering myself on my improvement——"

"You take me too seriously," he broke in.

"You *were* serious," she insisted.

"Serious—yes; in so far as I was afraid you were tired. I didn't even mean it as a qualification of my tribute; it was only genuine concern for you."

"How stupid of me!" she exclaimed. "I ought to have felt that atonce."

There was another spell of silence; he intensely absorbed in his brush, she obviously considering.

"I am not really like that," she said at last.

He stood away from the canvas, glanced critically at certain points, levelled his mahl-stick at her, took up a rag, and wiped a bit out. "Like what?" he asked.

"Like women."

"But you are. You see, it is sticking in your mind." He smiled wickedly.

"You fight too hard," she pleaded.

"I'm sorry," he said remorsefully. "I shall not do it again."

"Oh, I'm not a bit hurt," she protested. "I was only thinking the point over."

"I want to hear what you were thinking." His smile and tone were meaningly affectionate, as if they would add "little child."

"I meant that I should never really be hurt by qualifications. I have never been used to having nice things said to me. I certainly do not deserve tributes, but I know I deserve all possible qualifications."

"Oh, if you please! I'll not allow even Miss Robinson to say such slanderous things about so valued a friend of mine."

"So I have been slandering a friend of yours! I'm so sorry. Forgive me."

"I suppose I must—though I find it hard—very hard."

"I do believe you are paying me a tribute," she laughed. "Now for the qualifications. You shall see how stoical I am."

"Qualifications—none!" He threw down his brushes and palette, as if to emphasise the declaration. "I'm tired first," he sang out gaily. "Let us rest."

"There!" she exclaimed. "What a triumph for me!"

"But you say it so gently that it is a pleasure to concede you the victory. You are an ideal foe."

"Oh, if you please, I don't want to be a foe. ... How cold it is!" She stooped and held her hands again to the fire.

"No, child," he said gently, "of course we aren't foes. We are very good friends indeed, aren't we?" He held out his hand, as if to clench the understanding, so clearly and warmly acknowledged.

She was all a-flutter again, though, as was her habit, she covered it up with a smile. "Very good friends!" she returned, with conviction, and she put her hand in his, and let it linger there. "I have always lived reserved and to myself," she added thoughtfully. "You may think it strange, but I have never had a friend before—not even a woman friend."

"I can well understand your shrinking away from people. No doubt most people would jar on you."

"It would hurt me if I thought that. I should not like to despise anybody. I should have loved to have friends: only I have never had the gift of making them. Sometimes I am thankful that I am not brilliant—I might so easily have become unendurable and full of self-conceit."

"Ah, you are something better than brilliant," he exclaimed. "It needs an exceptional spirit to appreciate you. You are so much out of the ordinary in every way, in looks——"

"No, no," she interrupted in protest. "I have no looks. I have no illusions about that."

"Look at your own portrait," he insisted. "I say it is the kind of beauty it needs a gift to appreciate. In beauty—as in everything else—the crowd runs after the obvious and the commonplace."

"You are the first that ever thought I possessed good looks. You have given them to me."

"I have not even done you justice. I have omitted more than I have suggested. My sister thinks you are beautiful; all my artist friends who have seen the picture share her opinion."

She was silent, almost distressed; she could not meet his gaze, but turned her eyes away.

"It gave me pleasure to hear you appreciated," he continued. "You are above conventional compliments. I withdraw what I said before. You are *not* like other women."

Her breath came and went as she listened, but she smiled bravely.

"At any rate I am not like *some* women. I never could take any of the deeper aspects of life in a merely frivolous spirit. With me it is a loyal, deep friendship, or nothing."

He took her hand again. "Believe me, dear child, the friendship on my part is equally loyal and deep. It is for life."

"For life," she murmured, suddenly grown pale.

He dashed in, determined to strike home.

"I prize you at your full worth, since I am one of those who can measure it. I have the deepest affection for you. I believe I could make you happy. Don't you understand? I offer you my whole life—that is, if you think me worthy."

"Worthy!" she echoed, in dazed distress. "How can you think me worthy of you! I have lived in narrow retirement. I am nothing."

He seized both her hands now. "No more of this. I ask for your promise."

"I love you with all my heart and soul. But I am not good enough for you."

"I thought we agreed you were not like other women, and yet there is this stiff-necked obstinacy." He drew her nearer to him, and kissed her on the lips. "It is settled—you are to be my wife."

His domination seemed to hypnotise her. "Yes, I will do my best to make you a perfect wife, dear," she murmured, as if bowing to his irresistible will.

He held her hands tighter, and looked into her face as if proudly. She met his look with glistening eyes: she was deathly pale now, and her lips, too, were colourless. Then abruptly she drew her hands from him, and, as if impelled on some tide of womanhood that rose in high music above all hesitations, above the fluttering timidity of her whole life, she threw her arms round his neck, and kissed his lips with a long abandonment.

"I am now almost afraid of your sister," she whispered presently. "I shall feel on my trial."

"But she has fallen in love with you already," he reassured her again. "And Mary is the sweetest and gentlest soul in the world."

"I know I shall love her," she said. Her head hung down a moment in meditation. "But let us continue the work now, dear. I know you wish to have it finished to-day."

But he had little now to add to it, and he had made his last stroke before the dusk of the afternoon overtook him.

XIV

Wyndham's career as an engaged man began amid a radiance of enthusiasm. When his prospective mother-in-law arrived for the tea-party, she was enchanted at the news, declaring, after the first joyous surprise, that it was the wish that lay nearest to the hearts of herself and her husband. And, presently, when Mary appeared, and was introduced not only to "the original of the portrait she had so admired," but also to "a very sweet Alice" who was to be her sister, "I guessed it," she broke out, kissing Miss Robinson impulsively. "I am so delighted."

Heigh, presto! In a trice the three women were chatting away like a group of old neighbours! Wyndham became discreetly busy with tea-things.

Of course the Robinsons insisted on Mary's dining with them, and so there was a happy little reunion in the evening. Mr. Robinson thrilled visibly with the honour of having Mary at his board, and he congratulated Wyndham with pathetic cordiality, his voice husky with emotion, his eyes streaming with tears.

Such was the auspicious beginning. But the universe seemed to vibrate to white heat as a wider population entered into the jubilation. Mary was the first to spread the news, her letters reaching the Hertfordshire circle express. In the twinkling of an eye, as it appeared to Wyndham, a flood of letters poured through the slit in his door. He had done that which makes every man a hero for the moment, and dim figures with whom he had been out of touch for endless years started up again on the horizon, palpitatingly actual, athrob with goodwill. In the Bohemian world, too, confirmation of the former rumour was not slow to be noised abroad, and Sadler hastened to Hampstead and burst in upon him, the massive head enthusiastically aglow; declaring that he had never for a moment taken Wyndham's denial seriously, and roaring out his congratulations and envy with an exuberance of virile expletive.

At Aunt Eleanor's the Christmas festivities were struck in a gayer key in his honour. Odes of welcome and triumph were in the air. And he was glad enough to be among his own world again; living in the way that meant civilisation to him, and breathing homage and consideration—lionised by his equals! It was as though the fatted calf had been killed for him, after his prodigal riot of penury. He expanded in this atmosphere of adulation, amid all these manifestations in honour of the brilliant artist and the Prince Charming who loved and was loved idyllically. His engagement seemed to him now most admirable—the world's sanction had invested it with warm and pleasant lights. Certainly nobody deprecated or criticised the projected alliance; though it was known to be with middle-class people who were not in Society, but merely quiet folk of wealth and respectability. Mary's enthusiasm had gone a long way in anticipating any possible caste objections, and the word of approval went round from one to another in the usual parrot-like way in which public opinion has formed itself since creation. There seemed in fact to be a very conspiracy of approbation. Wyndham had done wisely; and voices dropped impressively to dwell on the Robinson millions—with the obvious implication that that is what wealthy middle-class people are for—to have the most promising of their kind promoted into the upper classes.

But the Robinson fortune, though not inconsiderable, was not the romantic one of rumour. Mr. Robinson had already performed his duty of writing to Wyndham on the financial aspect of the alliance, and in so charming a way that Wyndham had at once paid him the tribute of "jolly decent." Since they had not had the opportunity of disposing of the subject *viva voce*, had said the old man, he conceived it perhaps to be an obligation on his part to do so without delaying further; after which these matters would of course pass entirely into the realm of Wyndham's private affairs, where he was well content to leave them. Alice's fortune, such as it was, had been placed under her own control absolutely when she had attained the age of twenty-five, and probably now, with certain accumulations, amounted to some thirty thousand pounds. She was a wise and prudent child, well capable of controlling those money matters that were naturally distasteful to so gifted an artist, and in that way he would no doubt find her a most useful companion. However, he now left it to him and Alice to plan out their future together, and wished them all good luck. At the same time, if Wyndham had no objection, he would like to give them as a wedding-present any house they might fancy, and his wife desired to furnish it or give them a cheque for that purpose.

Wyndham was in reality deeply moved by so much considerate kindness and rare delicacy. He wrote Mr. Robinson a charming note of acknowledgment; though he touched just briefly on the main theme, diverging into a chatty account of his visit, and letting his pen run on and on till he had covered several sheets.

Each morning during his visit a letter from Alice awaited him on the breakfast-table. For a week or two the chant was timorous, uncertain; of a pitch to soothe his self-complacency, to stir no ruffle in his holiday mood. But towards the end of his time she found herself—she tuned up, and adventured. And then followed Wyndham's awakening; taking him with the force of cataclysm, and dashing him out of his drowsy mood of contentment. Evidently the poor child was not living in this world. If her feet touched earth, her head at any rate was in a heaven of its own. She poured herself out with a lyric fervour that was like the song of a lark for rapture. All the years of her life she had saved herself for this, not frittered her emotions away in flirtations or frivolous love-affairs—as the soberer Wyndham now reflected. Her ideals were as unsullied as in her childhood. Her spirit soared up with a tremulous eager joy—without doubts, without cynicism, with a simple sure faith in love's paradise. Reserved, shrinking away from men, her heart yet held rich store of treasure, and she poured all out at his feet. Timorousness had vanished; the soul that had woven its own music in solitude had been translated to a higher universe. There were no barriers now, nothing but this joyous, confident life into which her womanhood had passed at that moment when, swept onward by the flood, she had thrown her arms around him.

"Dearest," she wrote, "my whole past life seems like a half-slumber from which I have awakened into a world almost too dazzling with light and joy. Yet who am I that this joy should have come to me? When I think of the years when I lived alone with my own thoughts, it seems wonderful that your love should have been granted to me. The world is full of pale ghosts that come and go, not knowing what life is, and it amuses me to wonder if any of them will ever turn into real people.

"Oh, my dear love, you are so far, far off. I want you here, here again with me, happy that you love me, happy that I love you, wanting no other life than this with your arms round me and your heart beating close to me. And yet I like to think that you are happy amid your own family, in the place where your childhood was spent. I love, dear, to dwell on the thought of your childhood, and fancy I see you now, a beautiful child in velvet, with a feather in your hat and a toy sword. And I see myself a child again, playing with this fairy little prince in the meadows. How beautiful if we were children like that! Impossible does it seem? Yet is anything impossible in this enchanted world?

"Think of me, dearest, with the deepest and truest love of your heart, as I am thinking of you every moment of this wonderful life."

And another time: "It is strange to feel how everything is transformed since you came into my life and made me understand what this great happiness is. I laugh gaily at nothing; yet tears come into my eyes quickly at unhappiness or suffering. It seems as if I were born to love you with a yearning and a passion that sometimes frighten me, yet which I would rather die than live without. When I first loved you, I did not know that this would come, that I should not be able to imagine it to be otherwise. The thought is frightful; indeed, if anything were to happen to change the present, I think my heart would give one great, great throb, and all would be over. I draw my breath hard at the thought; there is a deep pain at my breast; my teeth are set. But how morbid I am to-day! how ungrateful for this splendid gift of your love that has been bestowed upon me! But somehow I feel frightened; I don't believe that anybody will be allowed to keep such happiness on this earth. So come to me quickly, dearest; you seem so far, far away from me. I kiss your dear letters, I wear them near my heart, at night they are under my pillow. I love you, I love you."

And this heart-cry broke down all the strong fibre of the man. Poor Alice! He must take care of such a child; he must cherish her life and make it perfect! Not in the least detail must he fail in his duty. Never for a moment must she think that this was—he flinched now before the words—an engagement of convenience!

An engagement of convenience! He slipped away to his room—away from the rest of the world!—and sat staring into the dusk. He knew now that he was face to face with the actuality that lay before him in all its horror. An engagement of convenience! He would have given the world to recall it. His eyes saw clear again—the enthusiasm that swirled and whirled around him had thus far sustained him: vibrations of romance had arisen within him, had resounded with a certain music. But these letters of Alice, this crescendo series, each soaring beyond the other, had illumined the horrible poverty of his own emotion. The freshness of her note was a revelation and yet an agony to him. If only he could have piped with half the thrill!

He could see at last that in his specious reasonings he had somehow assumed a largely passive attitude on her part. Indeed, egotistically preoccupied with his own side of the case, he had scarcely bestowed a thought on hers. This reality—immense—overpowering—of the romance in her heart terrified him. He had given her empty words, and she had given him—love! And what else, indeed, but empty words had he to offer her now?—had he to offer her in the whole long vista of their future? At the best a studied kindness, an acceptance of duty. He had entered on a rôle of mockery, and he knew now he was utterly unfitted to play it. His whole nature rose and cried aloud in revolt.

XV

At the beginning of the New Year Wyndham hastened back to town, and was soon at his post striving to adapt himself to the outlook of his life. He had tried to steel himself to confess the miserable truth to Alice, to lay it before her with a fidelity as unswerving as Nature, merciless both to him and to her. But her letters continued to shake him, and he had not the strength to face the inevitable wreckage. To break was to punish her: to continue was only to punish himself. His course was obvious: he must play the game *à outrance*. Yet he sought temporarily to escape the actuality by immersing himself desperately in routine.

So, for the present, his days were mapped out simply enough. He was up early, for the winter hours of light were precious. Braced for a great effort, he found himself drawing on unexpected stores of vitality; he flung himself on his masterpiece like a Viking into the mêlée of battle, and had the reward of splendid conquest. This sense of power, this subjugation of his material, made his old foiled strivings and strivings incomprehensible, incredible!

Meanwhile the domesticity of the house at the corner invaded his studio, and surrounded him with comforts and attentions that but threw up the more vividly the issues he sought to preclude. But he kept stifling down his rebellion; struggling to accept the position unreservedly, though sick with the sense of hypocrisy. He laughingly surrendered to Alice a duplicate key of the studio in token of their good-fellowship, and she and her mother devoted themselves to the loving task of smoothing his path, letting no point that might ruffle his inspiration elude their vigilance. Their whole life and activities seemed to converge to the studio. Mrs. Robinson kept discreetly in the background, though her brain planned and her tongue discussed, and she often went joyfully a-purchasing. Shortly before one o'clock Alice would march across, attended by a servant carrying his lunch, of temptations compact, imprisoned in shining caskets; and by the time Wyndham was ready to sit down, his table would be nicely set out, and the temptations spread to his view.

Many precious minutes were thus saved for him, and his train of ideas was luxuriously unbroken. This tact and thoughtfulness was characteristic of all the devotion that was cherished on him. Wyndham deeply appreciated its quality, and despite the pressure—with sending-in day looming barely three months ahead—gratitude no less than conscience drove him to acknowledgement, to contrive that the artist should not entirely swallow up Miss Robinson's future husband; though her expectations were considerately of the slightest. Thus his negative policy was answering effectively. With the passage of the days, he found himself sliding into a lethargy of acquiescence in the position. The mere physical fatigues of his labours dulled the unrest within him, and his brain fermented incessantly with the problems of masses and values which his great canvas still pressed upon him. He was glad he found it possible at last to be accepting all outer things so calmly. He told himself repeatedly: "Your revolt is over. You have decided there can be no break. So be as decent and affectionate as you can."

Thus his attentions seemed to her gallant and charming, to hold their touch of poetry. Flowers and bonbons, a book of verses or a novel were frequent tributes: after his work was done they went into town occasionally to a concert or a theatre, and if his conversation was of the theme with which his mind was most saturated, she did not regard that as otherwise than a compliment.

And so these winter days sped, and January was running its course. And out of this not unsuccessful routine there came to him the sense that his life was very full and singularly complete. Of perturbation or unforeseen excitement there was never a thrill. The only moment that held a flutter for him was when Mr. Shanner descended on the Robinsons, grey, decorous, and austere; congratulated the pair with an ashen smile, in the honeyed accents that had charmed so many diplomatists; and bestowed solemn formal attentions on the engaged lady throughout the evening.

The whole plot of his drama had in verity been revealed, was Wyndham's frequent reflection; and with that final comedy-scene the curtain had seemed to fall, and he knew all that there was to know.

But his own wretched money affairs were soon to give him food for pondering. Alice's portrait had gone home in a splendid frame to find a temporary resting-place before being tossed to the Academy; and Mr. Robinson, though seeing him face to face almost daily, delicately sent his cheque by post. Wyndham grasped it with relief: but it proved merely the illumination that accentuated the darkness. For overdue rent and many other calls made it melt away with terrifying swiftness; and Wyndham had indebted himself to the family jeweller for presents to Miss Robinson. Impecuniosity approached him again with no vague menace; kicked him brutally out of his ostrich-like attitude. Nevertheless he shrank in terror from the definite thought of pressing forward the marriage; though, in the clear light of these latter self- communings, money was the sole reason why he had sought it. Not only did he fear that life of simulation with a sickness immeasurable: but he foresaw endless money humiliations at the very outset.

He would fulfil his promise honourably, whatever the spiritual cost of it! But he could not face money humiliations in the eyes of his inferiors! A thousand times "no"! He must trust, despite all, to his own strength and performance!—he would do brilliantly with his pictures in the spring!—he would follow up the success and conquer London! He waved aside all his past disasters: he saw his good star in the ascendant, shining—he fixed his eyes on it fanatically. It was an irony of ironies that, after his great surrender, his pride should still flame up unconquered. Before the moral tragedy of love yoked to mockery, he might bow his head in resignation; but Miss Robinson's fortune loomed up as a ridiculous and contemptible complication in a situation already nigh impossible.

The metaphor of the vulture was often back in his mind now! The heap of carrion!—he had stooped for the sake of it, and it was now even more loathsome than his former morbid perception of it. His poverty seemed suddenly unbearable. In the past he had endured it. Now, for the first time, he was ashamed of it.

So he spoke to the Robinsons of a six months' engagement or thereabouts—which, to their ideas, was reputable and in order; and then felt he had time before him to fling down the gauntlet to fortune again.

But in estimating his resources he had counted without his new allies. Alice whispered into her father's ears her conviction that he might easily influence commissions for her *fiancé*; and, after thinking about it, Mr. Robinson felt he would like to have a try.

A rich, powerful Insurance Corporation had voted a portrait of its retiring president for the adornment of its board-room. Mr. Robinson set to work astutely, and the commission came to Wyndham. Item, three hundred guineas. But, before this new portrait had progressed very far, Wyndham had fascinated his subject—a tall, white-bearded merchant prince who sat to him with mysterious insignia, and resplendent chains and emblems. "A marvellous young fellow," he confided to Mr. Robinson. "I must really congratulate you on him—it's a treat to be in his society. And gifted! That great picture of Hyde Park Corner is worthy of Raphael." And for the pleasure of his company, and out of admiration for his talent, this bluff, good-natured president had at once arranged for paintings of himself and his wife for his own dining-room.

He generously and spontaneously made the fee seven hundred guineas. "There are two of us this time, and why should I get off cheaper than the Insurance Company?" he asked genially; in a spirit rare enough in the twentieth century, but nothing out of the way in the days of the grand patrons. "Besides, you're worth it," he roared out bluffly. "And the privilege of going down to posterity in your society can hardly be appraised at all."

Wyndham relished the compliment, though wincing inwardly at the thought that the wind that blew him good came always from the same quarter: yet in view of other important sitters he began to think of a more accessible studio.

"Why not a house with the studio?" suggested the Robinsons. "You could move in now, and furnish the rooms at your leisure, so as to have them ready for the marriage."

Wyndham fell in with the idea. He thought the locality had better be Chelsea, somewhere near the Embankment; a long distance from Hampstead, it was true, but an ideal situation for an artist. Somehow the sense of the distance, as he lingered on it, was not unacceptable. Alice flinched. "We could still look after you," she murmured bravely.

"Besides, I could easily cut to and fro in a hansom," put in Wyndham.

So off the old pair started at once on the quest, drawing some renewal of zestful youth from its absorbing interest. One day they reported a stroke of fortune; they had come upon the ideal thing. The rent was not impossible, and the tenant could have the option of purchasing the freehold. The next evening they took Wyndham to see it—a charming artist's house in Tite Street, with a broad frontage and a luxurious and unconventional interior. On the entrance floor— an unusual hall and three fine rooms. Above—a great studio and another excellent room. Below were the domestic regions with many household refinements, and bedrooms for the servants. Wyndham and Alice were enchanted.

Mr. Robinson was anxious to purchase this property outright as his promised wedding-gift; but Wyndham, again shrinking inwardly, diplomatically deferred the project. So the lease was signed, and the removal at once effected. Wyndham's belongings were swiftly installed on the upper floor of the house, at the loss of only a single day to him; and, leaving him to his labours, the others, in the enjoyment of their unlimited leisure, saw that the hall and stairway were made presentable for callers.

But at this point Wyndham came to a dead stop with his labour-canvas, to which he had of late devoted his mornings entirely, keeping the afternoons for his sitters. He saw that it was imperative he should now make some fresh sketches on the spot. But to regain his exact vision he must have access to the old window in Grosvenor Place. Yet the very thought of the house and the memory of those former visits had a strange shattering effect on him. And some warning voice rose sternly, bade him not renew these old associations.

He reasoned the matter out, and hesitation seemed absurd. For the sake of his picture, it was essential he should occupy a certain point of view. Though he had let the acquaintanceship lapse entirely ever since Lady Betty's marriage, access to that point of view was no doubt a simple matter. A mere letter of request, and the old earl would readily give his permission. This time he would probably come and go without seeing anybody at all.

Wyndham sat down to write the letter, the interest of the composition ousting for the time his irrational misgivings. He recalled himself to the earl's recollection, explained that the picture for which he had made the former sketches had unavoidably been put aside; but now that he was at last able to take it up again he desired to make some fresh sketches, and begged the use of his old post of vantage for a few mornings. He concluded with the hope that the earl was in the best of health, and sent his respects and remembrances to his daughter, should the earl be seeing her just then.

It was the merest courtesy on his part to show he had not forgotten Lady Betty! After all, their lives were so entirely alien now!

He addressed and stamped the letter; then his strong instinct against the whole proceeding reasserted itself. He rose and paced about. The warning voice said, "Keep away from Grosvenor Place. No good will come of it." "But it's absurd," he said aloud. "The thing's an absolute necessity—I can't throw over the picture at this stage. My whole artistic future depends upon it. What harm can possibly arise from my going there? Lady Betty? Why, she's a matron by now! And probably not even in England. And if she were, what is she to me now? And at any rate I am certainly nothing to her. If I stumbled up against her the very first morning I went there, we should still be far as the poles asunder. She was certainly a wonderful girl, and I of course fell headlong in love with her. Put any impressionable fellow with poetic ideals in the way of a lovely, clever girl and I suppose he's bound to feel cut up when somebody else marries her. But it's all as dead as King John now. I'll go there and do my work and wind up with a letter of thanks."

He put on his hat and coat, and took up the letter. "Don't go there," repeated the voice. "No good will come of it."

"Rubbish!" he said. "I can't chuck up the picture. It's all right."

He went downstairs and out into Tite Street, a little confused by all this current of doubt and reasoning, and by no means absolutely sure of himself. But, annoyed at realising this, he began to go forward sturdily, and flung the letter into the first pillar-box he encountered.

XVI

As Wyndham read the reply to his letter, it seemed as if the kind, bluff voice of the old earl were itself speaking. "A few mornings! Come along and make your nice little sketches for the next half-century. We have often thought of you, and wondered what you were up to. I think we may say with truth that we've missed you. This is a dull house now, and I suppose I'm getting old and dull myself. At any rate I've many a twinge in the joints, and am inclined to shut myself up in my library, though I'm never much of a reader." Then there was a PS. "Somebody or other tells me that you are contemplating matrimony. Well, you're a brave young fellow, and I like you for it. I congratulate you, and wish you luck."

As the next morning turned out fairly clear, Wyndham took his materials with him into a hansom, and rang the bell at Grosvenor Place at about ten o'clock. Not only had he decided that his misgivings were entirely morbid, but as a matter of course he had been quite open with the Robinsons about the arrangement. He had indeed explained to Alice some considerable time ago that he should in all likelihood find it necessary to make these fresh sketches on the very scene of the picture. It did not seem anything out of the way to her; she regarded it as a pure matter of work. It was sufficient that she understood his disappearance from the studio in the midst of these busy times. And as he had made it a point that she should possess a key of the new house just as she had had one of the old studio, she and her mother could come and go as they pleased in his absence, and proceed with their engrossing business of embellishing his hall and stairway.

But as he set foot in the house at Grosvenor Place after this long interval of years, Wyndham could not maintain his reasoned conviction of the simplicity and insignificance of the occasion.

He had the very real thrill of embarking on some extraordinary adventure; even of stepping outside his own existence—that theatre where he had been the spectator of his own fate, whose curtain—fire-proof—had already fallen on a played-out drama. But here was a strange theatre, with a curtain to rise, fascinating with promise of other drama to be revealed; yet the stillness and the dim light cast some spell of awe upon him.

A hand seemed to clutch at him and pull him back out of the house at the last moment. He was penetrating here against the warning of his deeper self; his heart beat fast not merely with the consciousness of imprudence, but of downright disloyalty to the settled destiny before which he had bowed his head so profoundly. The warning voice, too, was stern; but the sense of daring, of courting and facing some unknown delicious danger, lured him forward.

His lordship had already gone across to his club, the butler informed him; but he had half-expected Wyndham and had left orders in case he should present himself. As he followed the man up to the room he had used of old, he felt, despite the lofty well of the staircase, that the air hung heavy in the great house, muffled and silent with gigantic hangings, and thick carpets underfoot. Wyndham stood at the well-known window a leisurely moment, then arranged a chair or two, and unpacked his materials. The butler helped him to open the casement at the side of the bay and to rearrange the curtain, then asked if there was anything more he could do for him.

"Oh, would you get my hat again?" returned Wyndham, as a current of wintry air flowed in. He laughed; having forgotten he could not work uncovered.

When finally the man had complied with his request, and left him again, Wyndham looked out on the scene before him, his eye lingering for a moment on the royal gardens, then trying to catch the exact view he had painted. But as yet his mind was in too great a turmoil to concentrate itself sternly on the business in hand. "I shall be acclimatised in a minute or two," he reassured himself. "The atmosphere of this house is so oppressive—it upset me the first moment." He stood gratefully inhaling the fresher draught that streamed against his face; and when he had calmed down he took a turn or two about the room, observing it with interest. He had scarcely received any impression of it yet, but now he perceived that it was greatly changed in some respects. A new fireplace, and a mantel of a dainty cabinet-like design, replaced the former streaked framework of marble that had enshrined a great rococo grate. The double leaf door that led to some adjoining room had had its hanging stripped away, and the beauty of panelling showed naked and unashamed. The former carpet had gone; there were now soft Eastern rugs on the floor lying closely side by side, and covering it entirely. But though the Chippendale bookcases and the rest of the furniture had been left untouched, there was somehow a more intimate personal note about the room; accentuated perhaps by the trifles and photographs clustered about the mantelshelf. And then Wyndham came to an abrupt stop as if some sheet of flame had flashed by and seared him. There in the centre of the mantel, next to a tiny clock shaped like a Gothic arch, stood the silver easel bearing the framed photograph of his old Academy picture— his wedding present to Lady Betty!

Why was it here in this house? he asked himself, trembling. Had she left it behind because she esteemed it so lightly? Or was there perhaps some special significance in the fact; something his thought groped for wildly and blindly as if in panic?

He staggered back to the window, astonished to find how overcome he had been. The air revived him, and then a new and sterner spirit came upon him. Was he going to waste his whole morning by yielding himself to these idle and futile emotions? Resolutely he prepared his palette, and bent his mind by force to his task. He was pleased presently to find how exactly his eye recovered his scene; he felt he could almost lay the one he had painted over this one, and that it would fit like a transfer. Slowly and carefully he let the view sink into him, estimating the tones, the masses, the spaces; peopling it in his mind with all the figures and accessories that went to build up his great symbolic representation. Then he set one of the smaller canvasses on his knee, and started his note-making. Soon he was absorbed in the work, glad that he had forced himself to begin, and that the little wheels of his mind were turning so smoothly.

At eleven the butler appeared with wine and sandwiches, moved a little table over near Wyndham, and set down the tray within reach of his hand. Wyndham was glad of this refreshment; he had been in too uncertain a mood to do more than gulp down his coffee at breakfast, and the raw air had roused a craving for some sort of sustenance—a desire for stimulation rather than a keen hunger. He swallowed a glass of the wine, then began to nibble a sandwich slowly; but his mind was still in his work. He half-knew that the great folding door at the bottom of the room had opened, that somebody had entered. But it was as in a dream, and he did not look up. He considered his results, then poured more wine, and was in the act of raising it to his lips. God! what was this gracious, willowy figure, with the wonderful sheen on the fresh hair, and the girlish rounded cheeks! She was smiling at him, her eyes strangely alight under their long, soft lashes, her lips half parted; she was advancing towards him with outstretched hand. He put back the glass on the table and rose hastily, holding his sketch suspended from one hand; but his wits left him and he stared as at a ghost.

"Lady Betty!" he stammered.

"I am not an apparition," she reassured him; "but only a simple flesh-and-blood creature. Won't you put down your picture?" She smiled again at his embarrassment.

He laughed, and stood the sketch on a chair.

"Your presence certainly startled me," he confessed. "I had an idea you were thousands of miles away." They took hands—a good, comrade-like clasp. "Fortunately the idea was erroneous."

"Fortunately," she echoed, laughingly capping his gallantry.

"Oh, but how stupid I am! Forgive me!" He almost swept the hat from his head. "You see how I was scared; how ill prepared to cope with apparitions."

She laughed again. "You are to keep your hat on," she commanded. "My presence is easily accounted for; out of sheer restlessness of spirit I thought I should like to try London again—I had shunned it like the plague for ever so long. As all the nice little hotels were full, I descended on my father here, and practically appropriated this room."

"I fear I'm an intruder," he stammered.

"You had my permission; it was obtained in due form. Only I insisted my name was to be held back. I wanted to play the apparition, and my father entered into the whim of the thing. It seems like old times again."

Wyndham tried to transport himself back along the years. "I wonder whether there's anything better in life than to repeat the best moments of the past," he said pensively; "that is, if we can catch them with all the original magic in them." He saw her head drop a little; her expression was full of musing, half-sad and tender. Then he remembered that things had indeed changed since those old days, that Lady Betty had a husband! It was strange, but the apparition, besides the rest of the mischief, had momentarily driven the fact from the store of his knowledge. He had had absolutely the delusion that this was the brilliant Lady Betty, still unwed, to whom no suitor might aspire save with yachts and palaces.

"I have been calling you Lady Betty!" he exclaimed. "The delusion of old times was very strong."

"Please to keep on with the Lady Betty—I come back to it so easily. It quite pleased me when it slipped from your lips. You have stepped out of the long ago; I step back to meet you. You must still think of me as Lady Betty."

"And Lord Lakeden?" he murmured, though he felt the inquiry was rather a belated courtesy.

She stared at him, her cheeks white, her eyes growing unnaturally large.

"Your husband—I hope he is well," he explained, bewildered by this new expression that seemed to hold mingled amazement and horror.

"My husband!" She laughed—a weird peal that filled him with a fear as of blinding flashes to come. "Did you not know? I thought the whole world knew. I have no husband!"

He looked at her. "I don't understand," he stammered.

"I really believe you don't," she said, her face still blanched. "My married life was a short one. Lord Lakeden met with an accident on the Alps—the summer before last. He went out without a guide. The details were in all the papers. It was one of the sensations of the silly season." Again a nervous laugh, but more than ever it was full of unnatural echoes.

Instinctively Wyndham took off his hat again, and stood with his head bowed. "I am sorry. My condolences are late, but they are sincere."

"I somehow expected you would write to me at the time. Hosts and hosts wrote to me—till my head went dizzy; but never a word from you." She was speaking with greater command of herself now, but he felt in her words a world of reproach.

"I was living as a hermit at the time. I saw nobody for—shall I say it seemed to me a lifetime—save the poor old woman who came to turn out my studio once in every three months perhaps."

"Ah, you were unhappy!" Her face softened, telling of a swift, spontaneous sympathy.

"I was nigh starving. I never saw a newspaper unless by chance; my pennies were too precious."

"My poor friend!" Her eyes gleamed as if tears were about to come.

"I played the game up to a certain point with all my strength, but everything went against me from every quarter. I know there are men that would have risen triumphant above all these evils and difficulties. But I was not one of those men. I was beaten—smashed—utterly and hopelessly. I had not the smallest reserve of power to carry on the fight. I lived cut off from the world like a man in a tomb. I am ashamed to think that I kept myself alive——"

"No, no," she interrupted, shivering. "I can't bear it."

"I am ashamed that I did not die," he persisted. "It is the truth. It is the first time I say it either to myself or to another. In order to live I stepped below myself."

She covered her face with her hands. "I know you are misjudging. You are harsh with yourself. I hold to my faith in you."

"I lived on the earnings of my sister, who stinted herself in food and went shabbily clad that she might foster my work. Yet, for terrible months and months, I deceived her. I did no work. My will was dead. As a man I seemed to collapse physically and morally."

"You were not responsible. There is a limit to human endurance. You needed a delicious rest in some blue sunny place, in one of those earthly paradises where the orange-trees are golden in the sun. Your sister's love consecrated her sacrifice. She saved you for a great future. Her reward is yet to come."

"You see everything in so sweet a light; I can only hope that the issue will be as you say. It is on my future work that I have staked the redemption of my manhood in my own eyes. My work! That is where my real heart lies. Outside of that my life will be a mere appearance."

"But you have somebody else in your life now," she broke in, pale as death. "We heard a rumour that you were about to marry. Is it not true?"

He gasped at the bitter reminder. He hung his head. "It is true," he breathed.

"Then you have given your affections: you are happy?"

He wavered for a deep instant, the whilst her eyes rested on him gravely. "I have given my affections—I am happy." To himself he added: "I must be loyal to Alice, if indeed I have not gone too far already. But Lady Betty has made me see the truth. I understand now what I felt only obscurely—I bartered my life to the Robinsons, kind as they are, that I might repair the hurt and wrong to Mary."

"I congratulate you from my heart." She held out her hand again with a wan smile. He took it limply; feeling he held it on false pretences, that the sudden check he had put on his impulsive outpouring had raised a barrier between them.

"But forgive me for my stupid egotism. Here am I, a great strapping fellow, pitying myself because of a very ordinary sort of dismal failure; more than commonplace by the side of the great sorrow that came to you."

"Great sorrow!" Again that wild peal of laughter. "It was a great joy, the greatest joy I have ever known. When they brought me the news, I went out into the garden of our chalet, and, sure that no eyes were upon me, I danced on the green in the sunlight—with the blood pulsing so deliciously through my veins. I was free—I was free! The world seemed so beautiful! the sky and the mountains so exquisite! Life was such a gift! I was free—free!"

She stood up straight, all her muscles tense, her limbs quivering. The pallor had gone; her face glowed with an exultation that was almost of triumph. He stood spellbound at her revelation, unable to find a word.

"Ah, you don't understand what it is to be free again! Degradation! I tasted it to its depths. Yours was no degradation! You know nothing of it. I was tied to a brute—no, the brutes are decent and lovable. He was lower—he was lower."

Her voice broke in a sob, though no tears came. Wyndham was still silent; he would not seek to penetrate her last reserve. "Don't think me too horrible," she pleaded. "You are the only living being to whom I have bared my soul. You were the one to whom my mind flew as my friend—I have waited for this moment. You must not set me down as a monster."

"A monster!" he exclaimed. He was thrown off his irksome guard, and the instant was fatal! "Oh, no, no! I shall always hold you for what you are, for what you have always been to me—a rare princess!"

"I have always been to you—" she echoed, then broke off, her bosom heaving, her eyes flashing out with the full comprehension of his almost unwitting avowal. Then she went pale to the lips again. "You never spoke," she breathed, "and I did not guess."

He realised, half in a daze, that his secret had escaped him; yet—with swift change of mood—he was recklessly glad that she understood at last: even as, standing before her, he, too, understood at last—reading her distress, treasuring her implied reproach for its clear significance, though it put him on his defence.

"I was not even on the footing of a guest in this house. The very bread that kept me alive was not my own. It is the law of the world."

"You were wrong. There is no law."

"There is the law of pride," he argued. "We men do not stoop to happiness, we stoop only to degradation…. And then I feared to break the spell," he went on, seeking a lighter strain. "The wonderful princess would disappear, and I should be left rubbing my eyes."

"But it was you who disappeared. The princess thought you shunned her, and she was left—to weep—"

He hung his head like a broken reed. He had no longer anything to hide; he had already sufficiently disclosed to her that his marriage was to be a loveless one. She would understand and respect his first desire to keep his true relation to Alice sacred from her gaze. But Lady Betty's revelation of tragic experience had swept him off his feet. He had responded to her great emotion; had confessed his allegiance to her through all and despite all. His life seemed linked to hers with a mystic, enduring passion. And yet were they not hopelessly sundered?

"'Men must work and women must weep,'" she quoted. "Ah, well! we never can win our ideals; life is always a compromise. Perhaps it's a blessing to see our clear obligations."

"Yes—if one has the strength to turn one's eyes aside from the dreams; but saddening otherwise."

"Saddening otherwise," she echoed pensively. "But I thank you that I am still the wonderful princess, even after my terrible confession."

He took a step forward, and seized her hand impulsively.

"Never believe otherwise, no matter what you may hear of me. Whether this be the last time I see you or not, whether I fail and be broken again, my last breath shall proclaim my allegiance to—the wonderful princess! Listen, the woman I am marrying is more than goodness itself. I cannot pretend to match her; my manhood falls below her womanhood. But into the inner chamber of my life she can never enter. Out of loyalty to her I gave you to understand that I had given my affections. That is true, but not in the sense I led you to believe. There is no reason why I should not be open now; it would be a poor compliment to you after all this mutual confidence if I could not bare to you the absolute truth. And the absolute truth is—I have sold myself for safety, for the sake of my art, and for the sake of my sister. It would be unendurable were there not the mitigation of the esteem I have for the woman I am marrying, and for the many qualities of kindness and goodness in that whole household. But she is not my true mate. Unlimited as is her virtue in a hundred ways, she herself is yet limited. My work must find inspiration entirely apart from her. May I think of you, princess, as my inspiration?"

"She is a good woman. You must be loyal to her."

"It would be no disloyalty; I should be cherishing the ideal."

She was smiling and radiant again. "I can scarcely stop you—I see it would certainly be rash to try. Well, goodbye now; I have a thousand little neglected things crying to me. And your moments, too, are precious. You will be here again one of these mornings?"

"To-morrow," he said. "For the present, we may be friends?"

"Till the tide sweeps us apart."

"The cruel tide!" he murmured. "But you will always be the wonderful princess," he insisted again.

"I shall try to be worthy of the title."

She gave him a charming curtsey, flitted away down the room, threw him yet a smile, and disappeared behind the panelled door through which she had come.

XVII

For some time Wyndham stood with his head still bowed as Lady Betty's voice lingered in his ear. Her figure was still there before him, her lovely girl's face radiant with the smile with which she had vanished, her slender form in all its upright grace; a nymph of whom Botticelli had caught a glimpse on a spring morn when the world was rediscovering beauty.

He tried to recall the scene that had just been enacted, and dizzily held it all in a flash. He and Lady Betty were in love with each other! The fact that he had always cherished the thought of her held a deeper significance than he had known! Throughout all his sufferings—throughout all her sufferings—an ideal friendship for each other had subsisted in their minds. He had supposed her as indifferent as she was unattainable; that his love was one of those secret, mocking dramas that sometimes play themselves out in the souls of men and women. Yet it was to him that her deepest thought had turned! She had enshrined him in her heart! And he lying the whilst in darkness and misery!

It was precious now—this new sweetness that had come to him. Sweetness! His thought broke off at the word. Rather was it a bitter irony! Lady Betty and he had been cheated by life. Could he be even sure his eyes would behold her again? Was she not the soul of honour and rectitude! For a deep instant they had been swept towards each other; but at once her attitude towards his marriage had been clear and pronounced, and she might even now be bitterly regretting their meeting.

He sat down at last, and took up his work again; but his mind was utterly unfitted for concentration on any task. Better to get back again to his own studio, he told himself. So he stowed away his materials in a corner, and presently slipped downstairs; telling the butler, whom he met in the hall, that he would be there again at ten the following day.

At Tite Street men were tacking down a thick green length of Turkey carpet on his staircase, and Alice was superintending the operation. Here was his comfortable future in active preparation! And already he felt the atmosphere swallowing him up, claiming him body and soul.

He stayed a moment on the landing, affecting an interest in the proceedings. When he turned into the studio Alice came after him.

"You hardly seem well, dear," she said, observing him anxiously.

"You surprise me," he returned. "I am not conscious of any aches or pains," he added, with an implication of gaiety.

She did not seem convinced. "This malarial air must have affected you," she insisted.

"I don't say I find it pleasant." He seized the poker, as if glad to make a diversion, and stirred the fire energetically. "I'm a little bit disgusted, too; the day wasn't as clear as I hoped—there was a good deal of mist about."

"Better luck to-morrow!" she said.

He struck hard at a knob of coal, making a dreadful clatter. "I hope so, indeed," he answered, thinking it curious that Alice should now be expecting him to go to Grosvenor Place as a matter of course. "At any rate," he added, as it struck him Alice might reasonably be hoping for some account of his morning's visit, "they were kind to me—just as of old. Lady Lakeden sent me refreshments, and afterwards came herself to see how things were progressing."

"I suppose Lady Lakeden is a sister of the earl," she conjectured.

"No, his daughter—a mere girl," he explained, with the flicker of a laugh. "It was a great surprise. It is only a few years back that I was asked to her wedding. After that, I got out of touch with them, and I did not know she had lost her husband very soon after the marriage. He met with an accident on the Alps."

Alice was blanched. "How terrible!" she whispered.

There was a silence. Wyndham held his hands to the flame he had been at such pains to create. He hoped he had satisfied her interest sufficiently; for, of course, the whole scene between himself and Lady Betty must be kept from her inviolate. Was it not for Alice's own sake and happiness?

"It makes me afraid!" said Alice, breaking the silence. "Perhaps nobody is allowed to keep too great a happiness."

He winced. "She was always kind to me," he said, evading the train of her reflection. "I spent many hours at my post in those ancient times, and there were always unobtrusive attentions that made my work the easier."

"I should like to know and love her," said Alice pensively.

Wyndham was silent. Her words startled and embarrassed him, since he had been taking it for granted that she and Lady Betty would never come into contact. Besides, in a way, Alice had given utterance to more of a thought than a wish, so that a response hardly seemed necessary. They lunched together, and Alice went off soon after, leaving him to receive his sitters—the president and his wife, who were both to arrive that afternoon.

"Of course, you won't expect me at Hampstead," he reminded her. "You remember I put my name down for a club dinner to-night."

"Of course I remember," she said. "But I shall write you a letter instead. Please look for it when you come home to-night."

But Wyndham did not dine at the club after all; at the last moment he decided to spend the evening alone at his studio. It seemed a long time since he had had a few quiet hours all to himself. Moreover, it was strangely a boon to hear no other voices for once, and he lay back pleasantly in his chair, though conscious of an uncommon degree of weariness. And, in the calm and solitude of the studio, intensified by the echoing of his occasional movements through the empty rooms beneath him, the Robinsons seemed indeed a long way off up at Hampstead there, and for the first time it seemed a positive bondage to him, this constant duty of journeying across town to dine with them.

The nine o'clock post brought the promised letter from Alice, but from amid the little heap in the box he picked out another eagerly. The writing was Lady Betty's. He had never seen very much of it in the old days, yet he recognised it at once.

He remembered just then a shrewd dictum of Schopenhauer—that, if we wished to learn our real attitude towards any person, we should watch and estimate our exact emotion at catching sight of the well-known handwriting on a letter we are just receiving. He certainly could not help observing the contrasting emotions with which he welcomed these two letters. Alice's, at his first glimpse of it, had given him a deepened sense of the irrevocable. Yet there went with this a kind, affectionate thought in which was a world of appreciation. But he knew pretty nearly what the letter would contain; it could well be read at leisure.

He tore open Lady Betty's at once, and read it feverishly as he stood there in the hall. "MY DEAR FRIEND," it ran—"My father was so disappointed when he got home at hearing that you had been, and had already flown. He suggests that you should stay to-morrow and join us at luncheon, and he asks me to bend your mind well in advance to the contemplation of such an ordeal —as he seriously considers it. The present cook doesn't meet with his approval, but be reassured! It was only a new sauce sent up one day with pride; but that unfortunate sauce has since flavoured everything. My father has naturally imagination; at his age he has prejudices. Could even a Vatel face the combination?

"And now that I have performed my filial duty, I will add a few lines for my own pleasure. I humbly proffer a request. An idea has come to me that seems most charming—before we part again! Since you are working here, won't you make a small sketch of me?—a tiny, typical thing, hit off all in a dash—and give it to me as a souvenir of your work? Nothing that would steal much of your time. I understand that every moment is precious just now, with the exhibitions so near, and I wish you not to do it if you are very pressed. In return I shall have a souvenir to give you—a strange, strange thought of mine. Please feel very curious about what it is to be, for you are certainly not going to be told till the time comes. *Au revoir.* Your friend, BETTY."

Wyndham mounted the stairs again slowly, and in the studio he re-read these precious lines, lingering on each individual word, and setting a marvellous price on it. He was happy yet terrified at this flash from fairyland into his strenuous existence.

But her words, "before we part again," rang in his mind, lurid, persistent. Yes, Lady Betty would vanish out of his life soon enough; even though her letter confirmed the respite which she had indeed seemed to grant that morning, but which nevertheless—anticipating regret—he had scarcely ventured to dream of! There could clearly be no question as to her attitude towards his marriage; he told himself that even the crime (flashing splendidly through his brain) of cutting himself free from the Robinsons with one heroic stroke in order to throw his whole life into this wonderful romance would be futile. Would Lady Betty ever consent to happiness purchased at such a price?—woo her as he might!

But this sweet, dainty dream of her brief companionship—was he called upon to turn away from it? Surely, no; else she had been the last to dazzle him with it. Her lead could be trusted to be beyond reproach. And, however she regarded it in her heart, would there not be for him a little of strangely deep happiness; something to remember always, to leave a smile on his face at the moment of death?

The charm of the thought won him almost irresistibly. Lady Betty was his inspiration for ever; nay, that ideal elusive face would have been his inspiration even if he had never encountered her again. The harm—if harm there was in their meeting again—had been done irreparably in the past!

All would be over soon enough! What could emphasise it more than this very letter of hers he held in his hand? Was it not Lady Betty's underlying thought in this desire for an exchange of souvenirs?

All would be over soon enough! Life would bear them apart, but the touch of sweetness would remain as an illumination. He could never be cheated out of that.

What was this souvenir she intended for him—this "strange, strange thought" of hers? She had in truth piqued his curiosity, and he foresaw her delight at his admitting it. What, indeed, could it be? And, occupied now with this fascinating speculation, he languidly took up his other letters, his fingers turning them over with an extreme indifference. Presently, with a sudden decision, he broke Alice's envelope, and began to read her note. Three of the sides out of four were exactly as he had anticipated, but towards the end he lighted on a passage that unnerved him abruptly. "I have been thinking of your friends in Grosvenor Place. My heart goes out to Lady Lakeden. How hers must lie broken and bleeding! To lose a husband after only a few months of wedded life! I shut my eyes and try to think that such a thing cannot happen! And she and her father have always been so kind to you. My love for you is so great that I love everybody that spares one little thought specially for you."

Wyndham threw the letter down. That was enough; he must sacrifice all to the duties he had undertaken. He and Lady Betty must not see each other again. Could he not hear her dear voice saying, "Life is always a compromise. Perhaps it's a blessing to see our clear obligations." Well, he at any rate saw his clear obligations. He would reply to Lady Betty; he would enter into the situation in all sincerity. He would paint her some little thing for the souvenir, and send it to her, and perhaps she might care to send him hers in return. His meeting her to-day and this loving exchange of gifts would remain in his thought as the most poetic episode of his life; but an episode that must speedily be closed.

She would understand and approve. Was she not the very spirit of chivalry, of honour and goodness? Since fate had given its decree, let them both bow to it!

XVIII

But the next morning he dressed with care, choosing with fastidiousness among his flowing silk ties, and went off to Grosvenor Place, stopping only on the way to get a new canvas for Lady Betty's portrait. It was as if some great arm had encircled him irresistibly, and hurried him out of his studio, and jerked him into a hansom.

The first thing that caught his eye as he entered the usual room was a travelling easel opened out at its full length, brass-jointed, proudly agleam; and he marked his appreciation of the significance of its presence in equally significant fashion—by standing the newly-acquired canvas upon it. Then he installed himself at his window, and after a little preliminary fumbling he found himself well under weigh. At last he had struck the clear, even light he wanted, and he worked rapidly with his note-taking till the time the butler appeared with refreshments.

He sipped his wine, with one eye on the folding-door and the other maintaining some interest in the sketches before him. But the more vigilant eye of the two soon found its reward. Lady Betty appeared on the very stroke of noon, and came to him all fresh and smiling, in sunny contrast to his sense of the dull wintry universe.

"You seem a trifle thoughtful," she observed.

"I was speculating about the mysterious gift you promise."

She laughed merrily. "I observe, then, it is a bargain." She nodded towards the easel.

"I have had a charming idea as well," he said. "Could you give me two hours a day till the end of the month?"

"By all means."

"I should like to send you to the Salon."

"That is indeed a charming idea. But you must not risk your big work," she reminded him. "That, too, has to be ready in a few weeks."

"I shall have the whole of March for it exclusively. I am finishing my portraits this month."

"Your sketches are satisfactory?"

"One or two mornings more, and I shall have as much as I need. My difficulty with the picture all these years has been that I have had to build it up largely out of my own mind. My actual scene has of course never really existed in nature—though once or twice I managed to catch something of the kind here on the spot. But that was quite tumultuous and indiscriminate, whereas I wanted to catch the essence of the thing."

"You frighten the poor little amateur out of her wits."

They both laughed. "I had to snatch bits as best I could. Whilst striving to suggest the tumult and movement, I yet picked my material so as to give contrast and symbolism. Then I had to get my workmen and all the other kinds of folk to pose separately in the studio. Fortunately my old studio opened at the back into a little glass-house, and so I was able to pose the model as in the open. Naturally with the work on so huge a scale, I was wrestling with almost every drawback that could be conceived. It was no doubt a great mistake to have planned it at all, but I have learnt lessons I shall never forget."

"But you have conquered at last."

"Honestly, no. But it will succeed. My first idea was that the whole scene should be bathed in sunlight. But this, by throwing a vibration and glow over everything, would have submerged the social contrast of Fashion and Labour —would have made the whole thing primarily a piece of pure technique, and weakened its human significance. I did not want the sunshine to be the motive of the picture; I wanted the human side to stand out first, and speak with its full force. I therefore chose a dull light, so that the smartness of Fashion glows in relief against the drab tones of Labour. I am afraid though I am exaggerating the contrast more than I really like. That, however, will help it with the great public."

"I don't think I approve of such sentiments. I want you to strive for the highest."

"That is the future. But here it was a question of extricating myself from wreckage. As art it is far from perfect. But its success will help me to higher things."

"On that ground only we must pass it this time. But I have been wondering how you will use these last sketches you have been making." She examined them attentively awhile. "To me they are not very intelligible, though I have a vague idea of their purpose."

"They are mere notes," he explained. "If you will come here by the window and get the point of view, I think I can make them perfectly intelligible."

She came and stood by his side, and one by one he took up the little canvasses, explaining his tones and masses and relative values. As he spoke his words seemed to evoke a strange life from the blurs and brush marks. A splash of colour changed before her eyes into an omnibus; a darker blob into a brougham; vistas and spaces, buildings and foliage stood revealed out of chaos. She listened with a pretty interest, her lips daintily parted, her breath coming lightly, yet her features composed into a characteristic stateliness—of which catching a sudden glimpse as she brushed close to him, he mentally registered the judgment "surpassingly fine!" He was glad he had caught that aspect; it summed her up in a way so perfectly. There was his Salon picture!

"And while you have been listening I have been studying you," he confessed, as he placed the sketches aside.

"I should have thought you knew me by heart."

"You are not so definite and limited. Beauty is always flashing surprises on the eye that can see."

"I think I like that," she said gaily. "I must bear it in mind…. It's only a toy easel," she flew off as he drew it forward. "In spite of its excellent preservation, it is a relic of my childhood: in the family I was supposed to have talent, so an aunt gave it to me for a birthday present, pegs and all, to take into the country and sketch all sorts of pretty bits. There was a little stool that went with it."

"It will serve admirably—without the stool," he added, with a smile. "I should like you to stand with the folding-door as a background. I think we're lucky to have such an interesting stretch of panelling in the room. We must get all the light on it we can."

She tripped down the room gaily, and stood as he indicated. Then he manipulated the blinds and the curtain till a clear, soft light, melting gradually into the surrounding greyer tones, fell on the wood-work, and Lady Betty stood illuminated with a suggestion of airy phantasm.

"The face a shade more to the left," he commanded. "There! Now I have caught you again."

He worked with an appearance of rapidity. "A very dream of elusiveness!" he exclaimed presently. "I must seize it whilst I'm in form."

"Ah, I was just thinking it over," she said gravely. "I am not sure that I am really so pleased at being 'elusive.' If my features are not to be seized, how are they to be remembered? Definite women have the best of it—they are less easily forgotten, I should say."

"That would be true if one had any desire to remember them," he returned. "But no," he corrected himself; "it is not true in any case. Where there is only one definite set of features to forget, it is forgotten wholly and absolutely, once that point is reached. But the woman with the elusive features has so many sides that it would take a long time to forget them all. And then a man is always so entrancingly occupied calling up her picture. You let all the fleeting phases float around you. What more engrossing than to choose among these rival gleams of loveliness, yet find them all enchanting and precious?"

"You convince me of the absolute unforgetableness of the elusive woman," she laughed. Then, abruptly, she grew grave again.

When he stopped work for that morning, they both inspected the canvas critically. "I think I have made the right beginning—you see the spirit of the idea is all there."

"With the help of the lesson you gave me before," she ventured.

"If I continue equally well, we shall find oceans of time before the end of the month. Wouldn't it be splendid if the Salon received it!"

She was full of joyous delight at the prospect, but, glancing at the clock, gave an exclamation of horror. "We are forgetting lunch!"

A minute or two later Wyndham was shaking hands with the old earl, who was gazing into his face with apparently affectionate interest.

"This is very pleasant," said the earl. "Why, bless my soul, I haven't caught a glimpse of you for—let me see—three or four years is it? What has been amiss? Genius starving in a garret?—eh?"

"Pretty good guess," said Wyndham.

"You look fat enough, and sleek enough," laughed the earl. "On the face of things, I should have taken it that you've done very much better than I have. Now, if you had had to put up with my scoundrel of a cook— —"

"There was only one sauce on one occasion, father."

"So you insist, so you insist. Well, you seem pretty straight on your feet again, my boy; so all's well that ends well."

They sat down to table.

"Making lots of nice little pictures?—eh?" recommenced the earl genially.

"Oh, the one I am making sketches for here is rather tremendous—the size of a wall!"

"The size of a wall!" echoed the earl. "My gracious!"

"And now Mr. Wyndham has started a tiny one of me," put in Lady Betty.

"I'm going to stand to him an hour or two every morning, and we'll send it to the Salon next month."

"Bless my soul! That'll be a very pretty little thing."

"It's only one side of me. Mr. Wyndham thinks I've so many sides, and he selected just one of them."

"Mr. Wyndham's a genius, but, with all deference to him, I don't see that you've any more sides to you than I have or Mr. Wyndham has. We have each two sides and no more." He raised his tumbler of egg-and-milk and whiskey, and drank deeply. The others laughed.

"Oh, Mr. Wyndham thinks I'm so many persons rolled into one," explained Lady Betty, "and that you can take your choice."

"Many persons rolled into one! You are!" said the earl emphatically, setting down his glass. "Only I never *can* take my choice. If Mr. Wyndham has succeeded in doing so, I offer him my congratulations. Oh, by the way, talking of congratulations, it is true, I suppose, that you are going to be married!"

Lady Betty looked down and manipulated her fish.

"One of these days," said Wyndham lightly. "There is no date fixed yet."

"Ah," said the earl. "How is your *fiancée*?"

"Perfectly well," said Wyndham. "First-rate."

"A Miss—er—Llewellyn—wasn't it?"

"Miss Robinson," corrected Wyndham.

"Oh, ah—Miss Robinson! Yes, yes, that was the name—perfectly!" said the earl. "Mind you give her my compliments and respects.... By the way, Betty, did I tell you I'm sick of the climate? We shall have thrown out the Embankment Bill by the end of the week, and then I can turn my back on the House. It'll be Egypt or a voyage to Japan—why, I might meet Mr. Wyndham on his honeymoon!—eh?—what? I'll go across to Cockspur Street this afternoon, and see what's sailing."

"Shall I come with you, father, and help you to make up your mind?"

"If you'll be so kind," said the earl. "It was my intention to suggest that you should accompany me a great deal further than that, but I changed my mind just now."

"That is very considerate of you, father."

"Not at all, not at all." The earl made a movement of deprecation. "You couldn't come till the end of the month, so I simply make a virtue of necessity."

"You horrify me, father. You are making Mr. Wyndham think you are sorry I am standing to him."

"It's only my fun, little girl. You don't really suppose I want my own daughter trotting behind my tail, and keeping her watchful, charming eye on all my doings. No, no, no! I had it in mind to suggest your joining me as a matter of form. You might have liked it, and I wanted to do the proper thing. But I'm only too glad of the opportunity of having you off my hands. Mr. Wyndham was really providential. Meanwhile I shall be proud to think of the nice little picture of you—I beg your pardon, of one side of you—hanging in the Salon."

"If you take one of the long voyages, I presume you'll be away some months," ventured Wyndham.

"Probably till the autumn. I assure you my daughter long since washed her hands of me. She carries off her maid and disappears for years at the time. When I think she's in Paris, somebody says, 'I saw your daughter last week at Baden-Baden. How well she's looking!' When I imagine she's in Baden-Baden, somebody says, 'I met your daughter at Florence last week. How well she's looking!' Nowadays I never speculate as to her whereabouts. I give her absolutely *carte blanche*. I'm prepared to hear and believe anything of her, and what's more! to approve of it and give her my blessing. On one point, you will observe, the testimony is unanimous: 'How well she's looking!' That's the one settled thing about her—and the sides of her. For I suppose no two people ever do see the same side of her." He scrutinised her beamingly.

"Very well, father. It shall be goodbye till the autumn. We shall part friends."

"So far as I see at present. We've to get through the week yet. You'll lunch with us these days, Mr. Wyndham?"

Wyndham murmured his acceptance, enchanted at being so cordially recognised as a friend of the house.

XIX

Wyndham told Alice of the happy chance that had presented itself of a dash at Lady Lakeden's portrait, and held out the possibility of the Salon's finding a corner for it.

"How delightful!" she exclaimed. "Wouldn't it be brilliant to be in the Salon as well as in the Academy?"

"It's just a dainty little study, and of course I'm doing it for the pure pleasure of the thing. But the committee may not consider it important enough for serious consideration, though that depends on what I make of it. In any case I'll present it to her afterwards in acknowledgment of all their past kindness."

"It's the nicest acknowledgment you could possibly make them. I am so glad you thought of it." Her approval of the idea was generous and eager. And she was excitedly interested in the Grosvenor Place household. She plied him with questions. Was it an old peerage? Was there a great country house? Had Lady Lakeden a brother? Then who was the heir to the title?—would it pass to a collateral line? He enlightened her on all these matters, sketching out for her the grooves which the lives of such people generally occupied. And he threw out the reflection that it was lucky indeed the renewal of his relations with Grosvenor Place had not been delayed any further. He had gone back there in the very nick of time, for the house was going to be shut up; the earl leaving in a week or so to take a long sea voyage, whilst Lady Lakeden meditated departure as soon as the portrait was done. Alice remarked that they seemed to be fond of roaming about a great deal, and Wyndham pointed out that Lady Lakeden and her father were exceptionally placed, were to a great extent emancipated from the "swim." The earl had practically retired from society, and his daughter, as a young widow, naturally sought distraction in her own way, though of course she could float brilliantly back into the world whenever the mood took her.

Since the portrait was going to the Salon, he was naturally compelled to tell Alice about it. But the intense way in which she seemed to be fixing her eyes on the Grosvenor Place household disconcerted him beyond measure. This fresh interest of his had become her interest too; she had fastened on it out of all proportion to its visible importance. At uneasy moments he asked himself if she suspected that something lay behind this apparently simple and innocent acquaintanceship; for her insistent and almost morbid return to the subject on the following days indicated its amazing hold of her.

Yet, obviously, it was impossible that she should be cherishing any ideas of that kind. He flattered himself that his demeanour towards her, in this trying and difficult period, was perfect; that he was as tender in all their relations as if his heart were truly hers. Nay, he was devoting even more of his leisure to her than ever before. And for the very reason that the evening journeys to Hampstead had become distasteful, he was the more careful that there should be no falling off in his attendance there. In no wise could he have betrayed himself to his affianced wife. No, she could not possibly have any suspicion of the truth: he was satisfied that her preoccupation with the Grosvenor Place household all arose out of womanly sympathy on her part; that Lady Lakeden's tragic widowhood had touched the depths of her imagination.

Poor Alice! How simple and trusting her surface reading of the facts! How ignorant of the brutal complications, as grotesque as incredible, in which Nature often wrapped up human unhappiness!

What a terrible tangle it was for them all! Were he free now, how gladly would his princess have placed her hand in his! In the old days the possible marriage of the brilliant girl had been hedged around with extraordinary limitations—to which he too had bowed as to something in the order of nature. But, as a widow, she would naturally be expected to please herself when matrimonially inclined. By common social understanding, even the noblest and richest of widows may permit herself a considerable latitude of choice, and no word of criticism can lie against her unless she has travelled rather far out of the conventional grooves. A marriage between him and Lady Betty now might raise a flicker of interest beyond what was usual— considering his notorious poverty—but it could call down nobody's censure.

But all this, alas! was but an idle speculation now. The time sped; the earl bade him goodbye; and he realised that the end was fast approaching. The few days that remained to him of Lady Betty's companionship became trebly precious, to be counted with despair! Though only an hour or two out of the twenty-four was spent in her society, his whole heart and mind, his whole life, were concentrated there. Each day he brought her a bunch of lilies of the valley, which she fixed in her bosom and insisted he must include in the picture. And during the enchanted time they were together, they talked freely and in perfect trust. It was more than a friendship—more than an exchange of confidences; it was more than the intimacy of a soul with itself—for that is not always honest even at its most courageous moments. In this free, splendid realm of communion with her, he stood up in all his manhood: rising to that simple truth which is yet of the heavens and the spaces; measuring himself against great standards; seeing and regretting his egotisms, vanities, self- deceptions; valuing himself humbly. The depths of Lady Betty's sympathy were indeed profound. She could enter into his life, appreciate motives barely realised by himself, and, with charming broad humanity, understand and forgive his actions even when he felt ashamed of them as unworthy and discreditable. No comedy of sentiment here—no playing of the saint on either side; but a noble simplicity, a serene good faith, a spontaneous self-revelation!

He recounted to her, as naturally as everything else, the whole history of his acquaintanceship with the Robinsons. He spared himself not a detail: how he had first dallied with temptation, his moment of panic, his specious reasoning, his ignoble surrender! He laid himself bare as with a scalpel. Yet of Alice he spoke always with reverence and loyalty, dwelling on her devotion, on the little she needed from him to give her happiness. And Lady Betty caught his appreciation of her. "I seem to know and understand her well," she said. "She is a delicate, untarnished soul. She seems more real to me than people who have lived near me all my life. And so her heart has gone out to me! I feel I could never bear to meet her—the moment would be too terrible! Ah, why did you not speak in the old days?"

"I repeat I had not the right. And then I did not dream I was worth one single thought of yours."

"I gave you all my thoughts. You were so serious. You sat with knitted brow, sternly in your work, and I hardly dared to come near you. You seemed remote from women; grimly devoted to your purpose—to triumph or to die! At poor me you scarcely deigned to look. And then you disappeared, and I knew you would not return."

"I disappeared. I left happiness behind me, and retired into my living tomb."

"My heart bleeds for you." There was a pause. Her eyes were full of pain. But presently she broke the silence, as if discovering some crumb of comfort. "This time at least you will not be going to privation."

"In my heart of hearts privation is preferable."

"Ah, no. Remember it is the call of duty. It is the sacrifice we must make for Alice's sake. She is a good woman. Her life must not be broken."

"I promise I shall try to make her happy—whatever the cost. But think how happy we should have been together, you and I, darling."

"We should have been happy together," she said in a low voice. "It would have been a perfect union. But I say again that life is a compromise. Our demands are great; we have to accept the little that is granted."

"Yet the door still stands open," he mused. "We may yet take our fate into our own hands."

"The door stands open, but we turn our backs upon it."

"We are too strong," he groaned. "I am tempted to pray for weakness."

She drew herself up, her face alight with a noble radiance. "Let us both be proud of our strength. We have set right above everything."

"But suppose we are mistaken—" he urged tensely.

"We cannot strike her down! No, no, we must not take away her great happiness—you have given it to her! I depute you, if you love me, to guard her welfare—on my behalf and on your own. Remember, too, she is happy with so little!"

"I shall be a loyal husband. But, in the realms that lie outside her penetration, you have promised that I may cherish the thought of you as an inspiration."

"To speak to you with my own voice—to help you to the strength that cannot falter!"

But the end was close upon them. He could not linger over the picture, even had he wished. As the last days slipped by his face saddened visibly. Lady Betty begged him to bear up. He was so changed in aspect that Alice could not fail to notice it.

"There is no danger," he returned. "She has already spoken of it, and I have put it down to fatigue. She has seen how desperately I have been working for months on end, and she is satisfied I need rest."

One day, he ventured to question Lady Betty about her plans, but she replied that they were vague. She only knew that she would travel for the present; she would not make up her mind as to details till the last moment.

"But even then I should not tell you," she added, with a wan smile. "Our parting must be decisive. I shall read of your career, and my mind shall be always with you in your work; but I shall not cross your path again. There is one last thing I suggest. When you have finished the picture, let us spend the whole of our last day together."

"I shall set it apart. We shall consecrate it with our farewell."

"I shall give you the souvenir I promised. I shall keep it till the end; and then it will be goodbye."

"Goodbye?" he breathed. "Oh, it is cruel!"

He was shaken again. Some wild rebellion was rising in him, and vainly Lady Betty tried to calm him with pleading—even with tears. But she revealed only the more her own anguish.

At last she had command of herself again, and put a stern inflection into her voice.

"For Alice's sake you must conquer yourself. No, let it be for my sake. I put it as the test of your love for me. Otherwise I shall believe that your love is selfish."

"I promise I shall conquer myself, but I must have time."

"You make me terribly afraid—you may wound her by a chance word."

"That is impossible. Her mind is serene—no word of mine shall disturb it."

But Lady Betty's fears were by no means allayed. She wrote him long letters, imploring him to keep command of himself, else she would regret bitterly that they had ever met again. They had both fought this terrible battle: they were neither of them emerging unscathed, but their wounds and hurt were the price of honourable victory. She was sure of herself; but was he—the man!—to shrink back when the supreme moment came? The thought of loyal duty accomplished would bring equanimity hereafter.

"Ah, if all were only a dream!" he exclaimed sadly, as he lay thinking of nights. And then he would try to believe that he had not met Lady Betty again, had never even heard of her since her wedding-day. He had never made the acquaintance of the Robinsons, had never set foot in their great ugly house at the corner. Were not all these things the fancies of a disordered imagination, and was he not still here in Hampstead, in his narrow iron bed up on the gallery? To-morrow he would jump up and make his miserable breakfast as usual, would think of working without being able to raise a hand, and would potter away the hours. And at six in the evening he would see his prosperous neighbour from the City go past with noiseless, gentle step, bearing a plaited rush-bag with a skewer thrust through it. Yet what a relief to throw off the illusions of these latter days, and find himself again as of old, free of all the tangle; even though the problem of bread still faced him, and the vista of hopeless days stretched away endlessly!

Alas! the morning light, filling his panelled bedroom and revealing to his eyes the many luxuries of these prosperous days, testified only too convincingly to the reality of recent developments.

And yet, as he turned up the well-known Hampstead street of an evening on his way to the Robinsons, he would still struggle again to recover the illusion that the old days were yet. Approaching the house as it loomed in the near distance through the wintry mist, he would imagine himself supremely unconcerned with it. And then he would stop outside his own former door, and fumble in his pocket a moment as if to find the key. Like lessons learnt after the mind is set, all these later accretions to his existence were ready to drop away, to have a shadowy relation to him. It made him realise with astonishment how easily he might cut the Robinsons out of his life, and proceed as if he had never known them. His bond of obligation was more real to him than the people to whom he was bound!

He was shrewd enough to see that in his heart of hearts he was sullenly and perpetually angry that so much had come to him from so extraneous a source. Where his own strength and gifts had failed, these people from a world that was not his world, either in thought or mode, had come in and brought him prosperity. This galling sense of absolute dependence on the Robinsons seemed the deepest humiliation he had known. They had given him food when he was nigh starvation; they had given work when the prospect of work had vanished—had showered on him benefits and kindnesses innumerable. They had restored him to society and to the world of art and letters. He owed them the confidence of his bearing before the world, the manly swing of his step, the pride of his glance.

That this should be his destiny was horrible! He rebelled and cried out with all his might. Oh! to wield the sceptre of destiny himself!—to shape the evolution of a brilliant career and merit the crown of a great love by his own power and performance!

And yet at the back of his troubled mind there lay in terrible calm the stern determination to stand by his obligations. His promise to Lady Betty was in no danger. All this feverish agitation was but as the surf beating on a granite shore. He knew that he would bow his head in resignation; that, after the parting with Lady Betty, he would settle down as the most attentive of husbands; acquiescent of an atmosphere of physical well-being, yet paradoxically living from hand to mouth, so far as his deeper life was concerned; thankful for any morsel of good each day might bring him, and looking not beyond its horizon.

Alice should have her happiness, never guessing what turmoil and torture two souls had voluntarily undergone for her.

XX

In the silence and privacy of her room Alice was sobbing her life away. Like an opium eater, she had sought magnificent dreams, had surrendered herself to beautiful illusions, had duped herself supremely. But the awakening was fraught with fever and suffering.

On that memorable afternoon when her father had brought home the wonderful announcement that Wyndham was to follow him, Alice had looked at herself in the glass, and though her favourite dress lay ready for her, she knew he would not of his own impulse bestow a second glance upon her.

The evening had come and passed. As by some enchantment Wyndham had appeared, was seated at the same table with herself, engaged in intimate conversation with the family, left alone to wine and cigars with her father; rejoining them in the drawing-room, listening to her playing, singing to her accompaniment! Then, lo, he was gone; and she was left to ponder on the swift,surprising turn of events. After all these years of emotion, the acquaintanceship was an accomplished fact. She was to penetrate within his door at last, to become, for the time being, part of the very business of his life!

She retired that night still with the sense of miracle; yet infinitely grateful to her father for his charming concession to her whim. And her first subtle move had been crowned with success! At least there was work where work was needed so sorely; work, too, that brought her so near to him, annihilating a distance she had reconciled herself to think of as impassable, and opening up potentialities of service which her fertile wits would not be slow to seize upon. Would it not be a joy to help him to a firm footing again, to raise this gifted life of which she had watched the long slow sinking! It was miraculous that this privilege should fall to her! But everything must appear to flow naturally to him of itself; he should never suspect that the unseen hand at work was hers, any more than he should ever know that this was what she, who loved him, had for years worked out in fancy.

And she!—she should have no thought but the unselfish desire of serving him! What matter if she carried in her heart the cold conviction that he could never love her—since all she had dared aspire to had fallen to her lot! For who was she to cherish vain hopes? She had not the commonest touch of beauty; she was hopelessly out of his sphere. She felt herself appallingly ignorant and inexperienced. In her easy shelter the years had slipped by in monotonous quiet. In the world outside there beat a life that was strenuous, entrancing, dramatic—the struggle of the realm of affairs, the pomp and colour of courts and society, the important events of politics, the field of view that opened in the novels, or lay spread behind the footlights of the theatres. Wyndham belonged to all this brilliant universe, had walked with firm tread amid it all, breathing its airs with an assurance born of right and nature. No poverty could destroy his inalienable privileges, could render him less by a hair's breadth; indeed, save for the manifest inconveniences of the former, poverty or riches seemed irrelevant on that plane of high humanity; where differences of fortune were obscured by the highness of the humanity, however fertile in distinctions these differences might be in a lower world.

But as the acquaintance ripened, as she tasted of the gracious intimacy of the long sittings, his perfect kindness, his chivalry, his constant solicitude began to undermine the attitude with which she had embarked on the adventure. They had become such good friends, and she could not blind herself to the fact that he was pressing his personality on her beyond what mere courtesy and friendliness demanded. But she still fought to stand firm, and her humility was her strength. It was even more than her strength—it read for her his doubts and hesitations.

Not that she crudely supposed that, in his conduct to her, he was swayed by ulterior considerations. She saw that he had genuinely an affection for her, more kind and brotherly than a lover's affection; she knew that he was trying to like her better, to raise her in his estimation far higher than the truth. And she conceded that his hesitation was natural, that she was no mate for him, that his world would openly despise her. No, he must not marry her for the safety her fortune would bring him. She would marry only for love, and, as that she could never win, she would consequently never marry.

She dreaded now lest the situation should take a more definite turn, lest he should begin to woo her in earnest. She wished to be left in contentment with her deep secret happiness which could never be effaced from her life. She had had her way. It was she who had brought him the succour he needed; she—of whose existence he had never dreamed, whom he had often met face to face yet never glanced at. It was she who had rescued for the world's benefit this splendid genius that the world had rejected. This was joy enough. To anything else the end must be disillusion.

For awhile she lived in terror lest he might speak. But as the work progressed, and he became more and more enthusiastic over her portrait, she could not but fall a victim to the subtle implication, and begin to believe that he must really think more of her than she had ever dared to imagine. It was then that her stern control of herself began to slip away. Wilfully she shut her eyes to all that she understood only too well, and surrendered herself to the spell and wonder of the vista that opened before her. It was the best thing that life had brought her, she told herself, and in an impulse of pagan desire she was impelled to wring from it the last drop of passionate happiness it could afford her. Her love for him reached out into new depths; the dull, despairing, impossible love of before became a fever, a frenzy, a great yearning passion that must pour itself out or kill her.

Then came the supreme moment in which she let the belief that he loved her seize entire possession of her. Must he not have for his mate a woman who would love him and make him a perfect wife? He was a being apart from his own world, devoted to serener and higher ambitions. Had she not seen the glow with which he expounded his ideas and purposes, forgetting she was a humble, uninstructed listener, and surrounding her soul with the sweet unction of the implied perfect equality? Perhaps it had dawned upon him at last that devotion greater than hers the world could not hold. In his consecration to his high calling he did not need a wife to figure brilliantly amid social pleasures and functions, but a helpmeet whom perhaps he could not so easily find in those exalted spheres; one who needed no pleasures for herself, no triumphs; who had no purposes of her own, no desires, save the supreme end of self- sacrifice on the altar of his happiness and achievement. Only a woman absolutely capable of such self-effacement could understand the perfect bliss of it. If every man could find such faithfulness at his own hearth, how the world would thrive and grow blessed! And she thanked Heaven for the little fortune she could bring him, for this precious money to establish his life on a safe and sure footing.

And when he had spoken at last, she, casting away the last doubt, had thrown herself headlong into the dream. With her arms round him, and her lips to his, she felt that she had always been destined for this high bliss, that rendered by contrast the quiet stream of her life a mockery of life.

The joyous period of intoxication was all too short. With the sobering of the world to its work again in the new year, she, too, sobered a little, and the old questioning revived in her. Was it really the truth that he loved her? Where was the note of passion she herself had poured out so recklessly? His personal magnetism, his urbane, affectionate friendliness, the caressing vibrations of his voice, his delicate and considerate dealing with the gaps of ignorance she daily revealed—all this held her in an invincible spell. But the deep, irresistible conviction for which her heart yearned was unmistakably absent in his whole relation to her.

Perhaps some terrible struggle was going on within him. Was he recoiling in terror sometimes from the thought of the mate he had chosen? Surely at times he was arguing himself into acceptance and contentment. What meant the strange, furtive glances he sometimes directed at her?—not the soft glances of love, but glances bewildering, baffling! She watched him with a supernaturally sensitive insight, appraising his every expression, following the imagined see-saw of his doubts and reassurances.

Yet when he had told her of his meeting with Lady Lakeden again, and of the new portrait he had engaged upon, no shade of jealousy had arisen in her. Her sense of the calamity that had befallen Lady Lakeden was so infinitely distressing that she could have fallen upon her knees and prayed. To lose a dear husband after only a few months of wedded happiness!—what more crushing grief could a woman's destiny hold? She shut her eyes and shuddered, as she tried to realise the depths of its meaning. It seemed to her that no wife with the least spark of womanhood could recover from such a blow; that sorrow and weeping must be her portion for the rest of her days.

She redoubled her devotion to Wyndham, suddenly full of fear lest she should have been betrayed into injustice to him out of mere morbidity. And her mind lingered gently on the figure of this other woman whom she had never seen, but to whom her heart went out in an impulsive flood of love and pity. If only she could know her, and let her understand how deeply she realised her grief! But Wyndham had made no response to her first involuntary expression of this desire, and she was too diffident to recur to the point again. Perhaps if she waited patiently he might suggest such a meeting of his own accord. But the days went, and Wyndham was silent.

And not only silent, but changed. "Yes, yes. He is changed in a hundred ways," she cried, "though he does not know he has shown it."

If, for a moment, she had been willing to take refuge in the belief that over-sensitiveness and diffidence had been leading her into distrust of the situation, her eyes were suddenly too wide open to allow of any further indulgence in comfort of that kind. There was no mistaking this unprecedented self-abstraction, the curious, far-away expression that was almost stereotyped on his features, the continued inattentiveness to her words that often required her to repeat her remarks and not unfrequently ignored them, so that she was continually shrinking into herself, too wounded to insist again. By the side of this, his former attitude, little as it had satisfied her, seemed impulsive and passionate!

His face was grave and sad for the most part, but sometimes it shone with a rapture which she knew had not been inspired by her! He was not himself in any way; his smile and laugh had not the old spontaneous charm. Every note of his affection rang false. And yet, in form, his solicitude and loving care for her remained the same as always. But this could not blind her; she knew he was trying his best, but his heart and mind were not with her. Ah, well, if he cared for anybody, it was certainly not for her!

"Who has drawn him away from me? Who has robbed me?—who has robbed me?"

For days she had pondered and pondered, her mind faltering, her lips dreading to whisper the name. Wyndham was painting Lady Lakeden. She was young; she must be interesting and beautiful.

"He is in love with Lady Lakeden!" It escaped from her lips at last, and then she remained ashen—trembling.

Nay, surely he had loved Lady Lakeden in the old days—loved her secretly and despairingly, seeing her often, but too poor to woo her! Moreover, Lady Lakeden had then loved another. "Yes, yes, that is the truth—the truth!" she cried; "And now he has been seeing her again daily, and the old love has been reborn!"

A pall descended over Alice's spirit. What a cruel situation! Here was Wyndham pledged to a woman he could not care for, yet in love with another whose whole heart was with the dear husband that had been taken from her. "He is struggling bravely to be true to me—I see it all now—he is breaking his heart. It is my duty to release him from his word—ah! no, no!" She shuddered and covered her face, shaken and shaken. "Even if I gave him his freedom," she argued presently, clinging on to the wreck with might and main, "it would only be freedom to find despair. Lady Lakeden loved her husband. I know she is great and true. She knows he is mine. I trust her—I must trust her—I will pray for strength to trust her. Heaven help me!— Heaven help me!"

A terrible pang of jealousy smote her. Detesting herself for it, she tried hard to repress the flood of bitter hatred she felt rising in her against Lady Lakeden. Poor Lady Lakeden! She had suffered enough and was blameless. She could not help it if Wyndham loved her.

An overwhelming curiosity to know what manner of woman Lady Lakeden was, took possession of her. Of course, she was young and beautiful. But what colour were her eyes? Were they large and deep and brilliant? What expression had she habitually? What colour was her hair? And was it abundant? And how arranged? Was she slim and tall? How did she dress? And in what costume was Wyndham painting her? Were not these the questions that had been a thousand times on her lips, and yet remained unuttered?

And why had she not asked of him these questions as clearly and boldly as she had thought them? Had there been some obscure suspicion in her mind all along, and she had feared to embarrass her affianced husband?

Poor Wyndham! She told herself she had the most perfect understanding of his mind. She held him in honour as a noble gentleman, and knew surely that he would fret his heart away rather than wound her by word or deed. She would have put her hand in the fire for the certainty that he would never withdraw from the compact; that he would go through with the marriage, and die rather than relax the effort to simulate perfect happiness in their after life.

Could she accept such a sacrifice? Could she spoil his life for him, when she had only meant to set it straight, and had asked for no greater privilege? Would that she had been able, by some miracle, to help him from across the old impassable distance without coming into his life at all! It was for her to choose—to keep him and all that the future with him might hold, or to tell him frankly that she thought it best to set him free and return to the simple paths of her old existence.

But, ah, no, she could not give him up—she could not give him up! She had possessed his lips, she had possessed his thought and solicitude. The echoes of his voice caressed her. Break with him! She shut her eyes and shuddered again; her whole soul grew sick, and she writhed in agony.

XXI

Calling one day and finding her alone in the drawing-room, Mr. Shanner, after some moments of unruffled demeanour and honeyed conversation, abruptly launched into a piteous outbreak.

"I tell you, Alice, you've made a fine mistake with that swell of yours," he exclaimed, his eyes flashing with resentment.

Alice stared at him in deep distress. Ever since the engagement Mr. Shanner had been all decorousness and deference. As he broke now through his ashen shell of propriety, his sedate person seemed to relapse, to stand limp, a trifle greyer, a trifle less well trimmed.

"Oh," she gasped at last, "you are under some misapprehension."

"Come, come, Alice," he said; "don't you suppose I've two eyes—and wide-open ones, too?"

"I don't really understand what you're alluding to, Mr. Shanner," she returned as coldly as she could find it in her.

"I am alluding to your engagement, of course," he insisted. His tone showed he was determined to force the subject on her. "What do you suppose the fellow is going to marry you for? Men of his class do not come out of their way to look for a wife amongst people of our class. You mustn't mind my not mincing words, but it's clear to me he doesn't care a fig about you, and that your money is the attraction. There, that's plain!"

Alice felt herself turn scarlet. Mr. Shanner suddenly stood revealed to her—of roughness and coarseness unendurable.

"I don't understand you," she exclaimed, feeling she was floundering, and with an acute sense of her lack of social skill to meet the contingency and cut short the interview.

"Oh, yes you do, Alice. Only you are too proud to say so."

"You are mistaken. My intended husband and I are on the best of terms. I am very much surprised to hear this from you."

"You mean that for a snubbing, no doubt. Well, I suppose I brought it on myself." He smiled uneasily and bit his lip. "Only I did think that, being so old a friend of the family, I had the right to give you a word of advice when the happiness of your life is at stake."

"Oh! please, Mr. Shanner—I'm very sorry," she breathed, all gasps and palpitations. "But really, truly, you're mistaken."

"I have used my eyes and head. I am not mistaken. Everything's all wrong, and you know it, Alice. I have been reading it in your face of late—I tell you you show it. Give up the swell before things go to the devil."

"I'm sorry, Mr. Shanner," she said, with all the kindness in her tone that she could muster, "but if you will get these extraordinary ideas into your head, I certainly am not going to fight them."

He smiled wanly, droopingly. "Another snubbing, I suppose. But you needn't take it in such ill part. I don't profess to belong to the aristocracy: I do profess to be a friend, one of the sort that's to be trusted. And I think you'll come to recognise that in the long run. Whatever happens, John Shanner's your friend, and when the time comes, you'll find him ready to hand. But I earnestly advise you not to delay. Throw up all this business before there's mischief."

Alice smiled bravely. "I repeat that Mr. Wyndham and myself are on the happiest of terms, though I am sure you mean your advice for the kindest."

She took up her stand behind this simple assertion, so that he could not beat down her refusal to be drawn into a deeper discussion. By degrees he pulled together his decorum, recovered his frigidity, and ultimately retired with the dignified utterance, "Well, I hope you are not going to be disillusionised, my child, but I have my doubts. At any rate, as I say, I stand by you in any case. Only promise me one thing, that if ever you find my warning was not mistaken, you will do me the justice to admit it."

She thanked him gravely, and assured him that she fully appreciated his kindness, and willingly made the promise. She was glad indeed of the chance of winding up the interview thus amicably. Yet, when he had gone, she felt panic-stricken at this revelation of how openly she had been wearing her heart —as if veritably on her sleeve. How fortunate her parents had observed nothing yet! But they, of course, were taking the perfection of everything so entirely for granted, and were so happy themselves over the beautiful romance which had transformed their household and their lives, that it was difficult for any suspicion to enter their heads. Certainly they had never read any expression in her face save that of rapture and contentment.

She must try to control herself. If only, like other women, she were more practised in assuming a surface self that won acceptance, that none could penetrate!

But Mr. Shanner was so absolutely in the right. Was it really worth while going on as at present? Could anything be more unhappy than all this uncertainty and perplexity? Something must be done. Things must come soon to a crisis.

And then, one morning, some two or three days before the end of the month she received a letter from Wyndham, who had dined with them the evening before, announcing that he would be absent from the studio the whole day practically, as he had made club engagements for the entire afternoon and evening. As, too, he would be lunching out, it would not be worth her while to come to the studio at all on that day. He was sorry he had forgotten to mention all this when saying goodbye, but he was scribbling the note immediately on entry, and in a hurry to catch the post.

This letter gave Alice food for reflection. She did not attach any significance to the alleged club engagements; she had never grudged him the occasional evenings he spent in that way, since it kept him in touch with the art-world. But in this present instance there was certainly a suggestion of anxiety on his part that she should keep away from the studio over the day. "Ah—I understand!" she flashed, clenching her fingers; "Lady Lakeden's portrait is to be brought there to-day, and he does not wish me to see it! She is beautiful—beautiful!—he fears her beauty will sting me to jealousy."

He had never wished her to see the portrait! Had he not always turned the conversation whenever she had mentioned it? And only last night, as if in anticipation of so natural a desire on her part, he had had to confess that it was finished, but had added that it was going straight to Paris, as he preferred to feel it was safe there in the hands of his agent. He had thus led her to conclude that the picture would not be passing through the studio at all; but, with his letter now before her, she felt certain that his aim was to get the portrait framed, to touch it up, and then send it off without showing it to her.

But she had the right to see it, if she so desired, she told herself bitterly. If the Salon accepted it, nothing could prevent her going to Paris with her mother; though so enterprising an adventure was quite outside the habits of their life —a consideration on which he was counting, perhaps. But the Salon might not accept it, and in any case two or three months might elapse before such a possible visit, and in that time who could say how things might turn?

Entrance to the studio was a privilege that had been freely bestowed upon her. He had not forbidden her to come; he had merely tried to stop her by suggestion and diplomacy. But she would not be denied.

She would meet strategy with strategy: she would take care to arrive late in the evening, so as to be alone there. In the afternoon, or earlier in the evening, there was the danger of just catching him between his engagements, since he would no doubt come home to change.

She would see the portrait at her leisure; she would at last study the features of the woman—the beautiful, brilliant woman—who had unwittingly robbed her.

"And I have no beauty," she sobbed; "I am plain and insignificant. I have no cleverness, no experience; not one little weapon to fight with, to win him back to me!"

XXII

Wyndham had finished Lady Betty's portrait on the previous morning, and had taken it back with him to his studio. To-day the frame, a copy of a fine old Venetian model, came early in the morning, and Wyndham had soon fixed the canvas within it. He was enchanted with the effect. If the Salon had only a corner to spare for it, he was certain they would not turn it away. And— entrancing idea!—why should not Lady Betty deign to come here on this last day, and snatch a glimpse of herself in this charming setting which he had selected with such loving interest. There was a long day before them, and he might well seize the mood and the auspicious moment.

He lingered before his picture, then brusquely tore himself away from it, and sat down and wrote instructions to the frame-maker, who was to come and fetch it away on the morrow, and despatch it to Paris immediately.

For this was his great day; that was to leave with him for ever the memory of gracious companionship and irrevocable farewell! The day on which he would live for Lady Betty and forget all else! Then she would pass out of his life. He strove to face the stern decree. But only a blank met his vision. He turned his eyes away; his thoughts should be of the day only.

He had hardly considered what their programme should be. But now, on his way, he began to ponder it lazily, dwelling fancifully on possibilities rather than arriving at anything rigid or definite. They would roam about at random, like two sweethearts of the people; their evening they would spend at a theatre, no doubt something out of the way, and they would find their meals as the bizarre occasion might offer itself. They would invest this everyday London with the romantic light of their own spirit; they would wander as through a strange capital, and observe humanity with a new eye. And then, of course, he must keep before him the possibility of the visit to his own studio, in which Lady Betty had never as yet set foot.

At midday he rang the bell at Grosvenor Place, and was shown up into the great drawing-room. In a minute or two Lady Betty came tripping in. A glance showed she was ready to go out at once; her simple coat and skirt formed a costume unobtrusive enough for any expedition, and her hat and veil matched the occasion to a nicety.

She was radiant with an unaffected gaiety; he could hardly conceive the weight of sadness that must lie at the bottom of her heart.

"We shall have a happy day," she said, smiling at the thought of it;

"something to remember always."

He was quick to grasp her spirit. They were to have this happiness as if the day were one of many days, some past, more to come. They were to give themselves up to the joy of each other's companionship in simple acceptance of the passing hour; not dilating on the occasion as a parting; not letting it be overshadowed by the sense of what they had so tragically missed in life. Parting there would be; and then sadness would descend swiftly enough. Till that bitter moment—sparkle and enjoyment! He had come prepared to talk much of themselves; but he saw she was wiser than he, and at once fell in with her mood. There would be all the rest of his life to lament in.

"Have you thought of any plan?" he asked.

"None," she replied. "To tell the truth, I rather shrank from anything definite. 'The wind bloweth as it listeth.' Let us go on without end or purpose. That seems to me the ideal way."

"But we are bound to make a beginning. After that the game may play itself."

"Let us get away from the London we know; let us go to a romantic, wonderful London that we have never seen." She was almost echoing his thought. "We shall glide discreetly among the crowds as if we belonged to them."

"Then away!" he laughed. "To horse—or rather, to omnibus! Or is it to be hansom?"

"Everything in turn, and nothing long."

It was a cold day, yet though the sky was lightly clouded, the air was free from mist. As they stepped into the street a few patches of blue were visible, and a wintry sunshine filtered down with a pleasant sense of promise. The neighbouring houses were for the most part shuttered and silent, but the outlook on the great triangular space before them was cheerfully busy.

"How unlike the scene of your painting!" she exclaimed. "There is no suggestion of drama here, but just the average feeling of the London thoroughfare—busy people going their way, and a procession of omnibuses mixed up with carts and hansoms."

"Yet my own scene swims before my eyes—I have lived with it so long."

"You have still to live with it," she reminded him.

"If I do not die of it," he answered pleasantly. "Seriously, I came near to doing so."

"This omnibus is marked 'Aldgate,'" she flew off. "Now that makes me think of Aldgate Pump. I wonder if it goes near the Pump?"

Wyndham jumped on the foot-board, and put the question to the conductor.

"We pass within a yard of it," was the reply.

"Good," said Wyndham. The omnibus drew up, and Lady Betty mounted the stairway, and they seated themselves on the roof.

"Look!" he exclaimed. "The clouds are suddenly breaking; it will be all blue and sunshine soon."

"A grey ghostly blue, a cold, charming sunshine."

"Yet the promise is splendid after all this winter."

"The promise is splendid," she echoed; "and we are so happy to-day."

"We are so happy," he repeated.

He let himself lapse into a dreamy mood; he was enchanted to have her so near him, to feel the afternoon and evening stretching endlessly before them —a veritable lifetime of golden moments. Lady Betty's manner offered a marked contrast. Hers was a frank exhilaration, an excited gaiety, of which he had the full impression; though she kept it in a low key, like love's whisper intended for his ear alone. Soon, as he had predicted, the sky grew bluer, the sunshine warmer; the traffic and the bustle of the streets were cheerfully pleasant to the eye and the ear in the fresh day.

"Even the London we know seems delightful," he remarked.

"London, though sometimes impelling to revolt, is always wonderful—it has always the fascination of the unknown."

"And is as supremely problematic as the unknowable of the philosophers."

"But it is solid and real, comes to us through all the five senses. Look at that strange old man with the tiger-lilies. I wonder how he comes by them at this time of year."

"That is one of the wonders of London," said Wyndham. "One sees the flowers of all seasons at every season."

"And sometimes the weather of all seasons at every season. Has Aldgate Pump a history?"

He confessed to ignorance, though he had an idea that he had read much about it in his boyhood, an epoch when he had been fascinated by all the odd monuments of the town. He recalled, however, after a time, that there was a legend connected with it, not unlike that of the wandering Jew.

"Is it actually a pump?" she asked.

"Oh, it's a real pump," he assured her.

"Because I had a suspicion just now; it struck me it might be a sort of old coaching-inn or something of the kind. I've often been deceived like that, have gone off to see strange things, and have found a coaching-inn."

"At least there is the consolation of refreshment at the inn."

"Not a bad idea," she conceded. "It would be a thing to boast about for the rest of one's life—to have refreshed one's self at the Aldgate Pump."

Both laughed. The omnibus pursued its way with a steady rumble. They had turned out of Piccadilly and passed through Waterloo Place, and soon after through Trafalgar Square into the Strand, where the scene proved much busier. The pavements were thronged; people were pressing forward with an appearance of being very much in earnest. A sprinkling of tourists, clearly self-proclaimed by their holiday air and the style of their attire and grooming, paraded at leisure or gazed into the shop-windows. Here and there a young girl, in a picture frock and a big hat, tripped along daintily, holding her skirt with a touch that suggested Paris, and swinging her little bag from her free hand.

"Actresses going to rehearsal?" hazarded Wyndham, in response to his companion's interrogation.

"How charming they are!" she exclaimed. "And they are most of them frightfully poor. They struggle for years, and then drop out gradually. Fortunately we women have the gift of living intensely for the day. A few weeks' engagement, the guinea or two assured for the time being, and see how we bloom."

"Ah, yes," said Wyndham reflectively; "life for them, as for many others, is pretty much of a game of roulette. They stake their all on the table, fortune fluctuates during a few turns of the wheel, and then—everything is swept away."

"Away, please, with these sad reflections! Why look too searchingly at things? The world is pleasant; why spoil it by examining it? Why turn one's eyes willingly away from the good to see the evil?"

"And at any rate the good is as real as the evil," he agreed.

"We must make things contribute to our happiness while we may. All these crowds of people have no idea that they are there for our entertainment; they do not know, poor things, that we have willed they should be masquerading to please us. They have the delusion they are going about their own affairs, and they see only an ordinary omnibus, full on the roof—that is, if they cared to look at us. To them what more commonplace than a journey on an omnibus from Hyde Park Corner to Aldgate Pump? Yet, to us, what a whimsical universe it is!"

The omnibus rattled along with a not unpleasing vibration. They passed through the heart of the City, swept alongside St. Paul's, and then the humour of country cousins took possession of them. They pretended to be roused to excitement by all these guide-book regions and monuments, affected to be seeing them for the first time and to be recognising them from the engravings. Down Leadenhall Street they clattered at last, and presently to their surprise the conductor's head appeared above the stairway with the announcement of "Aldgate Pump, sir."

They descended. The omnibus passed on, and they stood hesitating, a little lost, but greatly amused.

"Here it is!" she exclaimed. "And a street arab in the very act of pumping! Why, it's real water."

They contemplated it for a moment or two. "Well, what do you think of it?" he asked.

"Thrilling," she admitted. "All pumps are interesting—in these days of universal taps. But look at those warehouses opposite, beyond the hoarding. Aren't they fascinating?"

"I believe the river lies beyond." Probably no existence had been less intertwined with the City of London than his, but he remembered the immediate neighbourhood pretty well from ancient wanderings, and he told her as an interesting fact that Mark Lane and Mincing Lane lay thereabouts.

"I think I have heard of them." Her face lighted with the pleasure of recognition. "Indeed, I'm sure I've seen them mentioned in the newspapers."

He tried to plumb her knowledge, but found no deeps. She knitted her brows prettily, or at least he imagined she did, under her veil. "A sort of Latin Quarter—an artist's colony?" she hazarded. "No, wait a bit, there was a wealthy, humdrum sort of man I once met, and everybody whispered he came out of Mincing Lane. He was not artistic. I give it up."

"He imported tea?"

"That's not unlikely," she agreed.

"That's what Mincing Lane is for. And Mark Lane is for corn and produce."

"How useful! What a good world it is! I think I like this part."

"Beyond is Eastcheap, famous for groceries, and beyond that again the water-side where all these things are landed."

"Let us come to Eastcheap." She was eager to see all the places he had enumerated, so he took her through the famous side-streets.

"I certainly do like this part of the world," she repeated emphatically. "And do you know, your talk of tea, and corn, and produce, and warehouses has made me very hungry. If we stumble up against a charming place, we shall lunch."

And, a minute or two later, as they strolled down Eastcheap, at the corner of a narrow winding lane, they came upon a sort of café, which nice-looking merchants were entering, besides a goodly sprinkling of brisk young women. Lady Betty peered in through the door. The place seemed pretty full, but a stairway led to regions below. In a box, at the head of the stairway, and busily taking the cash, was a charming old man of mildest aspect.

Lady Betty declared it all fascinating, especially the part below stairs, which had the attraction of the as yet unseen.

Wyndham hesitated. "There is smoking below. You may not like it."

"There are other women going down," she insisted. "I can't resist the temptation."

It was an average type of City lunching place, but Lady Betty had never before tried the sort of thing, so Wyndham fell in with her whim. Down the stairs they went into a spacious cellar, lighted with jets of gas, though the sun was still shining outside. Wreaths and clouds of smoke floated in the atmosphere, and a clatter of dominoes and crockery dominated the buzz of voices that rose from the chaos of people at the marble tables. The central tables seemed given up to chess-play, each game surrounded by onlookers, all with patient cups of coffee beside them. And here and there an exceptional table, laid with a napkin, and in possession of vigorous eaters, gave the note of the restaurant. Wyndham and Lady Betty found a snug place on one side from which they could survey the room; and a neat little waitress, scarcely more than a child, came briskly forward to serve them, handing them with a sweet professional smile a long slip headed "Bill of Fare." They were glad to note that their entrance had attracted no attention. Lady Betty studied the bill excitedly. They made their decision, and Wyndham imparted it to the waitress.

"Thank you, sir," she said; "And what'll you have to drink, please?"

Again an eager colloquy, with the prosaic result of "two ginger-beers." "A true old English beverage," declared Lady Betty, and her approval seemed to flash the æsthetic quality into it, to invest it with rank and nobility. "Small or large?" persisted the waitress, her tone and demeanour of the gravest.

"Oh, large," said Lady Betty, and the girl's face brightened at the definiteness of the information.

"Two large ginger-beers—thank you, ma'am," she said, and went off sharply, leaving them to their amusement.

Whilst waiting, they surveyed the place at their leisure. "I like it here," exclaimed Lady Betty again. "Look at the old chess player there, with the bald pate and the eagle's nose. Watch him considering his move, with his hand hovering in the air, hesitating, yet ready to swoop down to capture a piece."

But the hand did not capture the piece. Instead, the shoulders shrugged, an expression of disgust overclouded the face, and the hand descended, dashing all the pieces from the board with one sweep. A roar of delight broke from the onlookers, and mingling with it from another part of the room came a sudden fresh clatter of dominoes, rapidly shuffled.

"What fresh, frank enjoyment! So this is the strenuous commercial life of London—gingerbeer and dominoes!"

"A strange set of people!" commented Wyndham. "Study these faces—from each shines a different life. I almost want to put my enormous accumulation of art theories on the fire, and to paint only human faces for the rest of my life."

"Wonderful! There seem at least fifty different races here—to judge from the shapes of the skulls and the varying types of features."

"The thought often strikes me as I watch people in the streets or in omnibuses," said Wyndham. "No matter how dull or repulsive a human face at first sight, I believe it can always be painted so as to be interesting, and that without departing from truth."

The waitress reappeared with their lunch which had been simply chosen so as to admit of no possible failure, and in their present mood they were charmed with it. Lady Betty was enraptured by the experience, and chatted in an undertone, every now and then breaking into a spontaneous "I am so happy to-day," and flashing him a glance of light and radiance.

They wound up with black coffee, and then the little waitress made out the account, which, after leaving her demurely astonished with her big silver tip, Wyndham paid to the nice old man in the box at the top of the stairs.

"The sun is still shining—look!" she exclaimed.

Wyndham stepped after her into the air gratefully. "It is fresh and almost summery. Heaven smiles at us. Shall we stroll down this winding lane? I fancy it must lead to the water-side."

"Hurrah for the winding lane!" she said, and stepped out merrily. At the bottom they entered a street full of black brick warehouses with cranes at work, and huge carts with ponderous horses. "An antediluvian breed!" whispered Lady Betty. They strolled along, peering into dim doorways at vast interiors where a strange universe of life flourished in the glooms amid prodigious collections of barrels and boxes.

"We are almost on Tower Hill," he said suddenly.

"An unexpected fantasy!" she exclaimed, as the Tower of London itself came into view at the end of the narrow street, the grey far-stretching ramparts looming up ghost-like and romantic. "A mediæval mirage amid all this grimy commerce. I wonder if it will vanish presently! But let us try the opposite direction now—are we not vowed to-day to the unfamiliar and unknown?"

They retraced their steps, and, ere long, lighted on an iron gate that led visibly to the water-side.

"The gate is inviting," she said. "I hope it isn't forbidden."

"Ah, here is a notice. I see we shall not be trespassers."

They entered, and, passing through the preliminary alley, found themselves on a broad, open gravelled space beyond which flowed the water. Save for a couple of pigeons wandering about, they had the place all to themselves.

"This is a discovery," declared Lady Betty. "It is as interesting here in its way as the Rialto at Venice."

And indeed they had reason to admire. To the right lay the Bridge of Bridges, whose endlessly rolling traffic was at this distance softened to an artistic suggestion that by no means disturbed their sense of solitude. At the adjoining wharf on the left a Dutch boat was being unladen, actively, yet with a strange sense of stillness and calm. And over all the river and shipping hung a faint grey-blue mist, muffling and enveloping all things out of proportion to its density, and absorbing the sunlight into a haze that already seemed to foretell the chills of the coming twilight of the winter's day. They saw the sun, a large red ball, hanging extraordinarily low in the sky over a long squat warehouse with symmetrical rows of windows. And across the river, under the shadow of the opposite structures, lay strange families of craft and barges, moored in the water, or high on the mud; rusty and silent, some half-broken up, some swinging lazily, touched with the mellow decay of the centuries.

Lady Betty thought it would be ideal to stay here awhile, so they settled down on one of the garden-seats, and sat in quiet happiness, unheeding of the sharp touch of the afternoon air. More pigeons flew down from neighbouring roofs and walked tamely around them. And from all the mighty activity of surrounding London, that beat strenuous, feverish, far-reaching, there flowed to them only a serenity, an almost phantasmal calm: they were alone, supremely alone—far from their world of everyday existence.

The time slipped by deliciously. Their enjoyment was as spontaneous as of two children at play. And children they were in the perfect simplicity of their happiness. They watched the afternoon deepen, the haze of sunshine weaken and yield to greyer moods; they rose, too, and moved along the edge of the waters, and examined the shipping and barges. They spoke to the pigeons, gave them names, endowed them with romances; they spoke to each other endearingly, yet still as the two children who had played together always, who had wandered into this strange world, and were as enchanted with it as with each other.

At last they realised the light was already fading; the mist on all things was ghostlier, and damp in the throat and nostrils. Now and again a spasmodic wind caught up dry leaves and swirled them around playfully. Lady Betty gave a little shiver.

"Night will soon be on us," she said. "A million points of light will be springing up as by magic. It would be enchanting to stay and watch the darkness deepen and the river-fog steal down; to sit here through the mysterious hours, and study the shadows and silhouettes, and listen to all the strange sounds of the night, and watch all those lights glimmer on and on, till at last they show yellow in the pale dawn, and life again is swarming over the bridges. Must we go back, dear?—we have left our world ever so far away— and years ago, was it not, dear?"

A sadness had descended on them both. With the approach of evening, they could not but feel the precious time was fleeting; they could no longer immerse themselves with such wholeheartedness in the simple appreciation of the moment. The terror of the parting to come rose in the hearts of both. Yet they made a brave resistance.

"Come, darling," she said at last; "the hours still belong to us. We have indulged our day-mood. Let us search for something fresh now; our good star shall watch over us and send us happy adventures."

So they passed again into the street, and, absorbed in their talk, were scarcely aware whither they were turning. They knew they were in a network of by-ways, flanked by warehouses and offices, and sometimes they stumbled on terraces of decrepit old dwelling-houses. They were vaguely conscious that they were leaving the river far behind, and that they must have crossed Eastcheap again at some narrower part without recognising it. After some leisurely wandering they came into a more important thoroughfare with pretentious edifices, yet with archaic touches here and there, the relics of another epoch, worn and decaying, yet more suggestive of coming stone buildings to supplant them than of the glory of their own century.

At a street-corner, under the light of a lamp that was still pale in the gathering dusk, a shivering flower-seller with a red shawl over her shoulders stood with a basket of deliciously fresh violets, and Wyndham stopped to get a big bunch of them put together for his companion. Lady Betty was immensely gratified; she breathed in the odour of the violets with rapture, then fastened them in her bosom. She was herself again now, overflowing with good fellowship, and amused at every trifle. He caught her exhilaration. "We shall fill our evening with a whirl of gaiety!" he cried. "Rockets and fireworks; I wonder if the good star you spoke of will be kind enough to set down in our path some unheard-of theatre."

She suggested they should study the hoardings as they went along, and both undertook to keep a look-out. But they were absorbed again in each other, having only a vague pleasurable sense of the crowded roads into which their steps now took them. Eventually they were in a main thoroughfare, with bustling shops brilliantly alight, and endless lines of stalls a-blazing; the roadway full of traffic and tram-cars and amazingly gigantic hay-carts, the pavements thick with a working population pressing forward and forward in multitudes. It was night now, absolutely; but it had stolen on them so gradually, they were astonished it was so definitely manifest. The hours of light were fresh and vivid in their minds, they could almost hear and feel the unending clatter of the omnibus that had carried them across the town, and the riverside picture was still before them. The change that had come over the world, this transition to absolute darkness illumined by street-lamps and flaring naphtha, seemed mystic and amazing. And a subtle warmth from all this illumination and from all this press and bustle, from all these close- packed moving vans and cars and hay-carts, pervaded the wintry air; a sense of exhilaration, too; a sense of life in all its unrefined, joyous reality, intense and vigorous, accepting itself unquestioningly, too sure of the worth of the gift ever to doubt it—even as the hungry ploughboy does not speculate metaphysically about the fat pork on his plate, but simply falls thereon and devours it.

"Book-stalls!" cried Lady Betty, "and piled up ever and ever so high. And look, rusty Wellington boots on the one hand, and rusty tools and bits of iron on the other."

They stayed a few minutes, and turned over some of the books, as interesting and varied as those in any more pretentious bookman's paradise. They both grew selfishly absorbed, each striking out an individual path, though remembering the other's existence at moments of extraordinary interest. In the end each became the possessor of a volume. Wyndham's was a facsimile of the first edition of the "Pilgrim's Progress," a fattish octavo with the loveliest of wide margins, and the exact reproduction of the original engravings. Lady Betty's treasure was an old copy of the Dramatic Poems of Browning. Each paid the same one-and-sixpence, and as they bore away their prizes they discovered that each had been inspired by the same motive—of giving the other a memento of this wonderful day. Laughingly they exchanged their volumes, and the presentations thus formally carried out, Wyndham took possession of the Bunyan again in the mere capacity of carrier.

At last a hoarding with a great glare of light on it.

Wyndham let his eye roam over the posters. "The very thing," he cried. "A fine old-fashioned melodrama!"

"Splendid!" echoed Lady Betty, gazing at the many-coloured scenes that promised a generous measure of thrills and emotions.

"We shall have a box to ourselves," said Wyndham. "As you see, it is not so very extravagant. Only there is the problem of dining."

"What healthy little children we are!" she laughed.

"Oh, we must dine," he protested.

"I have faith," she declared. "Our good star has served us till now, it is not going to desert us. We shall light upon some quaint place presently."

The confident prediction justified itself, for, later on, they stopped before a Jewish restaurant that proudly announced itself as "kosher." And it proved immediately irresistible to the wanderers, who entered straightway, and found themselves in a simple sort of room with freshly papered walls, full of neatly laid tables, the very antithesis of the familiar formal restaurant of ornate intention. The place was empty of diners as yet—no doubt it was early for the usual clients; but the proprietor, a grave bearded personage in spotless broad-cloth and with the air of an ambassador, come forward bowing profoundly, and escorted them to a choice corner. Through a half-open door at the back they had a glimpse of a neat, comely Jewish woman busy amid pots and pans, whilst a boy and a girl, who both looked good and intelligent, were industriously doing their lessons at a side-table. The host waited on the adventurers in person, taking the dishes from a younger and shyer assistant who brought them from behind the scenes.

Despite the magnificent gravity of his presence, their host turned out to be an unaffected human being, whom they encouraged to talk of his own affairs, and who was pleased at their manifest interest in his homely establishment and in his little family. His wife and he worked together, and it was her cooking on which they were now being regaled. Their favourable verdict gave him an almost naïve gratification; a radiance and an illumination broke brilliantly across his features. He told them the Jewish names of the various dishes, but though they repeated them sedulously, the strange, charming words would not remain in their heads a moment. Meanwhile the kitchen was being stimulated to a display of delicate skill and finesse; the fish was as good, declared Lady Betty, as anything she had tasted at the Maison d'Or. A few other clients began to appear—a long-bearded Russian, carefully dressed, accompanied by a simple, buxom daughter of rosy complexion and deep, serious, aspiring eyes; then a middle-aged man, with a leonine mane that was dashed with grey and suggested the poor composer of genius; and finally a spectacled German in a threadbare cut-away coat, carefully brushed, who suggested unrequited scholarship. But all these, after the first distinguished bow and salutation on the part of the host, were left to the attentions of the assistant; the host himself being magnetised by the unaccustomed guests with whom he was deep in conversation. But, though he waited on them perfectly, there was yet conveyed in his bearing such a touch of distinction and courteous affability that they were sensible as of an honour that was being bestowed upon them. And that he was no mere small-souled tradesman was abundantly evident when he brought them a bottle of claret with the romantic recommendation that it had been grown on Palestine soil, and that, in its passage from the wine-press to their table here, it had never left the hands of his compatriots. He handled the bottle with pride and certainly emotion, and begged them to accept of it, and to allow him to fill their glasses. They were touched by the invitation, though they were naturally unwilling to accept such a gift from a poor man, but he understood their doubts and laughingly explained that, as he did not possess a wine licence, he could not possibly accept payment; a piece of reasoning which drew them into the laugh and disposed of their hesitations.

They made him join them, however, and they drank to the prosperity of the Palestine colonies, irrelevantly but charmingly coupling the toast with that of their host and hostess, the children and the restaurant. The other visitors smiled quietly, and, with conspicuous good breeding, scarcely turned their eyes towards this convivial table, the Russian conversing in an undertone with his daughter, and the musician with the scholar.

And at the end the host did not give himself any false airs, but made out their modest reckoning and handed Wyndham the change, all with the same courtesy and with a distinction of manner which seemed to lift trade to a higher plane than it occupies in Occidental prejudice. And as the wife appeared hovering with a shy smile in the kitchen doorway, she was invited to join the group, and warmly complimented on her culinary skill. Then Lady Betty asked for the children, and presently their bright faces were illumining the room with a warmer and sweeter light. Wyndham and Lady Betty spoke to them a little, then Lady Betty slipped a fragile ring with a single small fine pearl off her finger, and put it on the girl's. The little thing blushed and hung down her head. But the jewel became the tiny hand immensely. Meanwhile the boy's eyes were glued on the books.

"I can see you like books, little man," said Wyndham.

"Yes, sir," said the child, "better than anything else."

"His ambition is to become a scholar," put in his father proudly.

"He is to have the Browning as a memento," said Lady Betty. She handed it to the child. "Keep this volume carefully. When you are older, I am sure you will love and treasure it." Then she unfastened her big bunch of violets and pressed the flowers on his mother, who took them shyly but coloured with pleasure.

When they were in the street again they walked on silently for a while. Wyndham saw that Lady Betty had been deeply touched; that something wonderful had been revealed to her of which, perhaps, she had never caught a glimpse in her whole existence. Presently she turned to Wyndham with a quiet smile that was the natural reflection of her thought.

"You do forgive me, dear," she asked, "for my arbitrary disposal of your Browning, my own present to you!"

"You sacrificed my gift of violets, so we are quits."

"After this we shall scarcely need any memento of the day—who could ever forget?" Then with a little thrill of joy: "But I've my Pilgrim all the same." She touched the book lovingly as he held it, and he was aware of her movement as of a caress. It was his gift to her, and what a world of affection in this implication of the value she set on it!

XXIII

They found the theatre easily, and, from their snug box, enjoyed a most lurid melodrama, which amply redeemed the promise of the hoarding, and was played by a vigorous company who seemed in no wise dismayed by yawning spaces and a thin scattering of audience. Nay, the thrills were even more than the adventurers had reckoned on, for pistol shots suddenly rang out in the third act, and Lady Betty clutched hard at the curtain of the box. She presently realised, however, that the iniquitous foreign nobleman with the fur overcoat and large moustachios, whose veiled hand had directed the remorseless persecution of the good and righteous, had at last paid for his misdeeds, and with this passing of the villain Lady Betty found that her sense of poetic justice was abundantly satisfied; though the luckless heroine, appearing on the scene just then, and incautiously picking up the fallen pistol, was at once arrested as the manifest murderess. Then the curtain went down, and Lady Betty rose.

"We must not stay to the end. Our day is over, and I want to give you the promised souvenir of our brief friendship."

There was a catch in her voice, and he understood that the sob had been suppressed with difficulty. He felt it was for him now to be strong; to set the note of stoic resignation, even as she had led off their adventures with a mood that had made this day the most wonderful of all his life.

"Ah, your strange, strange souvenir!" he laughed. "You must admit I have waited patiently."

"It was very wicked of me," she admitted. "But I shall keep you tortured with curiosity till the moment I give it to you. I have it at home. We had better drive back all the way, if we can find a vehicle."

They slipped out of the box and along the corridor and into the open road. It was a keen night, but very clear. The perspective of street lamps stretched endlessly on either hand. There was a plentiful sprinkling of people about, and the tram-cars were still passing. At the kerb were a few cabs, waiting for possible clients, so they selected the smartest of the vehicles; and the driver, who had been standing flinging his arms about for warmth, climbed into his seat, stolidly indifferent that "fares" from the theatre should wish to go so far afield into the regions of the elect.

No doubt the horse was glad to be off, for they started at an astonishingly brisk pace. Outside lay the endless road and all the shuttered world of streets and houses, over which still hung the romance of their splendid day. Quietly they had their last glimpses, as if fearing to speak, and yet thrillingly conscious of their proximity to each other. Lady Betty was sunk in sadness; as if she recognised now that any affectation of cheerfulness was utterly vain. And Wyndham was thinking of the definite moment of parting. He had resigned himself to saying "goodbye" at the door of her home; not daring to suggest now that she should visit his studio, even for the first time and last— since the chance had not naturally arisen in the course of the day's wanderings, and she had not even expressed the desire for it. Indeed, in all these weeks she had thrown out no hint of such a wish, and he had felt that she considered the ground as within Alice's absolute sphere, and would not intrude on it. No doubt many mingled shades of feeling went to create this attitude of hers. Still, Wyndham, having dreamed of her coming there on this last day, was to that extent unsatisfied. Time and again the suggestion mounted to his lips even at this eleventh hour, but he had not the confidence to let the words fall.

Perhaps they had both fallen into reverie, for Wyndham found himself saying suddenly, "Why, here is the Bank of England!" And Lady Betty started, too, astonished at the stillness and the solitude here in the heart of the City.

"The night seems darker now, and how ghostly and silent the lights are!" she said. "The sky has clouded. Goodbye, dreamland," she added in meditation. "I shall never dare revisit the ground we have covered. I don't want to see it again; I couldn't bear it. But I shall always think and dream of it."

He dared not answer. The least false note, and she would be unnerved. Since the parting had to be, let them grip hands silently for the last time, almost without realising it; let them go off as if they were to meet again on the morrow—as in so many partings that life itself brings about.

And as they were borne westwards, signs of life began to appear again; as they approached the Strand they came full upon the torrents of population pouring out from their amusements. At Trafalgar Square the town was alive with masses of hansoms in motion that broke into jets and streams flashing and darting into all the avenues. They seemed to have returned into this familiar, dazzling London of the night as from a long journey. They were giddy with the impression of it all, and winced as if they had long grown disaccustomed to it. But, definitely, they were at home again; soon the houses of Grosvenor Place would loom up before them, though somehow their everyday universe had taken on some subtle quality of unreality since the morning.

And yet how small the distance they had gone afield, how soon annihilated! Up St. James's Street went the cab, alongside the Green Park, and in a few minutes it had pulled up in Grosvenor Place. Wyndham sprang out with a forced alertness, and helped his companion to descend. The house was quite dark. Lady Betty led the way to the door-step and produced a latch key from her purse. Wyndham stood by, strained and nervous.

"You must come in to receive your souvenir," she said. "You have well deserved it," she added with a brave smile.

He followed her in as she pushed the door open; then she switched on the light. "You had best wait in the dining-room, I shall join you again presently."

Wyndham stood alone in the spacious room, with a sense of chill and desolation. The thought of his marriage and life to come flashed on him with a stroke of terror. Suddenly he shivered. Ah, it was bleak here in this deadly, all-pervading stillness. The very lights seemed to flood the room mournfully. How tired he was! Everything seemed to swim before him.

And then he was aware she was in the room again, smiling at him and exhibiting a package. Her presence seemed to revive him.

"At last I am to be enlightened," he murmured.

"I am afraid you are doomed to be disappointed," she said, as she came and stood by his side at the table. "I have made such a mystery of it, whereas, no doubt, you will find it trivial."

"You said it was a weird idea. I am sure it is a charming one. Whatever it is, you know what it will be to me."

"I know, darling," she said, suddenly grave again.

She bade him cut the string and open the package. At last, as he was removing the many wrappings, "It is an old door-knocker," she said; "the figure of a lovely grotesque old wizard, wrought in bronze. I came across it on the door of a fifteenth-century house in Delft a year or two ago, and it so fascinated me that I bargained for it with the owner. It has ever since remained one of my pet possessions, and I at once thought of it for you. Tell me truly what you think of it!"

Wyndham held up the strange bronze man, slim and long, with fantastic bearded head, and grasping in one hand a rod that merged into a huge serpent that lay coiled round the body. The two legs were welded at the bottom into one big foot, the heel of which formed the hammer. It was a piece of grotesqueness worthy of the East, finely and subtly modelled, and quaint rather than grim in its suggestiveness.

"A masterpiece!" he said at last. "I have never seen anything of the kind to match it."

"I should say it is by an artist of at any rate the early renaissance," she ventured, her face agleam, for she had awaited his verdict with anxiety. "The modelling is so careful and scientific."

"Those were the days when artists still thought only of their work, and so much forgot their own existence that they took no pains to proclaim themselves to the world. The work of the so-called dark ages remains, the artists lie unknown and unheard of, if indeed they were known to the world at any time."

"You will set up my wizard on the door of your house. Every time you hear it you will think of me as floating there like a spirit. Isn't that weird? I have the idea that if an enemy should touch it, you would somehow know at once, and be on your guard. Oh, yes, I was convinced it was a magic knocker the moment I saw it."

He was still staring at it gravely, as if he, too, felt some eerie quality in it. She looked at him, then broke into laughter. "Aren't we a charming pair of children, taking our own make-believe so seriously?"

He laughed, too, though uneasily. "It is good to be children again."

"Like all good things, it is cut short so soon," she responded meditatively.

He replaced the old wizard in its wrappings. "It is true," he murmured, pale and haggard. "Time is flying."

"Ah, well," she said with a catch in her breath.

They were looking at each other brokenly. The air echoed and echoed with the "goodbye" that was not spoken.

He took her hand in his. "Princess," he whispered huskily, "I had dreamed of your seeing my studio ere we said goodbye. It would be for the first time and last, remember. Won't you come with me now, dear?—the merest glimpse—if only to see where your magic knocker is to hang—You understand, dear?"

Her eyes glistened. "Yes, I understand, dear. I will come with you."

"This is one of the kindest things that even your life will hold!" he exclaimed.

So again they were in the street, and the door swung to behind them. Wyndham was carrying his package, unexpectedly heavy, all concentrated weight, like a dumb-bell. The point caught her attention, and in a flash she changed again, was once more the amused laughing comrade, even though the sky was clouded now and tiny specks of rain flew in their faces.

"A midnight expedition!" she cried. "Let it be a hansom this time."

At the corner of Knightsbridge they found one, and they were off again at a trot; a fact so astonishing that they could hardly grasp it. And then, instead of feeling broken with fatigue at the end of a long day, they found themselves fresh and spirited, as at the beginning of a new adventure.

Soon they were cutting down Sloane Street, and then Wyndham suggested they should go the more interesting way round, so as to take in the Embankment, and drive into the Tite Street at the river end. It would leave a pleasanter impression with her, he argued, and Lady Betty readily assented. He gave the man the word, but straightway again the pair were deep in conversation, and lost all sense of the outer world.

Some minutes passed. Suddenly their driver gave a shout, the hansom jerked violently, and Lady Betty, clutching at Wyndham's hand, saw a woman just step back in time from under the horse's head. The driver cracked his whip and shouted something angrily, and then the hansom moved on again. Wyndham stared out into the night. He saw the line of lights gleaming along the parapet of the river, and recognised they were within a short distance of Tite Street. But the woman was already lost in the gloom.

XXIV

At the table that evening, Alice Robinson announced that she was going to meet Wyndham immediately after dinner. Had her parents not been accustomed to her departure at such summary notice, they might have observed the touch of embarrassment that accompanied it. For, although the expedition had been planned and considered for twenty-four hours on end, Alice found the initial falsehood singularly agitating. Painfully conscious of this lack of sangfroid, and fearful of betraying herself, she felt she must escape from the house as soon as was plausible. So, a little later, she rose in feverish haste from the dinner-table, and went to her room to put on her wrappings. No one was to wait up for her, in case she might be late, she said; she was taking a latch-key as usual. Then she slipped out of the house, and went down the street rapidly.

Some little time had elapsed before she had control of her wits and began to reflect. She had been impelled to start far earlier than she had calculated, and thus she undoubtedly ran the danger of finding Wyndham there, if she went straight to the studio. It was half-past eight; by taking various omnibuses she could fill out the time and be there by half-past nine. But even that seemed too early—he might be only just on the point of going out to his club engagement. No, to be absolutely safe, she would not venture actually to intrude till ten o'clock.

However, she decided to make the journey at once, and to pass the remaining time in that neighbourhood. So she mounted the first omnibus that came along, and, once settled down for the long drive, she drew a deep breath of relief. Now that she was definitely on the way, some of the stress and pressure seemed to leave her, and the expedition seemed less terrible. She pictured herself stealing down Tite Street, standing nervously on the opposite pavement in the shadow, and looking up to see if the studio were illuminated. Even if all were dark, Wyndham might still be dressing in the room at the back; for, from the state of the hall, nothing could be deduced, as often he would not take the trouble to light the oil-lamp on which he at present depended. No, it would be certainly more prudent to wait long enough for certainty. Should she once break in upon him, she knew he would take good care she should not see the picture; for no doubt he had taken measures against such a surprise visit.

Immersed in these reflections, Alice was dimly aware of the miles of streets through which she was being carried. Indeed, she forgot to change omnibuses at Oxford Street, and was borne some distance out of her way before she discovered the omission. The whole town seemed to her like a dream; the street and the studio at her journey's end were all that existed for her. And even when she gazed at the world around her, it refused to take on any reality; the people that were abroad, going their way and standing out brilliantly in the night wherever a blaze of light fell upon them, seemed all strangely irrelevant. The only figures that mattered were her affianced husband and the beautiful, sad woman of stately presence, whose loveliness and nobility had drawn him from her. She knew now she hated Lady Lakeden—definitely, terribly. It was shameful, it was wicked—to hate like that! Lady Lakeden was blameless, and had not the least idea of all this suffering which her loveliness had caused to a fellow-woman, and to Wyndham, too. Yet how good it was to let this mad fury against Lady Lakeden develop in her heart!

She pictured the portrait as standing with its face to the wall, unobtrusive, even lost, amid the hosts of other canvasses. With what terrible eagerness she would dart on it, turn it again, and let the light fall on it! At last she should gaze on the face, should satiate her consuming curiosity!

At Sloane Square she alighted, deciding to eke out the time by walking the rest of the distance. As she plunged into the heart of Chelsea, and was so sensibly near her journey's end, her pulse beat faster, her breath came irregularly, and again her whole mind was concentrated vividly on her goal. The streets through which she passed were almost deserted. The old houses, the gardens, the stretches of brand-new buildings, the great Hospital itself, were all vague silhouettes; above, the stars were keen, but her eyes were fixed rigidly before her.

At the corner of Tite Street she stopped to draw breath, for her heart was now thumping painfully. At the same time she felt almost afraid to set foot in the street itself. The hesitation was unexpected; she had imagined herself going straight to the studio, all of the same impulse. But here a sense of wrong- doing came upon her; the underhandedness of the whole proceeding stood out in that moment, curiously revealed, strangely impressive. A strong temptation assailed her to turn, to run off with all her force, to go back home. But she set her teeth, again. No, she must not go back without seeing Lady Lakeden's portrait. She must not yield to these moments of cowardice. It was stupid. Other women dared much greater things; would hesitate at nothing, however false and ignoble, to gain their own end!

She crossed to the opposite side, and flitted down the street like a shadow. She had so effectively lengthened out her journey that it was at last nearly ten o'clock. Wyndham's whole house was dark, and she had little doubt but that he was already out. Yet she wanted to be absolutely certain, so she moved on again, and sauntered off into a network of neighbouring streets. But she was too impatient to go far afield, and, after a few minutes, she retraced her steps till once more she found herself looking across the street at the silent house that lay all in deep shadow. How dark and deserted; how unnaturally still the whole quarter! Then tramp, tramp, tramp, came the heavy foot of a policeman, and she made him out dimly approaching her. She crossed the road, nervous indeed of any human scrutiny, and walked on briskly, only venturing to turn back when he had finally passed out of the street. Now, she told herself, was the moment.

With every muscle tense, her heart beating now with terrible strokes, so that she felt she might fall swooning at any moment, she approached the house, and mounted the few steps that led to the doorway. Her key was in her little purse-bag, and she extricated it tremblingly. At last she had the door open, gave a last, quick, furtive, glance around, and then stepped into the hall. For a moment she stood listening, her ears intensely on the alert for the least sound in the house. But the sense of absolute emptiness was too profound: the measured ticking of the tall hall-clock seemed to be sounding a curiously vigorous note. She let the door slam behind her, and moved forward a step or two, her feet sinking into the deep Turkey carpet that she herself had chosen; then she sank on a hard oak chair, and sat there gratefully, trying to master her breath, and waiting for her heart to thump itself through sheer weariness into a gentler measure. She unfastened her wraps and threw her coat open, for from head to foot she was burning. She did not note the time that passed, but when she rose again with a start she heard from some neighbouring church clock the single stroke of a quarter. She hesitated no longer, but determined to go up at once to the studio.

But first she lighted the hall lamp. Now that she was here she intended to take possession openly, as was her right. If he should come back suddenly, he at least should not imagine that she was there in secret. But the cunning of the reasoning gave her a twinge of shame; she knew that she was throwing dust in her own eyes in thus spouting of her right. Admit at once that this liberal illumination was a piece of craft, was intended to maintain the surface of innocence that was the cover for woman's guile from time immemorial. Well, so be it! She had been a child all her life. If perhaps she had been less truly innocent, even she might have kept the man who had slipped from her. She was graduating in womanhood now; how splendid it was to be unscrupulous, to do absolutely what you wished, yet skilfully maintain the blind belief and confidence of those you tricked! What great power, what joy could be gathered for yourself that way! Yes, that was the only thing for woman in this world; otherwise she was left to rot!

And, as if to emphasise the conviction, she deliberately lighted a second spare lamp that stood in the hall, so that the spaces were illumined resplendently. Then she mounted the flight of stairs, letting her hand trail along the graceful sweep of balustrade, and pushed open the door of the studio.

Peering into the darkness, her eyes at first could distinguish nothing save the objects in the spaces near her, as some of the light flowed up from below. But presently she was able to distinguish the familiar furniture, and cautiously felt her way across to the mantelpiece. Soon two powerful lamps were in full flame, and she sat down again to rest for a minute, whilst her eyes wandered round seeking for the portrait that was the object of her pilgrimage. She did not remove her coat and wraps, although, spacious as the room was, the atmosphere felt oppressive and the slow fire, banked up with ashes, seemed to give out an immense heat. Yet she felt singularly at leisure, in full possession of her purpose.

Obviously Lady Lakeden's portrait was not on any of the easels; nor could she distinguish any fresh unit amid these many canvasses, all individually familiar to her—like a card-sharper, she could identify any one of them immediately from its apparently featureless back. Her first feeling was one of astonished disappointment, and she rose now, ready to institute a closer search. The possibility of being baulked of her purpose stirred a sudden rage in her. She no longer knew herself. "I am mad—mad," was the thought that echoed through her brain. "But if I am," she reasoned grimly, "my sufferings all these weeks have made me so. I would sooner die than endure this all over again." Then she set about examining all the canvasses, turning them one after the other to the light, in the vain hope that her too accurate knowledge of them might prove in some instance mistaken. But in vain! Was it possible that the portrait was already on its way to Paris?

But wait, was there anything behind the screen so carelessly sprawling in the corner there under the great window? In a moment she had dashed across, and had half-dragged, half-flung it out of its place. Ah! she could almost have screamed with fury at Wyndham's cautious foresight—this unmistakable provision against an accidental visit from her. It was then true; definitely, absolutely true! The man whom she loved to madness, who had professed to love her for herself alone, belonged heart and soul to another woman!

A mist palpitated in the air before her, and the gold foliage and convolutions of the ornate Venetian frame shone through it distorted and terrible. But the canvas itself was a vague blur to her. She staggered over to the nearer lamp and bore it over to the corner, kneeling so as to bring the light full on the picture and her own face opposite Lady Lakeden's. And as now she saw this rare princess, bathed in a mystic light, this figure, full of a sweet dignity and a stately grace; as her eyes rested on the girlish face whose character yet shone out in a splendid illumination, though the rounded, youthful features were free from any stamp that might have touched the bloom of their spring-tide beauty, a cruel knife worked in Alice's heart, a knife that seared as well as stabbed. For a long minute she gazed at the portrait, letting it burn itself on her vision in its every shade and detail—the fresh sheen on the hair, the proud yet sweet tilt of the face, the wonderfully fresh and deep violet-grey eyes, the veritable rose-bud mouth that was yet so firm and true! This, then, was her rival! How could she, the plainest of the plain, hope to struggle against the irresistible might of this loveliness! A sense of absolute defeat, of complete hopelessness invaded her whole being; it was the same submissive acquiescence with which she had contemplated herself in the glass on that momentous evening when Wyndham had appeared in her father's house for the first time. But then the hope had never been roused; now the joy was literally snatched from her lips. But, though her intelligence saw the hopelessness, her heart was full of desperation. And while yet her eyes were riveted on the picture, fascinated, yet loathing it with a passion that seemed to flame and to dominate her as though her real self were too puny to stir against it, a wild whirling thought came to her that made her body rock and shiver, and she set the lamp on the floor to save it from crashing down out of her hand. What if this woman were as guilty as the man?

"I understand now," her lips broke out involuntarily. "They loved each other from the beginning, but she married another for convention's sake. Now they have resumed their old love, but I am in the way. He will not jilt me, because his honour is at stake, but as a man of honour he would not think it dishonourable to deceive me." She laughed aloud in bitterness. That was it! They would both deceive her, though he would never break his word. Had she not seen the point exemplified in a hundred books and plays?

Ah, this honour of the fashionable classes! And she had believed Lady Lakeden to be true; had, in pity and sympathy, set her on the highest pedestal of womanhood. How her belief in her rival's perfect goodness had blinded her! What a fool she had been, going through life with such simplicity! With a heart so open and trusting! No wonder nothing had come to illumine her existence!—that what had seemed to hold the promise was a cheat and a delusion!

And, as her mind ran back over the past weeks, a thousand things seemed to confirm her new inspiration at every turn. Ah, God! how she had been tricked! Was there another woman in the world who would have been so trustingly stupid? The blood seemed to surge all to her temples: everything before her faded. An impulse to give vent to her fury seized her. She longed to tear and rend the canvas, to crush and break it with her fingers, to bite it through and through with her teeth. And she would have carried the imperious impulse into effect, had not a new thought, like a zigzag of lightning, come flashing through her brain. Lady Lakeden had no doubt written him letters; there must be a whole packet of them somewhere here in the studio! She would read them; they would not lie!

Intent on this new end, she darted across to the bureau (of which the lid was permanently down and laden with papers and portfolios), and scrutinised the pigeon-holes. These were always open to her without restriction, but she had never thought of examining the contents, though she had often put away papers and receipts for him. She made a quick, feverish inspection of them now, not hoping to find the letters she sought in a place thus conspicuous, but yet fearful of overlooking them. The pigeon-holes yielded in fact nothing to interest her, and then with trembling fingers she turned out the little drawers, one at a time, replacing the contents of each carefully before proceeding to the next. She was reckless now, having no control over itself. She did not fear his sudden arrival on the scene; she would face him—she would taunt him with the truth!

Suddenly her physical powers seemed to break down, and she clutched at the bureau for support. And as soon as she had steadied herself, she was glad to drag over a chair, and continue her search with feeble, tired movements. And with this abrupt collapse, her crude, violent emotions seemed to have blazed themselves out. She felt now a poor forlorn, helpless creature; her eyes were wet with tears, and she was choking down her sobs. And it seemed to her that she was gulping down an infinite bitterness. "I have it," she said suddenly, a momentary illumination flitting across her features. He had once shown her in this old provincial French bureau a receptacle which he had spoken of as his secret drawer, a space neatly stowed away amid the other surrounding spaces so that its ingenious existence might remain reasonably unsuspected. She immediately stopped her operations, replacing things with a movement that was increasingly languid and feeble; and eventually opened the principal compartment in the centre which was on a level with the writing-lid. Removing all its contents, she inserted her nail in a little innocent slit, made the floor of the compartment slide along, then thrust her hand into the space revealed.

Clearly a packet of letters was there. She drew it forth—over a dozen of them, carefully preserved in their fashionable-looking envelopes and tied together with a broad piece of tape. A faint perfume of violets was in her nostrils as she handled them. And this packet, too, seemed strangely imbued with the personality of their writer, reminiscent of a world of dream and books. How remote from her they seemed! How remote from her, indeed, all the amazing history of these past months! That, too, belonged rather to a world of dream and books. What! these great tragic complications and emotions had sprung up in her simple, uneventful existence! had related themselves to a brick bow-windowed house in the suburbs!

She gazed at the packet again, conscious that her fingers were faltering. How mean, low, hateful to read letters that had not been meant for others' eyes! And what purpose would be served by her reading them? She needed no further proof of the intrigue that had been carried on in the shelter of her own credulity and simplicity. Besides, she could divine what passionate vows of love were written herein, and to pry into them would be to renew her tortures beyond human endurance. She feared and turned away from them as from a furnace heated seven times hot. The packet dropped amid the masses of papers that encumbered the desk. Her tears came anew, and she gave them full vent; a storm of hysteric sobbing shook her convulsively.

When eventually the attack had spent itself, she sat there listlessly, without the force to stir hand or foot. But her brain was working feverishly, definitely recognising that her life was spoilt. She had made her great cry of revolt in this mad dash and underhanded search; better perhaps to have made it in the silent depths of her heart! Ah, God, it was bitter, it was cruel! But what had she expected? Had she not known from the beginning that she ought never to accept one so far above her?—that she was not the ideal his heart would crave for, but that, at the best, a deep secret dissatisfaction would rankle in him all his life? Had she not steadily seen this, while yet a shred of sanity remained to her? But it had all happened in spite of herself; she had been stricken with blindness, and her clear-seeing mind had been possessed with inexplicable folly. She—Alice Robinson!—and the thought made her laugh out aloud— had wholly believed that this man sincerely loved her! She laughed again and again, seized suddenly by the pitifully comic spectacle she presented to herself—Alice Robinson, shy, awkward, devoid of all the graces, lacking *savoir-faire*, neglected not only by men, but even by her own sex: Alice Robinson, the granddaughter of a carpenter, seriously beloved by an aristocrat with all the graces and culture, an artist, moreover, for whom beauty was always the primal appeal! She—Alice Robinson—had been under this wondrous delusion! Was there anything more ridiculous since men and women were? Her laughter could not be repressed, but it rang out through the studio weirdly, with a strange note of hardness and bitterness, and somehow it echoed and re-echoed through all the house, coming back to her mockingly from the empty rooms beneath her.

Even when her laughter had died away she sat there brooding. And for the first time there was mingled in her emotions a touch of pity for Wyndham.

She was conscious now of a softening, in spite of all. Poor Wyndham! Had he not loved Lady Lakeden years before he had set eyes on the Robinsons? If only he had not possessed that terrible code of honour! He might then have come to her frankly and begged her compassion! She would have released him. But he could not break his word. His honour only allowed him to carry on an intrigue!

But time was passing, and she told herself she must not stay. She knew she was defeated and must accept it: she must leave him to his intrigue, whilst she herself stepped back into the old suburban existence!

She replaced the letters in the secret receptacle, and restored everything in the bureau as it had been before. Then she dragged back the screen before the picture, turning away her eyes resolutely so as not to catch sight again of that gracious figure gleaming out in exquisite radiance. The lamps were put back as she had found them, then carefully extinguished. But the difficulty she had with them revealed to her the tense nervous condition under which she was still labouring, though she had appeared to herself quiet and resigned now. She stood in the dark a moment, conscious of the suffocating closeness of the atmosphere. How good it would be to be out in the air again! She would walk on the Embankment for a few minutes, and then ingloriously go home as fast as possible—in a hansom! having yielded to ignoble impulses and played the rôle of a common spy. But in one way she at least had no regret She was enlightened, knew as much of the position as Wyndham.

She descended the stairs, put out the lamps in the hall, and stepped into the streets again. The cold air beat in her face deliciously; the stars were brilliant in the pure sky. She looked up to them now yearningly—their calm and beauty shamed the storm and fever in her own mind. The street, too, seemed so exquisitely still in the splendid darkness. She let her wraps hang loosely about her, and did not fasten her coat. She breathed the air greedily, and it seemed to allay the stress at her heart. Then somehow she turned her steps towards the river, wondering where Wyndham and Lady Lakeden were passing their evening! She could take that for granted now, she felt. How carefully he had built up the wall around his romance!

At the bottom of the street the river night-scene, scintillating with points of light, burst on her vision, and seemed to draw her into its own strange mood of mystery. It was as though a new universe of stars had come into being, wafting some fascinating message which baffled her reading. And as she stood in the great avenue, under the far-spreading arch of foliage, a deeper calm seemed to fall upon her. She went to the parapet, and looked over. The long stretch of water, all gleams and shadows, lay gently between the two gray bridges that hung suspended from their steel network in soft silhouette.

Alice strolled some distance down the bank, then turned and retraced her steps. She told herself it was foolish to linger here, that she ought to make at once for the busier streets, and take the first vehicle that offered itself. But it was so deliciously silent, so majestic, that it comforted her to stay here. Besides, somehow, she could not tear herself away from the neighbourhood of the studio. She looked at her watch; to her surprise it was nearly half-past eleven; she had been at the studio a full hour and more! Surely he must be coming home soon. Perhaps, indeed, he had returned already!

She found herself instinctively turning up Tite Street again, keeping as before to the opposite side of the road. But all was as dark and still in the house as when she had left it. Then the idea came to her that she would wait and see. It was a mere whim perhaps; but she could not go home till she had watched him enter. Still, she could not wait here in one fixed spot; she had almost the sense of being observed by she knew not whom. Besides, she must be cautious; she did not intend that he should suspect she was actually so near to him at that hour of the night. It gave her an anguished thrill to think he would pass close by her, and yet never give her a thought.

She was, however, loth to move away, for she could not know from which end of the street he would come. If she waited too long near one end, he might slip by from the other. And this, whether he came on foot or in a hansom. Feverishly she paraded the street, stopping here a minute, there a minute; keeping well within the shadow, and avoiding the encounter of every chance passer-by. Now and again she heard the ring of a hansom, the smart trot of a horse, and she held her breath with excitement. And there was even a minute when hansoms came dashing into the street one after the other; most of them to pass right through it, and only one or two to draw up in the street itself.

Midnight sounded, but still no sign of Wyndham. She looked up at the sky, but was surprised to find the stars were blotted out. A spot of rain fell on her upturned face. Her sense of misery reasserted itself, and with it came a sullen resolution to stay out till dawn, if needs be. Again she went to the Hospital end of the road and took up a discreet point of vantage. But again the tramp of a policeman scared her away, and accepting this as a sort of unpropitious omen she definitely decided to keep to the other end. She was like a gambler uncertain how to stake, but at last abruptly deciding for any irrelevant reason.

The minutes passed, infinitely long to her now impatient mood. The spots of rain kept falling. The neighbouring clock boomed out the quarters. At last another hansom—coming from the abandoned direction! Back she went again into the road, but it had stopped short farther down. The studio was still in darkness. Strangely disappointed and fatigued almost to the point of falling, she dragged her worn feet once more down to the Embankment, keeping her wits alert with a sustained effort, that grew harder and harder. This time she did not cross to the parapet, but walked under the great red brick houses, noticing idly their gates and doorways as they loomed on her. And her eyes were half closed in spite of her struggle. The trot of a horse, and the rattle and tinkle of a hansom sounded just then, coming smartly along the avenue. But she went on more and more as if in a dream, taking one step only because she had taken the last. Nearer and nearer came the hansom, louder and louder beat the horse's hoofs on the asphalte, but she pursued her meaningless way, without paying any heed to it. Her senses had almost left her. She opened her eyes suddenly, and, looking towards the river, saw that a greyish mist hung over it, that the pavements were wet and glistening. Ah, yes, the water lay below, dark and soft, full of an eternal peace. The message that had baffled her!—she understood it now! She had nothing to live for! In a flash all would be finished. Impulsively she stepped into the roadway to cross to the parapet.

"Hallo, hallo!" The horse's head was almost on her, and she drew back with a natural unreasoned movement. The driver shook his whip and shouted angrily, then went onwards. But a moment's vision had burnt itself on her consciousness as deep as that first sight of the portrait of Lady Lakeden. Wyndham was seated in the vehicle side by side with Lady Lakeden, his face turned towards her, whilst her hand clutched his convulsively. And in that same swift moment Alice had felt Lady Lakeden's face encounter hers with mutual intensity. The sudden backward movement had almost paralysed her muscles; an agonising pain racked her at her knees and ankles. She dragged herself to the nearest wall and leaned against it. The picture of those two side by side was always with her: of Lady Lakeden's eyes flashing full on her own.

She knew not how many minutes had passed when she was called to herself by the inexorable clock that had sounded its notes throughout this strange evening, and that now seemed to fling its boom through all the spaces of the night. Was the universe resounding with a peal of mockery?— disproportionately Titanic for so humble a soul as hers, so paltry a destiny? Ah, she remembered now her frustrated purpose; the instant when death had beckoned her imperiously and she had responded with every fibre of her soul and body. Why, then, had she not let the wheels crush her?

But she shuddered. Ah, no, no! Thank Heaven she had been inspired to save herself. How his life would have been saddened and embittered by so ironic an accident! She had meant only to help him; never to be a cause of grief to him! Since apparently it had been thus fated, better perhaps to live on. "I have others as well to think of—father and mother!" she murmured. "How wicked it was of me to forget them! Besides, as I never expected anything in life, why should I be disappointed now at getting nothing?" The argument seemed convincing, so painfully she began to hobble along the Embankment, moving again towards the familiar street, why she knew not. But her lips kept muttering, to herself. "She has gone with him alone to his studio. She is a wicked woman."

And opposite the house, that had held her brilliant hopes of love and wonderful happiness for so brief a period, she stood still again, and looked up to the great window of the studio that was now illumined with a warm light, though everywhere else the house was dark. She saw a shadow flit across the blind, and then another shadow. They were there together.

How they would stare if she boldly used her key and intruded upon them! How they would tremble if they knew she was there, straining for a glimpse of their shadows!

But she had no impulse now to disturb them. The game had been played, and she had been thrown out.

With a sigh she moved away, turning her painful steps up the street, more instinctively than consciously. She walked and walked mechanically, retracing the route she had taken on her way there. The rain descended in thin, sharp lines, but she took no heed. But suddenly an arm was thrust through hers, and she looked round with a terrible start. A burly flush-faced man with a ruffled silk hat was holding an umbrella over her, was speaking to her. Her eye noticed irrelevantly they were just by a closed dark public-house whose nickel reflectors caught the light from an adjoining street-lamp.

"Hadn't you better take me home with you, my dear?"

For a second she stared at him, then, with a hoarse cry, she shook herself free, and with a supreme effort rushed off like a frightened fawn. As she turned into another street she overtook a hansom going at a snail's pace.

"Where to?" asked the man through the roof, after she had got in.

"Straight home as fast as you can," was her strange answer.

The man looked down upon her. "Where's that?" he asked good-humouredly.

"I beg your pardon," she exclaimed, vainly attempting to control her breath. She gave him the address, and off they went.

At the end of the journey she paid him profusely, and he thanked her with as profuse a civility. She let herself in with her key, went up at once to her room, and threw herself across her bed. Her sobs broke out afresh. "Darling," she called; "I want you back again to be mine, and mine only."

XXV

Lady Betty did not let go the hand which she had clutched in terror, and her companion responded with a touch of caressing reassurance.

"My heart is still beating," she said, as they turned off the river bank into Tite Street. "Suppose we had crushed that poor creature. What a terrible memory it would have left with us!"

"Happily she wasn't in the least hurt," he replied. "She must have been in a fit of abstraction."

"I caught sight of her face," said Lady Betty; "and I shall not easily forget it. Such a wild, haggard look I have seldom seen. She must have been labouring under some terrible stress of emotion." She gently withdrew her hand, and appeared lost in thought. "I hope, dear," she exclaimed suddenly, "that there is nothing horrible happening."

"No, indeed! The thing has got a little bit on your nerves."

"You did not see her," she insisted. "She came full into the light of our lamp, though it was barely for an instant. My face was turned that way and yours away from hers."

"Naturally she was startled at the moment!" he ventured. He was certain Lady Betty's nervous imagination had deceived her, and that her alarm was groundless.

"It was not a startled look. It was a set look, something like the desperation of a hunted animal. Some man has treated her badly. Darling, you don't think she was going to throw herself into the river?"

"Seriously—I don't think anything of the kind. If she had wanted to take her life, would she have stepped back so promptly?" he argued.

"I daresay you are right," she conceded, though her tone was not wholly one of conviction.

The hansom pulled up, and he helped her down. They mounted the house- steps in silence, she unusually engrossed in thought, and with an unmistakable air of sadness, as if her mind still lingered on this woman's figure that had flashed on them out of the darkness.

They entered the hall, and after some searching and fumbling he lighted one of the lamps. His companion shook herself out of her abstraction, and surveyed the place with affectionate interest. He was anxious she should take away with her a very definite impression of his future home, and threw open the various rooms, and led the way into them, as he held the lamp aloft. They went, too, below stairs, and here Lady Betty's eyes beheld the many evidences of domestic comfort and foresight that the Robinsons had established in these regions where they had reigned supreme. Her face lighted in comprehension, though her thought remained unexpressed. At last, after they had completely explored the rest of the house, he led the way up to the studio, and soon had it brilliantly illuminated. Lady Betty refused the chair he wheeled forward for her. She preferred to be moving about, to be examining everything at leisure—his bureau, his great oak worm-eaten armoires, his long, low chests on whose panels Gothic Church dignitaries stood solemnly in high relief, his wonderful easels, his model's throne, his draperies and costumes, and, so far as it was possible by this lamp-light, his old canvasses. She did not ask for Miss Robinson's portrait, as she knew it was at the house in Hampstead, and would remain there till its despatch to the Academy. She saw, however, the large picture; and although she did not love it (for she knew at what a cost it had been brought up to its present pitch, and felt, moreover, that it was too sensational a bid for public attention), she yet recognised that there was much excellence in it, and that it would probably bring him the actual success which was of importance even to genius. Her ideal for him, she repeated, would have been the most absolute "no compromise." "But I agree that we must take a strictly practical view of the situation. It is not really compromise," she added, "but only a surer grasping of the ideal in the future. The idealist who does not know when to make his concessions in practice is just the one who loses his ideal altogether, and never comes down from the realm of abstractions."

He seized a favourable moment, whilst her attention was otherwise engaged, to fetch her own portrait from behind the screen and arrange it on one of the smaller easels. Then she turned with some curiosity to see what he had prepared for her, and gave a little cry of delight.

"You are pleased with it?" he asked, gratified.

"And touched—deeply," she answered. "You have chosen the setting with excellent judgment. But what pleases me most is the absolutely fresh impression I now get of the picture itself. Though I have seen it grow, and have lived with it every day, I am really seeing it for the first time. It is a beautiful piece of work—I speak for the moment as if I were entirely unconnected with it." She stood examining it in silence, and he watched her face and every shade of expression that declared itself.

"And this truly is your personal impression of me?" she asked, with a new flash of the joyous, eager comrade.

"My everyday impression of you! I have another which I keep for Sundays—something with more of the stateliness of an olden time, with a far graver outlook and a deeper thoughtfulness."

"But this one is thoughtful and dignified, too, is it not?"

"Most decidedly. But it is a real warm human being as well. To tell the truth, I stand a little bit in awe of the other one."

"Poor me!" she laughed. She stood yet a moment contemplating the portrait, then turned her eyes away. "Oh, well," she said. "It will be a happiness to possess it, but a greater one to feel that, in some measure, it has helped to gain you the recognition that must be yours—a little sooner, a little later, signifies nothing. But I leave you in perfect confidence as to your career."

He bowed his head. "I shall not dare to disappoint your confidence. To justify it is what I shall live for before all things."

"I am content," she said. "I ask for nothing better than that our hopes shall be realised. I am glad you have chosen so charming a home for your labours. I hope you will be happy here."

He did not reply at once, not trusting himself to speak. Lady Betty, too, looked sadly down.

"Ah, yes," he conceded at last. "It is an ideal home for an artist!"

There were bitter implications in his tone, and she made no pretence of not perceiving them.

"Darling," she said, "you know it would be the dream of my life to help you. That is the only meaning happiness would have for me—to live by your side and help your work and your life. Before everything else, I am not the solemn, dignified being—the thought of me you keep for Sunday," she interposed smilingly—"but a mere human being, a simple woman, for whom the love of the right man, once she has found him, is the principal thing in life."

"I can't realise that you are going away," he broke out. "I want to keep you with me always. Don't leave me, darling! Let us begin our life anew—now, this minute! An ideal home here! I hate and loathe it. Let us make a home together—a home of our very own—far away from all these associations. Let us laugh at all else. I am strong enough to throw over everything, to fight!"

She read the passion in his vivid face, in his terrible movement towards her. She stepped back, and held up her hands to check him.

"It cannot be," she said. "Perhaps we are to blame for delaying our parting. Believe me, I thought and thought about it after our first meeting till I feared I should go mad. I felt I had already made my great blunder—I had revealed the awful secret of my life. I had till then nursed it all alone, but when I saw you again, after those miserable years, I had to pour it out. I did so recklessly, unthinkingly; it was such a joy to feel there was one friend in the world to whom such things could be said, and I put no curb on myself. And afterwards I was bitterly sorry."

"No, no, darling," he interposed. "You hurt me."

"Don't misunderstand, please. It was splendid to think that you shared my confidence; above all that you had cared for me as I had cared for you in the old days. But yet I was tortured incessantly. You had contracted other ties; there were your duties to others, and the tangle was horrible! After I left you on that first day I was determined that, if I was to be an influence in your life at all, I must be the first to keep you true to your duties. You and I are enlightened, you see. We have the advantage over these simpler souls. Therefore we must efface ourselves to leave them their simple rights."

He stood humbly; silent before her gentle and unanswerable rebuke.

"I struggled terribly with myself. I felt it would hardly be right to see you even a second time, and I was almost on the point of leaving London at once, perhaps without sending you a single line of adieu. But then the thought came to me that that perhaps would be a worse blunder than the first. My intrusion into your life might in that case have disturbed it to no purpose. I thought my sudden departure might leave a bitter memory for years. So I determined to stay long enough to soften the parting for both of us—for me as well as for you. And during all the time I meant to influence you to be loyal to your engagements. I had made the first mistake; on me lay the obligation of mending things. I stayed only to mend them! That was my sincere motive in asking you to do the sketch. I know I have had my moments of weakness; it is hard to live with one's hand in the fire without flinching now and again. Darling, I must go—far away from you, and you must not follow me. Your honour, dearest, is precious to me. The thought of your perfect loyalty to Alice will help me. I only ask you to remember the high standard I have set for you. Strive for the best; let your watchword be 'No compromise!' You will let me go now, darling. Say you understand my motives, and forgive me if they were mistaken. Perhaps, instead of mending things, I have only added mischief to mischief. I throw myself on your generosity and magnanimity. Promise me you will be the truest husband to her, that you will do everything in your power to promote her happiness."

He seized her hands; his flesh burnt hers. "I love you, darling, I love you," he cried hoarsely. "I cannot let you go."

She looked him frankly and firmly in the face. "Don't break my heart, dear," she said gently. "It is as hard for me as it is for you. Think, darling, what it might be, if you gave her up. If she were to kill herself, our love would be a curse to us. Dearest, the face of that woman we saw on the Embankment still haunts me. It was the face of a woman whose heart had been broken. I tell you, dear, that if I had not of myself the strength to part from you to-night, the awful glimpse I had of her face would have given it to me. I have always seen where our duty lay; yet I read it in that poor face a thousand times more. Darling, it must now be goodbye. I shall often think of you here, and of this evening— and of our whole glorious day," she added, smiling. "Come, you do promise all that I ask of you?"

Her smile and her cheerful note won his surrender. "I promise," he said slowly and solemnly, yet with distinct decision. "All that you have urged on me shall be sacred, shall be the principle of my life."

"Thank you, darling," she said simply. "I believe you, and I trust you absolutely."

They gripped hands, looking each other full in the face. The neighbouring church clock sounded its preliminary change, then struck two sonorous notes. It recalled them to the sense of the night and the silent world without. "Come," he said at last. "I will escort you back."

They went down, and out into the street again. "The clouds and the rain have vanished. It is a beautiful night again," she said. "Even that helps to soften the moment."

He strolled along by her side; they spoke now of matter-of-fact points. If the picture were accepted by the Salon he was to send it eventually to her father's country-house in the North. She hoped, too, he would not entirely forget her father, but that he and his wife would call and see him at Grosvenor Place— they could count on finding him there most years during the height of the London season. And, by the way, she was curious to know how the picture would fare when it got to Paris. Was the Salon so considerate to foreigners that it took the trouble to open packing-cases and take care of them? Wyndham gravely explained that pictures were usually consigned to the good offices of a French frame-maker who unpacked and delivered them to the Salon, afterwards collecting them and sending them back to England when the show was over. Some of these people had a large foreign clientèle, and put only a moderate value on their services. Thus chatting in this trivial fashion, they were fortunate to meet a hansom, though they had abandoned the hope of one at that hour, and were prepared to stroll all the way.

"Let us say goodbye here," she insisted. "It is simpler, and perhaps easier. We part just as two friends who have met casually."

"Goodbye, then," he said huskily. "I wish you many happy days and dreams in your wanderings in the sun-lands."

"And I wish you the power to be as great in your life as I am sure you will be in your work." She held his hand with a gentle pressure. "You will be loyal to her," was her last wistful whisper. Then she gave him a parting smile, full of sweetness and affection, and he heard the driver crack his whip, and the horse started off briskly.

Wyndham was left standing on the pavement, his head bowed. For a long minute he did not stir, and when he roused himself again to look after the hansom, it was already in the distance, though the trot, trot, of the horse came sharply to him. He watched it till it was out of sight, then turned slowly and gently homewards.

XXVI

"Father," said Alice Robinson the next morning at the breakfast-table, "I want you to find some more portraits for us. This whole month has to be given up to the big thing for the Academy, and then we shall come to a stop for the present, at any rate so far as immediately remunerative work is concerned, and you must not forget we have a heavy rent to pay now."

"I shall certainly keep my weather eye open," declared Mr. Robinson, "and my ears too. Portraits in oils are rather the thing just now in the City, and I daresay we shall be able to find something for you."

"That is nice of you, father. I think I am just beginning to like you."

Mr. Robinson smiled, and looked across at her affectionately. "You know it is my greatest pleasure to work for you both," he said.

Alice bore his gaze heroically, sustained by the curious satisfaction she felt at having thus set the never-failing machinery in motion. But his trusting belief that all was well touched the tenderest chords of her nature. She longed to throw herself into his arms, to tell him the terrible truth. But why cause him suffering when she still hoped to avert it from everybody, and let the whole burden rest on her shoulders alone? She must do nothing abrupt, nothing to cause any trouble or scandal; above all, she must pay the most watchful regard to the peace of those around her.

For she had seen the quietest and simplest solution of the tangle; nobody but herself need suffer a single pang! Since she had endured so much, she might now as well offer herself for the sake of everybody else's happiness.

Such had been her dominating thought, as she had lain thinking through the night. And the moment had come when she held the solution clear in her mind. How glad she was that she had decided to live! Her parents had been spared a cruel grief, and her affianced husband would be left to his happiness without any alloy of remorse or tragic memories.

There was only one worthy and rational path before her. She must break with Wyndham and leave him free. Mr. Shanner wanted her; she would give herself to Mr. Shanner. His ashen figure, gray-clad, rose before her, wistful, pleading, pathetic. She remembered his touch of sentiment, his hint of deeper feeling—how he would have treasured her promise; how he would have looked forward to "the new light to shine in his household." He was good and honourable; full of kind actions. She knew that Mr. Shanner had not found felicity in his first marriage. After all, if she could bring somebody a little happiness she might as well do so; and she could make this ostensibly the ground for her action. She and Wyndham were unsuited to each other—could anything be truer? She had made a mistake, since she now found she cared for Mr. Shanner, who reciprocated the sentiment, and for whom, as regards upbringing and ideas, she would make so much more suitable a wife. That was less true, and, after her surrender of the evening before to her ignobler side, she now loathed the idea of playing a further part. But the fiction that she cared for Mr. Shanner, and her actual marriage with him, constituted in essence the sacrifice that the position demanded of her. To Mr. Shanner she could atone by incessant devotion—she would illumine the light in his household he had spoken of so yearningly; her parents would be spared all but the first painful surprise; to Wyndham the break would come as a splendid release. It would restore to him his honour and self-respect, since in his eyes, and in the world's eyes, she would be taking all the blame for his freedom.

Wyndham had told her that Lady Lakeden was leaving England indefinitely, and that he did not know when he was likely to see her again. But Alice now did not believe that. That was part of the wall he had been building behind which to pursue his romance; she had tested things far enough to feel sure of it. And even if Lady Lakeden was really going to travel for a time, there would be correspondence between them, and their relations would be renewed on her return. Since he loved this woman he should be free to love her openly.

And all the world would be left at peace!

In the days before she had come into his consciousness, had she not longed and prayed in vain for the joy of helping him to rise again; had she not dreamed of stretching out a helping hand across the abyss that separated them, telling herself that that alone would mean supreme happiness for her? It now came strongly upon her that that mission had been granted her, and the knowledge that she had achieved it should help her to be strong! Had not her love for him held a perfect unselfishness? Was not her goal his happiness before everything? Ah, there was far too much self in the earthly love of woman for man. This note of self, at first so carefully suppressed, had yet asserted itself insidiously. Yes, that had been the cause of all her suffering— poignant, shattering, almost beyond human endurance. It had been wrong of her; she ought to have kept closer watch over herself. She had not meant to be a source of pain and embarrassment to him. To burden his life with a marriage against his heart and true self were hate, not love. Let him mate with this brilliant, beautiful woman of his own world, who could tranquilly breathe the air of the great heights—of Society, of Art—in which his destiny had placed him. What more could she wish him than that he should find in life all that he desired?—all the joy, all the achievement, all the love! Was not this the supreme self-sacrifice of love?

And she must be content with the privilege of the high mission that had been hers, nay, she must be proud of it—to have entered into his life at his moment of blackest despair, and set him on the road to heaven! Let her go back into the darkness now with the ecstasy of sacrifice for a great love, keeping herself for such service to others as she might find to her hand.

XXVII

But her mission was not yet complete. She thought of his inadequate resources, of the uncertainty of the future, if his exhibition pictures were not successful with the Press and the public. She wished to see him embarked on the full tide of success before she retired, so that all joy should flow to him at once. Her retirement must cause him some little emotion, but the intoxication of success would soon thrust that aside, and the lapse of a day would find him in full appreciation of his freedom. The projected period of their engagement had of itself three full months to run; there was time to withdraw at any moment she chose. And these months that remained should be devoted to her finding more work for him, so that he should be left with a substantial balance at his bankers.

She thus attached some importance to his not yet suspecting any change; so she decided to go across to Tite Street at tea-time, and see him, and do things below stairs just as on a normal day. But she feared to face the experience alone; she did not trust her own sangfroid. As the afternoon proved a fine one, she pressed her mother to join her in the journey across town, throwing out the inducement that they would look at the shops in town *en route*.

They found Wyndham putting his brushes in order after his long day. He had risen early, he explained, and had started work with the light. A month was not too long to finish off this great picture; he really saw a year's work yet to be done on it! So therefore he was making a tremendous effort and giving himself up to it, body and soul.

"And I'm afraid I must claim your indulgence. If I appear neglectful, you will really understand, and put up with me. I shall make it up to you afterwards," he added, smiling.

Alice was surprised at her calm, once she had mastered the first tremor at the moment of arrival. It gave her confidence, too, for the future, since it was good to know she could trust herself.

And this strange, almost inhuman, calm which had succeeded to the tempests that had swept through her of late did not desert her. She knew that the storms had worn themselves out, and that she had found a strange, an almost baffling peace.

Wyndham, for his part, only rejoiced that she seemed so contented and happy; so ready to overlook his shortcomings in the rôle of affianced husband. Poor child, how good and devoted she was! If only out of his brotherly tenderness for her, and appreciation and gratitude for all she had planned and done to smoothe his life, he would take care that his promise to Lady Betty should be carried out, not grudgingly and according to the letter, but in a generously full and human way.

Perhaps now, in this last critical month, when every stroke of the brush seemed a stroke of fate, he threw more frenzy into his work than ever before. His mind struck deep roots in it, so that the passion of it was ever in him. Yet a sense of suffering and defeat stirred sometimes in him, so that he dared not be alone with himself. He spent some of his evenings in coteries where art and other things were hotly debated, and this, too, helped him, furnishing food for reflection and sending him to books as an interested reader in search of enlightenment and suggestion.

Thus the month flew away with almost unprecedented rapidity. Show Sunday arrived, and the great picture (on which he had worked till the last moment) was revealed to the world at large. The house was thrown open, the empty dining-room improvised into a commodious buffet, and the great studio arranged as a gallery, with the new portraits and the best of the old work all brilliantly framed and lining the walls. Alice's portrait, which had been brought across for the occasion, occupied a central place of honour immediately facing the masterpiece.

The function was eminently successful, and a great many people of the very pink of fashion came to lend it the light of their countenances. The Robinsons had worked hard the previous fortnight preparing for it, and had arranged the house and buffet, and had seen to the framing of the pictures, and attended to the catering arrangements, without taking a moment of the precious time away from Wyndham. Everybody said the house was charming and the pictures works of genius. People could be overheard asking each other, "Well, what do you think of it all?" and then eyes would be turned up in ecstasy, and faces would glow with enthusiasm, and the long-drawn "Beautiful," full of conviction, was the epithet most largely utilised. There was in the air the dominant note of triumph, the unmistakable feeling of Success. Alice, who flitted about quietly, showing herself as much as good taste demanded, yet by no means in the centre of the world's eye, was keenly sensitive to the prevailing spirit of the afternoon, feeling closely the pulse of the assembly, and she knew at last that Wyndham's barque was to sail in full career.

Mary, too, was there, immensely important as the host's sister, conducting special friends of her own round the walls, and talking ubiquitously in an unusual glow of zest and animation. If for Alice the occasion happily revealed the future, for Mary that future had emphatically arrived already!

And in the midst of all the crush Sadler arrived, extraordinarily smart in an immaculate frock-coat and a beautifully embroidered tie, his big powerful face shining with friendliness. "Gee! What a swell affair you've got on!" he shouted in Wyndham's ear. "I thought there'd be something of the kind, you old brute, so I rigged myself out."

"You are certainly fascinating," smiled Wyndham.

"Yes, it's a jolly good coat!" declared Sadler, glancing down at himself. "I gave the tailor hell over it. Gee! you've fetched them this time! We shan't be able to squeeze past your damned picture at the Academy!"

The crowd still kept surging up the stairs, and Sadler was swept aside. But Wyndham was not only receiving his visitors; with great address he was here and there, pointing out his Exhibition pictures, explaining his ideas and motives, accepting choruses of laudation. He had good reason to be elated with this afternoon of tribute and foreshadowing!

In the last two or three weeks, moreover, Mr. Robinson had been drumming up the further commission for which his daughter had enlisted his good services. He had heard that one of the great joint-stock banks meditated presenting their retiring general manager with his portrait; the gift to be made with full ceremonial at the next meeting of the shareholders. Mr. Robinson was himself an important shareholder, and two of the directors were his personal friends, but although they worked strongly on his side, he had a far more difficult task than usual in achieving his purpose. He was forced to expend his choicest diplomacy and pull enough strings for a piece of international politics, but the majority of the directors, who knew what was appropriate to the dignity of the bank, wanted a full-blown Royal Academician, and were strongly in favour of following the lead of another great institution, which, under the like circumstances, had approached one of the most learned of the body Academic, and had honoured him and themselves with their command. There were dissensions at several board meetings, but the opposition, sedulously fanned by Mr. Robinson, could not be beaten down. Academicians, they argued, sometimes went down woefully in the sale-room only a few years after their demise. Surely it was better to choose a genius, the connection with whom would be everlastingly honourable to the bank, whose insight might become historic. In the end a small sub-committee was appointed to investigate and report on the matter. The members of this sub-committee were invited to Tite Street for Show Sunday, arrived together, were received by Wyndham with charming urbanity, had every attention showered on them, and were greatly impressed by this society gathering. They were enchanted at their reception, and, being kept and marshalled together, stimulated each other's enthusiasm. This great display of Wyndham's work astonished and dazzled them. Above all, the amazing *pièce de résistance* of the afternoon won their obeisance to the genius. They stared at the vast canvas in wonder, at once conquered by this crowd of tattered labour intermingled with the silk hats and frock-coats of Bond Street, the smart brougham rolling along with its aristocratic occupant and her poodle, the pillared structure in the background, the vista of roadway, the trees and the foliage. At the buffet they talked it over among themselves, and presently Wyndham himself appeared again, and with a discreet introduction here and there to people of social importance, he quietly and swiftly sealed his victory. Such civility indeed was the only part that had fallen on him in the matter, and the commission was well obtained at that outlay of trouble, he told himself, since, with so fairly an expensive place on his hands, he could not yet despise so solid a piece of business. But with the new little heap of guineas to accrue from the month's work or thereabouts that would be involved, he felt he could face marriage and the beginnings of housekeeping with dignity, and yet carry out any artistic schemes he might next conceive. And he welcomed the work, too, as likely to keep him busily occupied during the time his great picture was in the balance at the Academy.

When Alice reached home after the reception, with the full confidence of his success in her heart, she realised the end was now fast approaching. The afternoon had excited and unnerved her again, and she had once more to reassure herself that she had the strength to go through with the coming breach. Since her memorable secret visit to the studio she had borne up with firm strength, but to-night she felt frail and broken! A storm of sobbing shook her, but when at last she had controlled herself she knew that she would never weep again for her lost dream of happiness.

And now all things began to go incredibly well with Wyndham. No sooner was he flourishing and doing work that was well paid for, than every other horizon opened out before him. The Academy received both his portrait of Miss Robinson and his great piece of allegory; and a couple of the other paid portraits found a niche in the New Gallery. The Salon, too, presently notified him of their acceptance of Lady Betty's portrait, but that he had really been counting on with an almost fatalistic confidence.

On varnishing day he was delighted that both his Academy exhibits were hung on the line. His Press, too, was unmistakably good; the critics seemed all to conspire to hail him as the man of the year. At the clubs those who knew him accosted him enthusiastically, came thronging round and pressing hospitality upon him. There were so many anxious to "get" him for this and that occasion, to take possession of him, and have the honour of dragging him here and there. New names and faces bombarded him, and even his own special coterie were anxious to intensify their various degrees of intimacy with him, contending for the privilege of entertaining him, of being able to boast of an almost proprietorial friendship. In Society, too, he felt himself the object of a curious *empressement*; on all sides he was courted and flattered, and rival dealers were inquiring the price he set on his wares. It was the stampede of the world to acclaim Success!

Well might his eyes be dazzled by all this glare of sunshine! Was not this success as persistent as the failure that had been his lot previously? It made him think of the run of red that sometimes followed a run of black at roulette. He was indeed a public personage now! And rolling in prosperity to boot!

A touch of worldly bitterness indeed lingered with him; there was the remembrance of the lean years behind him. But his nature was too mercurial, too affable and genial, to dwell on that aspect of his career for long. He took all this homage very seriously, and thought tremendously well of himself as an artist, walking through the world with elastic step and as one of the elect of the earth.

Yet in the still moments when he sat alone at night with his lamp for sole company, he would lose himself in reverie; and then he would feel saddened ineffably by the ironic side of the case, since the more brilliant the success that came to him, the deeper his sense of the mockery of things! How splendid if the woman he loved were by his side to share it all with him! How near too he had come to attainment, yet destiny had played him this shameful, this merciless trick!

And just as his absorption in work had helped him hitherto in the situation, so now this new excitement of business and the world coloured his everyday demeanour and conversation; wrapped the Robinsons, too, in the whirl of busy interests, and carried him safely towards the inevitable time when he must seriously discuss the date of the wedding.

XXVIII

One morning early, towards the end of May, Alice sat down at her desk, and wrote the following brief letter to Mr. Shanner.

"My Dear Friend,—I owe you an acknowledgment. When you ventured to raise the question of the wisdom of my engagement to Mr. Wyndham, you were right in one respect. He is in every way a man of honour, and I have nothing against him. But, as the time goes by, it grows upon me more and more that he and I have made a mistake, as you were first to see, and that we are not suited to each other. His world and his ideas of life are not mine, and I have decided that it is wiser for me not to attempt to adapt myself to them. I recognise this before it is too late, and I have determined, not lightly, but after full and serious consideration, to draw back. I promised you that I should let you know if ever I arrived at such a conclusion. I now carry out my promise."

She directed it to his office, carefully marking it "Personal and Confidential." Shortly after noon she was startled by the rat-tat of a telegraph boy. "Approve of your decision with all my heart. Please remember that I am the first applicant for the privilege." Such was the answer he had flashed back the moment her letter had reached him, and the perusal of it gave her the satisfaction that accompanies the realisation step by step of an elaborate purpose. "So be it," she exclaimed. "To-day I shall ask for my release."

Wyndham was expecting her to join him at the studio. They were to dine together, then go to a Paderewski recital. But now she decided she would not go. What good to face him personally? Besides, it was easier to feel that she had already seen him for the last time. She went back to her desk, and began the laborious composition of a long letter. On and on she wrote, breaking off only to join her mother at lunch, and returning to her desk at the earliest moment. She had covered several sheets, when brusquely she changed her mind. Perhaps this was not really fair to him, and, besides, he might feel he ought to come to the house to see her again. Surely they might at least shake hands and part as friends. So she tore up the letter, and went to prepare herself for the journey to Chelsea. "I have been brave all through," she murmured; "and I mustn't spoil it at the end by turning coward. I am taking all the blame —let me be strong enough to take it face to face with him."

And now she was impatient to have done with it all. Her mission was ended. So, although he would not be looking for her yet, she would descend on him, even at the risk of disturbing him. The commission from the bank had already been completed, and at present he was making cartoons and sketches for new pictures. But he would be all the more grateful afterwards that she had not delayed her coup.

She got into a hansom, which, choosing its route through unobstructed back streets, arrived at her goal wonderfully soon. She got down firmly, paid the driver, and walked up the steps unfalteringly. She felt her calm and self-control as a great blessing; she had so long schooled herself for this moment, and it was splendid to feel how actual a fact was her resignation, how completely ingrained in her this acceptance of the inevitable.

She let herself in with her key for the last time, and put it on the hall table lest she should forget to leave it afterwards. Then she went upstairs, and tapped gently at the door of the studio, though it stood half open. She found Wyndham in a mood that was even a shade more affable than usual. Indeed, he seemed almost light-hearted to-day as he came forward with a friendly alertness to greet her, and pressed his lips affectionately to her forehead, and wheeled forward a chair for her. She was in a close-fitting coat and skirt, of a heliotrope shade, and there were roses in her hat. But, in spite of this burst of spring gaiety, her face retained the marked pallor that had characterised it of late. He indeed observed it for the first time.

"You must have a little of this light Chambery," he said. "It clears the head and nerves. I remembered I used to have a glass at the Café des Lilas in the old days whenever I felt done up, so I laid in a few bottles."

"Do I seem so unusually flurried?" she asked.

She smiled, but he saw at once that the note was forced, and began to suspect that something was amiss.

"It's rather close to-day—the heat has come upon us all of a rush. It's sure to be crowded and stuffy at the concert to-night. Now do try my remedy, child."

"If you don't mind, we'll not go to the concert."

"By all means," he agreed. "We'll dine early, take a stroll on the Embankment, and if there's a boat going up or down, it doesn't matter which, we'll get on, and see where it takes us. Not a bad idea, little girl, eh?"

"I'm sorry," she said, "but I meant that we were not to pass the evening together at all. I came now, instead of later on, to see you and talk to you."

He looked at her hard. "You rather mystify me."

"I'm sorry," she said again. "I sat down to write you a long letter to-day," she resumed, after an almost imperceptible hesitation. "In fact, I really began it, or rather I wrote a good many pages, and then I thought it would be fairer and braver to come here to you at once instead."

He leaned up against the table for support. "My dear child, I don't in the least understand your drift—I am bewildered."

She smiled wanly; yet the smile of one about to set forth in a cool, reasonable way a case that needed exposition, and that necessarily must carry conviction. "I was writing to ask you a favour. Now I have come to ask for it in person."

"It is yours to command." He inclined his head graciously and gallantly.

"You are sweet to me, as always," she returned. "But, as you will see, I am quite undeserving of your graciousness on this present occasion."

He laughed. "Modest as usual, my dear child! I'm afraid it's going to be one of the tasks of my life to impress you with a sense of your own merits."

"Please don't say any more nice things to me," she implored. "Your kindness hurts me."

He looked hard at her again, then passed his hand across his face. "Let me see," he said; "where were we? I confess I'm rather confused. Ah, yes, you said you preferred that we shouldn't go to the concert."

She drew her breath hard; her bosom palpitated. "Because I want you to set me free altogether." Her face was suddenly on fire, but an exultation thrilled through her. At last the words had been spoken; she was near the end.

But she felt his eyes upon her; she saw his face set in a strange expression, half-vacant, half-surprised. "To set you free?" he murmured.

"To break off our engagement," she launched out. "Oh, I know it is horrible of me," she went on quickly, feeling herself giving way at this moment of trial, despite all her fortitude and all her schooling. She saw that his lips made as if he were about to speak, but, dreading to hear him yet, she gathered up her force and hurried on piteously. "Please don't think that I have anything against you, that you are in the least to blame. You have been chivalrous and kind throughout. The responsibility must all rest on my shoulders."

He winced at the pain she was visibly enduring, the expression of her eyes, the convulsive catch of her breath.

"But what on earth has come between us?" he exclaimed, in a sort of dull despair. He felt no joyous glow at the return of his liberty. The occasion seemed too miserably tragic, and his human association with her had made him care for her enough to be deeply distressed at the agony under which she was labouring. Even now, if it could have made her happy, if it could have induced her to withdraw all she had said, he would have taken her hand tenderly, and melted away every cloud between them. "Yesterday all was well, and to-day——" He gave a gesture of blank bewilderment.

"I have arrived at the conviction that we are not suited for each other, that I am not the sort of woman to make your life all that it should be."

"Oh, come," he said. "I am surprised to find such morbid nonsense running in your head."

She was taken aback at this resistance on his part; and she rightly set it down to pure fraternal consideration for her. She let herself go now; best to give her explanation at full length.

"It is not a sudden impulse I have yielded to, or a passing wave of depression," she urged, trying to conjure up the ghost of a smile again. "Believe me, I have seen the right path before me only after the deepest consideration."

He interrupted her with a gesture.

"But what has come between us?" he insisted again. "You do not say you have ceased to love me."

With a great effort she looked straight at him. "Yes," she said with steady voice, and no physical flinching. "I have ceased to love you. I searched into my heart before it was too late, and I found my affections had gone to another."

A flash of understanding seemed to come to him. "Mr. Shanner!" he exclaimed.

She averted her eyes. "He was my friend before I knew you," she pleaded, as if driven to defence.

"I see now you are perfectly serious," he murmured, hurt at last, and firmly believing her. "Does love come and go in women with such momentary capriciousness?"

"Perhaps," she said with a weird dreaminess. "It comes and goes like the blossoming of a flower in the sunlight—beautiful for the day or two it lives. My love for you is dead. I should not be happy with you, so why make the pretence? I should not ask you to forgive me, only I am not worth your remembrance for any reason. Let us shake hands and part not too bitterly."

He stood silent, his head bowed. There was no thought in his mind, only a sense of shame and of poignant regret.

"Believe me, it is for the best," she resumed, trying to smile. "And be assured, the guilty party alone shall be condemned, should the world discuss us!" She held out her hand. He took it and held it gently, in sign that he bore her no ill-will.

XXIX

In the first profound depression into which this unforeseen occurrence had plunged him, Wyndham remained totally indifferent to his freedom. His thought in a feeble way reached out, recalling her words, lingering on her crowning confession. Suddenly he laughed out aloud. How much greater the irony of his life than even he had imagined! For the second time he and Lady Betty had come together, only voluntarily to part that they might not disturb the happiness of this other life! How they had tortured themselves; how Lady Betty had sought deliberate martyrdom, staying near him only long enough to school him to perfect loyalty to Alice! "Whilst I was fretting my heart away," his lips murmured, "lest I should wound her with a chance word, she was vibrating again towards her own kind, and was planning her retreat. Surely the gods are pulling the strings and making us poor puppets dance for their amusement!"

And then he thought of the Hampstead street miles away, where he had passed so many years of his life in suffering and degradation; and the sense of its distance helped him. Were he still in the old studio, the sense of the Robinsons' house within a stone's throw would have been intolerable. He would hardly have dared to set foot out of doors for fear of the painful accident of stumbling up against one of the family. He desired no further explanations and apologies. He shuddered at the very idea. Here at least he could take shelter silently within his own pride.

And the thought of his pride made him rise up again, and pace to and fro vigorously. It was beneath him to admit that that had been wounded. But he came to a standstill, and the blood rushed to his temples at the abrupt remembrance that all the prosperity and success that must still remain his had come to him through the Robinsons. Were not the humiliating evidences here before his eyes? This charming house and studio, the successful pictures hung in the galleries, the money at his bankers, the promise of unlimited treasure yet to flow into his coffers, the acclamation of the world and his social lionising— how much of all this would have been achieved without the timely co-operation of the Robinsons? He staggered in moral agony under the burden of good they had heaped on him so lavishly.

Nothing of course could be undone. Wisest to acquiesce silently, and start forward afresh from the point at which he stood. But since it was now only the end of May, and the best of the season was yet to follow, he felt that to stay in London would be intolerable.

The world seemed to swarm with people, all intent on chattering about his affairs, on discussing and misunderstanding this sensation in the life of the lion of the season. A lovely titbit for the social gossips to relish! He could not possibly meet people, shake their hands, answer their stupid questions, listen to the hateful sympathy of the more intimate. He must shut up the house and fly from London. But where could he hide himself for the time?

He resumed his pacing to and fro, sometimes perambulating the studio to vary his movement. So far he was under the influence of the first excitement attendant on the rupture. Whatever his astonishment at having been ousted in the affections of a woman by a man whom he had more or less despised, whose rivalry he had brushed aside as easily as a cobweb; the bare idea that a broken engagement should figure in his life was so distasteful that it made the wound to his mere vanity a secondary matter. He could not at once extricate his mind from the contemplation of these immediate bearings of the event. His relation to Lady Betty, indeed, was present to him, but he had not yet turned the flood of his thought in that direction.

In the reaction of feeling, however, when the first sting and shock had somewhat lightened, it was natural for his whole soul to turn to Lady Betty longingly; not with the joyous impulse of one unexpectedly free to claim his true comrade, but like a bruised child to find relief for his hurt. But how to reach her again he did not know. So thorough had been their sacrifice that he had even promised never to write to her. Besides, letters would only follow her if sent through a certain banker, whose name she had withheld from him. And though now he felt that circumstances absolved him from the promise, he did not care that such a letter as he must write, once he put pen to paper, should go to her father's deserted house, and thence be tossed about the world in perhaps a futile pursuit, with the possible fate of being read in a dead-letter office, and finally returned to him. He would wait awhile. Perhaps, if the gossip got abroad, it might by some circuitous route arrive even as far as Lady Betty's ears, and then no doubt she would announce her whereabouts to him. The pressing problem before him was to decide on his own plans for the immediate present.

How stale and tired he was! How terribly he had toiled these past months, sustained by he knew not what mysterious energy. It seemed almost as if he had exerted a supernatural strength, and the work he had accomplished might well have claimed double the period. And now, something had suddenly gone snap. He was finished; a mere hollow shell of a man.

His mind turned again towards other climes and other skies. It seemed so long since he had crossed the Channel; so many years indeed that it was hateful to count them. It reminded him too much of the big slice of his life, the years of his prime, that had been so miserably sterile.

But his face brightened as his thought played again amid the haunts of his early manhood. Ah, those were happy times—the work in the schools, the discussions in the café, the pleasant camaraderie, the freedom to laugh, to feel master of one's own soul. The brilliance and green avenues of Paris beckoned him; his blood beat pleasurably. And then of course there was his portrait of Lady Betty in the Salon. What better shrine for a pilgrimage!

He would linger a little in Paris, then proceed further South. He was not of the great crowd that refuses to venture in those regions during the summer. He knew well how to adapt himself to the conditions, and the lands of the South would be soon in their full glory. His imagination dwelt on the prospect, and sunshine broke in on his mood. Perhaps, too, there was the hope, deep in his heart, that he might encounter Lady Betty somewhere—by some charming train of events! Heigho for the orange trees, for the old Italian palaces, the Venetian canals, the coast-line of Salerno! He would make a leisurely progression, working a little as he went—just a few distinguished sketches, odd impressions of light and beauty caught on the wing! Late in the year when time had done its work, when the wretched affair was forgotten, and himself recovered from the sordid experience, he might return to London. But never here to this studio again!

The prospect of departure stirred him! "Here I cannot breathe another day!" he kept murmuring to himself.

Then why not start this very evening?

He glanced at his watch; it was not yet four. There would be time to dash round to a local bank and provide himself with funds for the start. But on investigation he found he had enough to take him to Paris, so he could devote the whole time to his preparations and necessary correspondence.

And no sooner was the decision arrived at than he adjusted his outlook to it as an accomplished fact. Without any further delay, he got ready his trunk and dressing-case, and started his packing in earnest.

The train left at nine that evening. He had five good hours to catch it. So he worked deliberately and carefully, overlooking nothing in the haste of departure. Lady Betty's wizard, his most cherished possession, went down deep into the trunk, and he did not forget his cheque-book and his private papers. Otherwise, everything was in such excellent order that his task was comparatively simple. Whatever he lacked for his journey he could count on purchasing in Paris, where also he could renew his funds for travelling.

At last everything was ready, and he had ample time for his correspondence.

This was speedily disposed of, since his letters were mostly to cry "off" from invitations already accepted. Only one was of a more intimate character, and that was to his sister Mary. But even that was brief and to the point. "Dearest Mary," he wrote,—"I regret I have rather disagreeable news for you, but I trust you will not take too serious a view of it. Alice asked me to release her to-day, and of course I had no alternative but to accede to her wishes. I cannot bear to stay in London just now, so I leave this evening for a long stay abroad. Forgive this brief note, forgive me also for not coming to kiss you goodbye, but, as you may guess, I am off on impulse, time is short, and there were a few matters to arrange. Perhaps you may be able to join me later when your vacation comes, and then we shall have a happy time together. I am all right, so please don't worry about me. I shall write to you soon, and keep you posted as to my adventures."

He took out the batch of letters to the post, picking up a cab on his way back. In a few minutes his traps were on the roof, and he was being driven to the station.

It was a serene summer night, and the crossing was ideal. As he promenaded the deck, and looked into the spacious darkness, and let the breeze play free about his face, the sense of strain and fatigue, all the broken feeling that remained from the stress of his tussle with the world, seemed to be swept away. His early manhood, when he had gone to and fro as he listed, began to stir in him again, and the consciousness of mature power and ripe experience which were now added to it awakened an almost overweening sense of well- being and confidence.

The episode of his broken engagement already began to look absurd rather than tragic in this new spirited mood of his. The whole thing seemed beneath his dignity. Of course, in some ways, he would always look back upon it as a bitterly unpleasant incident; but, in this life, you were necessarily called upon to be a stoic in some degree. The point was to choose the degree yourself. In face of unpleasant things stoicism was no doubt the wisest; but where good things were concerned it was best to preserve all the fresh feelings of the natural human being.

The Robinsons were already receding into the mists of distance. Despite the reality and the closeness of his connection with them, they were taking their place among the shadows that peopled the past. His own vision was turned forward—ever forward!

"Strange," he thought, "how things and people cease to have any consequence, once you have turned your back upon them!"

The night passed like a dream. In the train from Calais to Paris he dozed lightly, and woke only at dawn. The sky was cloudless and wonderfully blue, but the sun shone as yet coldly over the landscape, and the fat fields sparkled with dew. Save for the quiet herds of cattle, the world was deserted. Immediately all his faculties were pleasurably alert again. He noticed with delight the hamlets and sleeping villages, the still wayside stations where moustachioed old women, who surely dated from the Revolution, stood on guard with flags at the cross-ways. At last they were running through the environs of the capital, and Wyndham tasted the sensation of entering the great city of light and intellect as keenly as in his jubilant boyhood.

The drive through Paris in the early morning was exhilarating and enchanting. At that hour the streets at first were surprisingly thronged, the roadway sometimes blocked with a heavy traffic of carts all converging to the Halles. But soon they were passing through quieter neighbourhoods, through stately avenues lined by vast hotels with far-stretching lines of shuttered windows. Wyndham surrendered himself to the charm of steeping himself again in this atmosphere, drawing freer breaths, subtly attuned to it, aided by golden memories.

The brisk buxom matron, who was already at her post in the hotel bureau, recognised her old client, and welcomed him with a cry of joy. Her face beamed with pleasure as he shook hands with her, and he had a joyous sense of home-coming!

"But one has not seen you for eternities," she exclaimed. "We had thought that you had quite abandoned us!"

"The loss has been more mine than yours, madame," he returned. "I should have announced my arrival beforehand, if I had not left London so suddenly."

Presently he took possession of his room, and, as it was not yet seven, he sank into an arm-chair and dozed for a time. At nine he awoke, washed, changed into more civilised clothes, then strolled out cheerfully on to the Boulevards, and had his morning coffee at a little table in the open, with a budget of French papers to look through, and the spectacle of the passing world in the sunshine for his entertainment.

He sat on for a long while in leisurely enjoyment, then proceeded to stroll by way of the Place de la Concorde (which looked vaster and finer than it had ever appeared to him) round to the great Palace of Art off the Champs

Elysées. It had sprung up during these years of his absence, and he wandered round it delightedly, examining all the façades, familiarising himself with all the points of view.

At last he entered through the nearest turnstile and went straight to see how Lady Betty's portrait was hung.

But Wyndham did not linger in Paris as he had intended. He had found Lady Betty beautifully placed on the line, and had returned to her daily, not to gaze at the painting, but at the features of the woman he loved. And then there surged in him a fever of impatience. He had not the least hope of finding her here in Paris—he took it for granted she had long since seen the Salon, and he had the strangely settled belief—he did not know why—that she was not then in France at all. And somehow he was unable to conceive of himself now save as actively in search of her. All the first impulsion towards holiday and repose that had swept him headlong across the Channel had mysteriously died away, to give place to this haunting, this imperious, idea of a mission. He must push on with it at once!

He chose his route largely haphazard, yet zigzagging through her favourite cities. His heart thrilled with hope as he was borne again through the outskirts, and Paris lay behind him. In this dash through Europe, the happy chance might perhaps befall him! He knew the quest in that way was wholly irrational, but it had its charm. He might pass within a stone's throw of her a score of times, and yet remain unconscious of the proximity. A billion to one at least against him!

Yet he pursued his journey feverishly; passing through Belgium swiftly, thence to Dresden by stages, then hurrying down to Munich, next on to Vienna, and passing further southwards; vibrating off the beaten path at every turn; staying here a day, there a night, rarely anywhere longer; guided by no principle, but darting about at random, often doubling back on his track, and yielding to every fantastic impulse that rose in him.

At Belgrade, where he found himself some four weeks after leaving Paris (though the days, packed with changing scenes and impressions, had seemed to run into months), he had an inspiration, and abruptly took the train straight back again. Might not Lady Betty gravitate once more to the portrait, before the Salon closed its doors for the season? Even though it was to be her own possession in the end, she might well desire to pay it that tribute. Had it not given them their brief companionship in avowed affection? He would haunt the Salon daily; he would wait and watch for her. He journeyed all day, all night, and all the next day, impelled by the same fever of impatience, which now oppressed him tenfold. He stepped out of the train in the evening amid the bustle and lights of the terminus. He was in Paris again! He breathed with relief as at a goal accomplished.

XXX

One blue summer morning, Wyndham, for the twentieth time at least, entered the Salon through his customary turnstile, and stood in the great central court, under the crystal roof, amid the gleaming display of statuary. There was already a goodly number of people about; not yet a crowd, but enough for the costumes and hats of the fair sex to colour the whole place like a flower-garden. He moved about among them for awhile, his eye keen and ready; then ascended the staircase, and entered the nearest doorway. He spent an hour or two in leisurely progression through the galleries, long since familiar with all the pictures, and staying only before the interesting ones, yet with attention ever on the alert.

At last he had set foot in the particular room, which was to him the shrine, the inner sanctuary, of this Temple of the Arts. It was already crowded here, and his first impression was of a mass of silk hats and beflowered millinery rather than of pictures. He hesitated in the doorway an instant, then began the slow tour of the room, pausing before every picture in turn, so as to indulge in the pleasurable make-believe of coming on Lady Betty again suddenly. Gradually he worked his way along and it was not till he had come again within reach of his starting-point that his own frame gleamed on his vision. He manoeuvred through a bevy of ladies, and then found himself side by side with a girlish figure in a light flowered muslin costume and a pretty hat trimmed with violets. He had stepped quite close to her out of the crowd, by which she had been entirely hidden; but, his eyes drawn imperiously to the portrait of Lady Betty, he was merely aware of his neighbour as one of the crowd, and he did not even look at her definitely. He saw just her gloved hand holding her catalogue, and, in a vague way, he wondered what she was thinking of the picture. He felt rather than saw that his neighbour had stepped back a little, as if naturally to make way for him. Then some mysterious impulse made him turn, and their eyes met. In all those winter days that were past he had never seen her so bright and gracious as she appeared now, clad for the summer, and in this sparkling universe. Never before had those violet eyes shone with so perfect a light, as of the full freshness of childhood. Yet her face was pallid and awestruck as she gazed at him. But a wild joy sang at his heart, and he felt his blood pulsing with a glad note that seemed to be at one with the note that sang to him from horizons of enchantment opening before him; at one, too, with the note that sang to him out of all this exquisite Paris!

"I am free," he whispered. "Do you understand? Free!"

"Free?"

He divined rather than heard the breathed exclamation from the movement of her lips—read the amazed questioning of her eyes.

"I have not broken my promise to you!" The crowd surged round them, struggling to see his picture, ejaculating banal words of admiration. "You do not doubt!" he whispered tensely.

The blood came back to her face at last. "No! But the how?—the why?"

"She sought her release!"

"She suspected the truth!" She was pale again.

"We cheated ourselves. She cared for one of her own kind. Our renunciation was an irony."

Lady Betty bent her head. Her brow was wrinkled for a moment in thought, and her hand trembled visibly.

"An irony—no," she said gently. "We were true to ourselves—the future lies the fairer before us."

The press around them grew closer.

"Mais c'est chic ça!"

"Un beau talent!"

"C'est exquis!"

She took his arm, as if seeking freer air, and they moved through the throng that continued its compliments, unsuspecting of the proximity of either artist or subject. They stood at last on the great balcony, and looked down on the splendid court agleam with sculpture and greenery.

"I have searched Europe for you!" he said.

"This great change in our lives—it is too wonderful to grasp all at once," she murmured musingly.

"I do not see why we should not stroll round to the Embassy now, and inquire," he suggested stoutly.

"Inquire about what?" she asked, her deep absent look changing to bewilderment.

"As to when they can marry us, of course!"

"Oh, I see," she said, with a quick smile; but her glance was inward again.

"You don't think me precipitate?" he asked uneasily.

"I am thinking of Alice," she returned. "I could have sworn she was the soul of constancy."

THE END.

UNWIN BROTHERS, LIMITED, THE GRAHAM PRESS, WOKING AND LONDON.